A FATAL ALL-NIGHTER

Lauren felt a rush of relief at the sight of Michael's familiar face. "Lauren darling," he was saying. "*What* is the matter? You look like the tormented heretics in the Sixth Circle of Dante's *Inferno*."

Lauren, who had gone to a public high school in New Jersey, and not to the Phillips Academy, had no idea what precisely went on in the Sixth Circle, but it sounded vaguely appropriate to her present psychological state.

"And where were *you* last night?" Michael was saying. "I knocked on your door at midnight, I knocked at one, and I knocked at two. Your roommate, I presume, was spending the night with that incredibly unattractively oversized shot-putter. But where were you? And who was *he*, you bad girl? Did he beat you, or did he just keep you awake all night, you haggard thing. You know, they say sex is good for one's skin, but I never really believed it, and now I know I'm right."

"I was sleeping with Emily."

Michael raised his eyebrows.

"No, I mean, I spent the night in Emily's room. And during the night, one of Emily's roommates—" Lauren broke off, and then made herself finish. "She was murdered."

Death of a Radcliffe Roommate

■

Victoria Silver

BANTAM BOOKS
TORONTO · NEW YORK · LONDON · SYDNEY · AUCKLAND

DEATH OF A RADCLIFFE ROOMMATE
A Bantam Book / September 1986

ISBN 0-553-25932-6

Published simultaneously in the United States and Canada

Bantam Books are published by Bantam Books, Inc. Its trade-
mark, consisting of the words "Bantam Books" and the por-
trayal of a rooster, is Registered in U.S. Patent and Trademark
Office and in other countries. Marca Registrada. Bantam
Books, Inc., 666 Fifth Avenue, New York, New York 10103.

PRINTED IN THE UNITED STATES OF AMERICA

KR   0 9 8 7 6 5 4 3 2 1

For sweet D.
the man in my life

1
Choosing Roommates

■

The prince who does not detect evils the moment
they appear is lacking in true wisdom.

Machiavelli

Lauren took a deep breath and said, "Emily, let's room together next year."

And just at that moment, as Lauren held her breath with anticipation, waiting to see what Emily would say, the silent pause between the two Harvard freshmen was shattered by a deafening, honking, hideous explosion of sound. And then, relentlessly, another and another and another as Lauren and Emily stared at each other, paralyzed, terrified, and Emily's little room seemed to quake and shudder with each horrible, mechanical shriek. In her head Lauren preserved the echo of her own last words, Let's room together next year, and she found herself thinking, A fine moment for a nuclear attack. Then, still holding that first breath, she reminded herself reproachfully that this was no time to be flippant.

"Fire," said Emily, and Lauren didn't so much hear the word as see it mouthed and obliterated by the clamor. "It's the fire alarm," said Emily. Lauren read her lips easily, because somewhere in the back of her mind she had known all along that that was what it had to be.

"Come on, let's get out of here," said Lauren, rising from Emily's bed, finally breathing again. Emily got up from the desk, took her black bowler hat from its peg on the wall, and placed it squarely on her prodigious, curly black hair. Very cool, thought Lauren, wondering whether, after all this was over, Emily would remember where they had left off—with Lauren's suggestion about rooming together next year.

Lauren opened the door of Emily's bedroom and stepped out into the inner hallway of Emily's five-person suite in Weld Hall. Emily went back to her desk for a moment to snatch up a framed photograph—her father, thought Lauren, her famous father, Senator Anthony Ravello of Pennsylvania— then joined Lauren in the hallway, where the brutal honking of the alarm seemed even more unbearably oppressive. They paused to look over the doors of Emily's four roommates: Helena, Debbie, Cookie, and the Princess.

Two doors were opening, and two remained closed. Helena was coming out of her room, clutching a pile of letters to her breast with one hand, arranging her beautiful hair with the other. Debbie also appeared, then disappeared out the main door, out of the suite, a book in her hand. "Hurry or you'll all burn up," she called over her shoulder, but it didn't sound as though she really much cared one way or another. The Princess's door was closed, but from behind it you could hear a male voice giving directions, the voice of the Princess's security guard. Cookie's door was also closed, and there was no sound from within.

"Cookie," cried Emily as loud as she could, "are you in there?"

"Coming, guys," came the reply from behind the door, unmistakably Cookie.

Now Lauren and Emily headed out of the suite, and again Emily held back, stopping in front of Debbie's door, which Debbie had left open. Emily ran in, picked up a package wrapped in brown paper at the foot of the harp, then rejoined Lauren, slamming Debbie's door behind her.

"I'll kill her; I'm going to kill her," Lauren heard Emily muttering as they moved along with all the other Harvard freshmen who were scrambling down the stairway to get out of the dorm, away from the deafening alarm, safe from the fire, if there really was one.

Lauren felt curiously detached from the scramble since it wasn't her dorm; she was only a visitor. If all of Weld Hall went up in flames tonight, Lauren would still be going home to sleep in her own room in Thayer on the other side of Harvard Yard. Cute, thought Lauren, as a male body in gym shorts and a sweatshirt passed her on the stairs, a track trophy in one hand, an obviously half-written paper in the other. And there was Emily alongside her, holding on to the framed photograph and the wrapped package. What was it, anyway, that Emily had taken out of Debbie's room that had made Emily so mad? Lauren looked down at her own hands to see that she was carrying her paperback copy of Machiavelli's *Prince*, the book she'd been trying to read on Emily's bed. Pretty pathetic, thought Lauren, to save from the raging flames a book I can't even concentrate on for five minutes.

Outside it was dark, past eight. Harvard Yard was illuminated by the lights from the windows of all the dormitories where students were studying or amusing themselves. Only from Weld came those horrible honking noises, muted now from inside, and only there was everyone huddled outside the dorm, anxiously sniffing the air for smoke. "I think it's a real fire," said a voice behind Lauren.

"It's just a drill," said someone else.

"The boys on the fifth floor were playing with the alarm," said a female voice.

"The girls on the fourth floor were using that hotplate," said a male voice.

If the fire was in my dorm, thought Lauren, what would I save? The diamond stud earrings? No, Lauren liked her earrings, but she didn't care about them passionately.

Photographs of the high school boyfriends she had left behind in New Jersey? Probably not. She hadn't really minded leaving them behind, and she had no intention of ever living in New Jersey again. A book, perhaps, but certainly not Machiavelli. Lauren was sentimental about books she'd read while she was growing up, and she'd brought several along with her from New Jersey to Harvard. *Gone with the Wind* she would rescue. She had read that now battered copy when she was eleven, and it had given her both her first role model and her first and most enduring sexual fantasy. And she would also grab that old hardcover *Wuthering Heights*, which, two years later, had given her a new fantasy of rival intensity. Face it, said Lauren to herself, Rhett Butler and Heathcliff are much more important to you than any of those New Jersey boyfriends. She would save two books, then, and also that gorgeous new mohair sweater she had worn only twice; it would be a tragedy to lose it now. Books and clothing, she thought, something for my fantasies and something for my vanity, a nice combination. And the mohair sweater, as it happened, would be useful, as well, if she were driven from the dorm.

"If Weld burns," said Lauren to Emily, "at least we'll be able to warm our bodies by the fire." In fact, everyone was shivering in the cold. That afternoon there had been a warm sun of very early spring, but tonight, unexpectedly, it was almost winter again, and no one was dressed warmly enough. Lauren, in jeans, was damn cold, but Mr. Track Trophy over there in the gym shorts was jogging in place with a sort of desperation.

"Whose body are you interested in warming?" inquired Emily, whose eyes had followed Lauren's.

"B-plus," Lauren graded him, thinking that in a crisis it was always best to resort to favorite pasttimes.

"Only a B," Emily disagreed. "If you lifted up your gaze for a moment, you'd see that he has no shoulders." She seemed to be easily enough distracted from the fire alarm, but from the way she held on to that package and photograph, Lauren could see that something else was bothering Emily, really bothering her. Lauren wondered, of course, but she knew Emily well enough to know that it was not yet the moment to ask.

Instead, she lifted her gaze, as instructed, and immediately forgot about the track team, for there, emerging from the dorm at last, was the Princess, escorted by her security guard. They called him J.B. because he looked so remarkably like the young Sean Connery as James Bond, and as far as Lauren was concerned, he was the most attractive man on the Harvard campus. He was wearing a dark suit, as always, and the Princess, at least, was warm, since she was wearing a fur too expensive to be left behind to burn. The Princess was from one of the oil emirates on the Persian Gulf, and J.B., of course, was British.

"Something about the way you walk when you're wearing a fur," said Emily. "It's really unmistakable." And putting down her package she walked a few steps in the night. It was tremendous, thought Lauren, Emily's talent for mime. You could really see the imaginary fur as she walked, an extremely expensive imaginary fur—there was no doubt about it.

"That's wonderful; what a wonderful talent," said a soft voice, and Lauren turned to see another of Emily's roommates, Helena, still holding tight to her letters.

"Thank you," said Emily. Her concentration interrupted, the imaginary fur disappeared, and once again she was Emily Ravello in a black bowler hat and a black turtleneck—the right costume for a mime but wrong for such a cold night.

Helena smiled at Emily so sweetly that Lauren immediately suspected Helena hoped to go on rooming with Emily next year. But would Emily consider it as long as Helena was such good friends with Debbie? What was the package that Emily had taken from Debbie's room? And was there a fire or wasn't there? If there was, where were the firemen, and if not, why couldn't they stop the alarm and let everyone back in out of the cold?

"Do you think it's a real fire?" said Helena. "I've saved *his* letters." There was no need to ask whose letters, and Lauren couldn't help wondering unkindly whether Helena wasn't the tiniest bit glad of a fire alarm, which gave her the opportunity to make such a public display of saving those letters. She had already, very shyly, very modestly, managed to let a lot of people at Harvard know that she corresponded with Augustine Wedgwood, that he had read the poems she sent him and praised her talent, that he had even last year written a letter of recommendation to the Harvard Admissions Office on her behalf. Even Lauren, who had never written a poem in her life and never intended to try, couldn't help being impressed that one of the great British poets of the twentieth century should have taken an interest in the poetry of a seventeen-year-old girl from Newton, Massachusetts. "I just got another letter from him today," said Helena, reverently separating one letter from the pile. "If you'd like..."

"Would you show it to us?" Lauren took the words right out of Helena's mouth, and Lauren felt as though she'd done her good deed for the day. What would it be like, she thought, to be Helena's roommate?

Helena looked at Emily expectantly, and Emily said, "I'd like to see it, if you wouldn't mind." If Emily intended any irony, she was too much of an actress for her face to give her away.

"Yeah, show us the letter," said another voice, an unpleasant voice with the unmistakable inflections of Long Island, and there, appearing out of the dark night and the nervous, milling crowd of students, was Debbie Doyle. Without even looking, Lauren could feel the sudden tension in Emily, the tension of real hatred. Emily lifted the package, but Debbie didn't seem to realize its significance (now I'll find out, thought Lauren, intrigued but a little bit afraid) and continued to talk to Helena. "You've got me so interested in Augustine Wedgwood that I'm reading this book about him." Debbie held up the book, and Lauren noticed the dark gloves.

"Oh, I could just tell you," said Helena with a lovely, silvery laugh. "I know all about him." There was something almost defensive about the way she said it, as if Wedgwood were her personal property and she didn't really want anyone, even her roommate, even her best friend, to learn about Wedgwood from anyone but her.

Odd friends, thought Lauren, who was generally curious about the way people chose the friends they chose. Helena was probably the most beautiful of the five roommates—though Emily, Cookie, and the Princess could all be considered beautiful—and Debbie was unquestionably the plainest. At night it was impossible to appreciate the shimmering golden highlights of Helena's long, artfully natural hair, but still she managed to hold her head in such a way as to present the most lovely silhouette. She was as beautiful in the dark as in the daylight. Debbie, on the other hand, even at night was recognizably plain, and that was because her plainness had nothing to do with her perfectly ordinary features. It could only be ascribed to deeper spiritual causes, to the unpleasantness of her personality. Beautiful and plain, best friends, they were both artists. Helena was a poet—Augustine Wedgwood said so. Debbie Doyle was a superb harpist, Juilliard trained, whose first thought was to protect her hands with gloves, even if the rest of her body shivered. Lauren had once peered into Debbie's room to catch a glimpse of her practicing and had almost failed to recognize her. There had been something almost beautiful about Debbie when she was playing her harp.

"Where's Cookie?" said Lauren quietly, almost to herself. "Did she come out of the dorm?" No one heard Lauren over the continuing alarm, and by the time she was about to repeat her question full voice, Emily was addressing herself to Debbie.

"What was this doing in your room?" Emily held up the package.

"What's that?" said Debbie, as if she didn't know.

"It's a package addressed to me," said Emily. Then she added, "From my father."

"Oh, that," said Debbie, as if she really didn't care. "It was delivered this morning, and I signed for it since you weren't here, and then I guess I forgot." She managed to give the impression that her forgetfulness was entirely intentional.

"This morning?" Emily demanded.

"Maybe it was yesterday," said Debbie, "maybe it was

the day before. I don't remember; leave me alone." Lauren
knew how intense, how volatile, was Emily's relationship
with her father, the senator. She also knew, from Emily,
that Debbie's parents were divorced, that Debbie hardly
knew her father.

Was that why Debbie had withheld the package? Was
that why Emily began to open the package right now
before Debbie's eyes? Emily passed the framed photograph to Lauren and set about unwrapping the brown
paper with almost ostentatious care. Debbie watched sourly,
unrepentant. Helena with her letters, now forgotten, looked
on with an expression of distress, nervously stroking her
beautiful hair; she was Debbie's friend and wanted to be
Emily's friend. Lauren looked at the photograph in her
hand: a little girl who had to be Emily, a handsome man
recognizable as her father, though much younger and
much less senatorial than his current newspaper photographs. She wants him to be just her daddy again, thought
Lauren, instead of being the nationally known Senator
Anthony Ravello of Pennsylvania. Lauren's father was a
doctor in the New Jersey suburbs. Emily's father, of
course, was often mentioned nowadays as a possible presidential candidate.

Emily took out of the box a long caftan and held it up for
everyone, especially Debbie, to see. You could only make
out the shape at night and the gold-and-silvery embroi-
dery at the neck that glittered even in the darkness.
Senator Ravello—as everyone in America knew—had recently
returned from Cairo, where he had been part of a Senate
delegation to consider Middle Eastern affairs, at the same
time cultivating his image as an international statesman.

"I had a fight with him last night on the phone," said
Emily to Debbie. "I accused him of never thinking of me,
of only thinking about his political career." Lauren thought
she saw a tear shining in the corner of Emily's eye; she
wanted to go over and hug her.

"I know," said Debbie. "We all heard." The five roommates shared the same phone, which sat in the communal
living room.

"And you had this package in your room the whole time and didn't give it to me."

"I forgot; will you leave me alone? I wish they'd decide whether there's a fire or not and let us go back in. It's cold out here." She paused and added, "And boring." Then she yawned, a rude, ugly yawn that was somehow intended to disparage Emily and her father. Emily, still holding the caftan, watched Debbie with hatred in her eyes, and Lauren held her breath, because she suddenly knew what was going to happen the moment before it actually did happen. Emily copied Debbie's yawn, copied it perfectly in all its rude ugliness, and did it while looking Debbie in the eye. For Lauren it was terrifying to watch, as if Debbie were suddenly being forced to look into a mirror that perfectly reflected all her inner unpleasantness. But Debbie was unable to look away, hypnotically compelled by her own image. And Lauren and Helena watched with a different sort of fascination, looking from Debbie to Emily and back again. The mimicry was perfect.

After ten long seconds Debbie broke loose and lifted her book in her gloved hand. "I'll kill you," she said to Emily, and everyone turned to see who had spoken, because just at that moment the alarm had finally stopped and there was silence. "I'll kill you," seemed to echo in the night air, and Debbie lowered her arm, turned her back, and walked away. In a moment, everyone's attention was distracted again, because a fire engine was now making its way into Harvard Yard, through the far gate, and moving toward them.

Back in New Jersey, in Lauren's hometown, there was a volunteer fire department, and Lauren had once spent a summer afternoon making out with one of the younger volunteers in the back of the fire truck. A romantic profession, Lauren always thought; she liked the idea of men who risked their lives for her. She was titillated now as the fire engine approached Weld Hall—though surely it couldn't really be a fire, and even if it was, everyone was out of danger. Then it popped back into her head: "Where's Cookie?"

"She must be somewhere in the crowd," said Emily, examining her caftan in the light of the fire engine's headlights. It was a heavy cotton, rich maroon.

"I don't see her," said Helena, looking around.

Emily looked up from the caftan and called out, "Cookie!" But there was no response, just a hush over the group and then the beginning of nervous murmuring.

Emily and Helena went to meet the firemen, to say that one of their roommates hadn't come out, was still in the dorm. And then, just as the firemen were ready to enter the building, the door opened, and Cookie appeared: a tall, blonde Los Angeles cheerleader, obviously all dressed up for a date. "Hi, guys!" she called from the front steps, waving as if the whole group had assembled just to greet her and admire her clothes. "There's no fire in there," she said to the firemen as they rushed past her into the building. "I was just finishing my makeup," she explained as she joined Emily, Helena, and Lauren. "I have a date tonight."

Surprise, thought Lauren, I would never have guessed. Cookie Fink always had a date, and therefore she was always dressed for one. Lauren had dates of her own, but she admitted to being dazzled by the success of this Beverly Hills cheerleader transplanted to Harvard.

"I like your new robe," said Cookie, eyeing Emily's caftan. Cookie had night vision when it came to clothes, and she clearly didn't like the caftan at all.

"I like your sweater," Emily reciprocated. The knitted polka dots seemed to glow in the dark, and Lauren guessed that Emily wouldn't have worn it in a million years. Cookie and Emily just barely stayed on friendly terms, and Lauren guessed that Emily would not want to room with Cookie again next year.

"I saw it in *Cosmo*," said Cookie, who arranged her wardrobe and also her life according to articles from magazines. Just now she was making the transition from *Seventeen* to *Cosmopolitan*, from all-American high school honey to sexually sophisticated metropolitan vamp. "Hey," Cookie said, changing the subject, "have you guys seen Debbie?"

"Yes," said Emily grimly.

"She's on her diet again; you can always tell. As soon as she tries to take off those extra pounds in the hips, her breasts disappear instead. Pretty funny, huh?" Cookie laughed, a mechanical, humorless, not quite human laugh. "I really hate her."

"Me, too." That was Emily.

Helena was about to say something, perhaps on Debbie's behalf, but Cookie was already talking again. "You know, me and Debbie used to be friends, and I used to give her tips about how to improve her appearance, like from the magazines, but now she doesn't give me my phone messages, and she stole my superlash waterproof mascara (which isn't gonna do her any good, anyway, because she always looks terrible, rain or shine), and last week she washed my contacts down the sink, just by accident, she said, and fortunately I had a spare pair, because I had a date that night and I like to be able to see the guy I'm going out with. But this afternoon she really went too far. You know, I have a chemistry midterm this week, and last week my chemistry section leader (he's a really geeky graduate student, and he's in love with me and wants me to marry him) brought me over some special stuff to help me study, and he left it with Debbie, and she didn't give it to me till today. Can you believe that? If I don't get an A on this midterm, it's gonna be her fault, and I'll rip her face apart." Cookie held up ten long, pointed fingernails, fluorescent pink.

She just might, thought Lauren. When Cookie Fink set out to do something, she did it, and Lauren respected her for that. Cookie wanted to have straight blonde Los Angeles hair; that her hair was naturally red and curly didn't stand in her way. She wanted lots of dates, and she had them. She wanted to get A's in all her science courses so she could go to the best possible medical school, and fall semester she got A's. If she decided to murder Debbie Doyle, she'd do it.

"Now there's nothing technically wrong with Debbie's nose," said Cookie, launching into her favorite subject. "Plastic surgery can't help her." Said with smug satisfaction and an air of professional certainty. "Now Emily, you could have your nose fixed to look like mine—I swear my nose used to be bigger than yours—and Lauren, you could have that little bump cut away and you'd be perfect." Like me, was Cookie's unstated addition. Lauren thought Cookie's nose was too perfect, a sort of technological wonder, again not quite human. Cookie believed that plastic surgery had made her what she was (perfect), and she was determined to become a plastic surgeon and help make other people perfect, too. I like my bump, thought Lauren, lifting a cold finger to her cold nose, and Emily's Roman nose is beautiful.

"Where the hell are those firemen? Why won't they let us back in?" said Emily, not eager to debate the merits of her nose with Cookie. "They're probably pawing through our underwear up there." Cookie looked momentarily alarmed, then realized it was a joke and gave her mechanical laugh.

"Who's your date?" asked Helena softly. Lauren had almost forgotten she was there. When Cookie got going, it was easy to forget that anyone else was around.

"It's David," said Cookie.

"Which David?" asked Emily.

"You know," said Cookie thoughtfully. "I can't remember. Those two Davids are my favorite dates, and I think I'm gonna choose one of them to be my boyfriend, but they have the same name, and they look alike, so I get them confused. There's David the premed and David the prelaw, and I hope tonight it's David the premed. I have a question about chemistry, and I don't wanna have to call that geeky graduate student."

"Don't look now," said Lauren. Everyone looked.

"Oh, no, I can't believe it!" exclaimed Cookie. "I must have gotten mixed up and made the same date with both of them." Two tall young men (exactly the same height) were approaching the group in front of Weld from different directions.

"They really do look very much alike," remarked Lauren as they drew nearer. "How *do* you tell them apart?"

Cookie lowered her voice. "There is one big difference

between them, something very private, you know. Do you think *that* really matters?"

But there was no time to answer, for the Davids were upon them. Cookie stepped over to greet them ("Hi, guys!"), brazening it out, and they looked at each other suspiciously. Just then the firemen came out of Weld Hall to announce that it had only been a false alarm and that everyone could go back in.

The group began to shuffle into the dorm, and Lauren and Emily lingered behind, as if by agreement. The fire engine drove off in one direction; Cookie, with a David on either side, walked away in another. Helena left Lauren and Emily, promising that she would show them Augustine Wedgwood's letter some other time. Lauren saw Debbie moving in with the crowd. And the Princess was a little apart, with her fur and her extremely attractive security guard. The track trophy and the gym shorts brought up the rear, but Lauren was thinking about Emily's roommates.

Emily Ravello, Cookie Fink, Helena Dichter, Debbie Doyle, Princess Yazmin. Someone in the Freshman Dean's Office must have thought they would make an exciting, diverse rooming group: a senator's daughter who was a brilliant mime, a nose-obsessed Beverly Hills cheerleader, Augustine Wedgwood's favorite teenage American poetess, Long Island's most irritating harpist, and an Arab princess attended by James Bond. Diverse, thought Lauren. Harvard loves to be diverse. But she was overcome by a sense of relief that she was not a part of that diverse combination. It was too much, too intense, too something— Lauren felt that something about that combination of five roommates was very, very wrong.

And then everyone had gone back into the dorm, and Lauren and Emily were left alone with each other in Harvard Yard.

"Lauren," said Emily at last, "let's room together next year."

"Yes," said Lauren, smiling, with a sense of relief. Relief that Emily remembered, that Emily agreed, mingled with relief that the fire alarm had been false, that Weld Hall was still standing before them, that Harvard Yard was peaceful again.

Every spring, the sixteen hundred Harvard freshmen who live in Harvard Yard choose roommates for the three years to come. Each rooming group of two or three or four or five students moves as a unit from the Yard to one of the Harvard Houses to live together in an upperclassmen's suite. Those spring weeks, when rooming combinations are being formed, are the most tense and traumatic weeks of freshman year. Even exam period does not generate the same excruciating air of anxiety and insecurity. Choosing roommates makes you realize who your real friends are. Someone might like you a lot but not quite enough to want to live with you. Someone else might want to live with you but not want to live with your best friend. Or you might find yourself trying to explain tactfully to someone that you wouldn't room with her in a million years. Every year a number of people find themselves friendless, forlorn, and hurt.

For Lauren the process was both tense and exciting. She made a list of all her friends and acquaintances who could even remotely be considered as possible roommates, and then she spent many fascinated hours sorting the names, ranking them in various orders of preference according to different criteria, annotating them with all the information she could bring to mind. This is what Lauren liked best about Harvard, considering, reconsidering, and speculating about her classmates, all those who like herself had been so selectively admitted into the most famous university in America.

And so, armed with her list of possible roommates, she had consulted her best friend, Michael. They had spent many hours lamenting that *they* couldn't room together, since freedom of choice was restricted by the proviso that boys choose boys and girls choose girls. Lauren and Michael had reviewed together Lauren's list of girls and then Michael's list of boys (ranked strictly in order of cuteness). Then Lauren consulted Carol, her freshman roommate in Thayer, and they agreed that although they had gotten along well freshman year, it would be more adventurous to look for new roommates for next year. And so, after much reviewing and consulting, Lauren had realized that the person she most wanted to room with (after Michael, of course) was Emily.

"Anyone else?" said Emily, for that was the obvious next question. Would they room together as a twosome, or would they put together a larger group?

"Don't know," said Lauren cautiously. And then, coming right out with the thing that was most on her mind, she asked, "What about your roommates?"

"Don't know," said Emily, also wary. "Were you thinking of one of them in particular?"

"Don't know," said Lauren. "Say, for instance, what would you think of rooming with the Princess?" She paused. "And of course J.B."

Emily grinned lewdly. Generally it was she who teased Lauren about J.B. rather than vice versa. Though they both agreed that he was gorgeous, A-plus, Emily's true crush object was a very distinguished professor of American history who looked, Lauren thought, suspiciously senatorial, rather like Emily's father.

"I think J.B. was upset by the fire alarm," said Emily. "You know, not as perfectly cool as usual. We had another alarm in the fall, and he reacted as if it were all part of a plot to kidnap Her Royal Highness. Her cousin, the heir to the emirate, was assassinated in Paris around then, so J.B. was especially on his guard."

"I'd like to catch him off his guard sometime," said Lauren.

"I'll bet," said Emily, "but you know, it's a little scary living with a roommate who has to be constantly protected from assassination and kidnapping, even if you don't think she's really in any danger."

"You don't?"

"No," said Emily, and Lauren suddenly saw that Emily naturally had a stake in believing that the daughters of important political figures were not really in danger. If Emily's father were to run for President, would she herself need security protection?

Lauren tried to change the subject. "If we room with

the Princess, then I get a shot at J.B.," said Lauren, "but if we room with Cookie, I think you'd have a good chance of getting one of those identical Davids."

"I thought you could only get them as a matched set," replied Emily. And then, seriously, she added, "Cookie is amazing, Cookie is a scream, Cookie is a laugh a minute—but I really don't want to room with her again. I'm tired of hearing about how I need a nose job. I can't tell anymore whether she means well or whether she's a bitch. There's definitely something wrong with Cookie, like she's a cheerleader without a soul or something, and on top of all that she's stupid and completely illiterate—she never reads anything except science texts, *Seventeen*, and *Cosmopolitan*."

"How did she ever get into Harvard?" wondered Lauren. "What's she doing here?"

"Cookie gets A's in her courses," said Emily.

"Which is more than can be said for you and me," finished Lauren. "Another reason not to room with her. What do you think of Helena?"

"She's sweet," said Emily, "and she's certainly not illiterate; maybe the opposite problem, you know, a little bit affected. But she does get letters from Augustine Wedgwood, so I suppose she's entitled to some affectation. I'm pretty impressed by those letters—and I don't even like Wedgwood."

"I don't, either, really, but still, he is Augustine Wedgwood." Lauren liked poets who rhymed. She liked Byron and Kipling and Doctor Seuss. She knew this was not the mark of sophisticated poetic taste, but she did not care. "Do Helena's poems rhyme?"

"No."

"Never?"

"Never. Another thing about Helena—she spends hours in the shower rubbing essences into her hair so it will have all those lights she's so proud of. If you room with her, you have to expect limited access to the shower."

"Hmm." Lauren herself had been known to spend quite a bit of time tending to her hair, long and dark. She was very vain about it.

"But the worst of Helena," continued Emily, "is that she's such good friends with Debbie."

"What does she see in Debbie?"

"Helena thinks art is more important than anything, and Debbie is an artist. I think Helena somehow imagines them as the sister muses, poetry and music, something like that. And I think that Helena might want to room with you and me *and* Debbie—and frankly I'd sooner die. I'm not even sure I want to room with someone who's friends with Debbie, because after freshman year I don't ever want to see her again. In fact, as far as I'm concerned, she can drop dead immediately." Emily was holding to herself the caftan and the photograph. And then she seemed to relent a little. "It's not just Debbie," she said. "I think it's all five of us. I think we bring out the worst in each other." And then, after a pause, "Did I ever tell you about the sixth roommate?"

"The sixth roommate?" Lauren was fascinated. Actually, she had once or twice tried to imagine herself as a sixth roommate in Emily's suite—but her imagination had failed her.

"Once upon a time," said Emily, "way back in September, there was a sixth roommate. She was a farmgirl from Iowa named Betty Jane or Mary Lou or something like that—I really can't remember—and anyway, Betty Jane or Mary Lou arrived at Harvard cheery and fresh, with pigtails and dimples—the easiest person in the world to get along with; she even volunteered to be the one to sleep in the living room. After two weeks with her new roommates—that is, with the five of us—she ran out of the dormitory in the middle of the night, screaming that she was going to come back with a hatchet. But instead she found her way to Stillman Infirmary, where she was sedated and put to bed for a week, after which Harvard managed to come up with a single room for her in the hope of preserving what was left of her sanity. The funny thing is, I don't think anyone was especially mean to her or anything—somehow just the way we naturally behaved was enough to drive her out of her mind. I guess that proves that the five of us really do deserve each other."

Lauren was thinking: When it comes to roommates, this year's or next year's, somehow men have nothing to do with anything. It feels like Radcliffe, like an all-girls school. Or more like the ghost of Radcliffe, since nowadays Radcliffe is only a name, and everyone, male and female, is really a Harvard student. Lauren, too, shivering cold in the middle of Harvard Yard.

"I'm really not sure I want to go on rooming with any of these roommates next year," Emily was saying. "I have a feeling it would be unlucky. If the five of us make it through the rest of freshman year without killing each other, I, for one, will consider it a triumph."

2
Down, Strumpet!

■

*One might well wonder how it was that Agathocles,
and others like him, after countless treacheries and
cruelties, could live securely in his own country and
hold foreign enemies at bay.*

Machiavelli

Lauren was reading Machiavelli, and Emily was reading
Shakespeare, two Harvard freshmen absorbed in their
Renaissance heritage. It was almost midnight, the next
night after the fire alarm, and they were lying on Emily's
bed in her little box of a room. Emily was wearing the
new caftan, one broad maroon sleeve draped over Lauren's
shoulder as they studied side by side. It was a narrow bed,
intended no doubt for one of those tall, skinny, chaste,
Puritan males who monopolized Harvard in dreary past
ages when the university could not even have imagined
the advent of Lauren and Emily. The little room was
virtually overwhelmed by the presence, at the foot of the
bed, of an enormous Indian sculpture: three deities, two
female and one male, almost life-size, copulating ingeniously
and exquisitely. Many years ago, when Emily was a child,
her father had been the American ambassador to Thailand.

19

Since then, her family had occasionally returned to southern Asia, and Emily had acquired this erotic masterpiece last summer in Sri Lanka.

"I just finished the last act of *Othello*," said Emily. "I think that final scene—when he kills her—is just incredibly sexy."

"Me, too." They were both silent for a moment, thinking perhaps about Moors. Then Emily had an idea. "Listen. Let's act out the last scene. The lines keep going through my head."

"Okay, let's do it," Lauren agreed, not suggesting that they act out Machiavelli instead.

"I'll go borrow Helena's copy. She's in the Shakespeare course, too." Emily rose from the bed, shook out the sleeves of her caftan, and stepped out of the room. Helena's room was two doors away in the same suite.

A minute later, Emily returned, laden down with the collected works of William Shakespeare in one very heavy volume. Emily herself had bought little paperbacks of the individual assigned plays, instinctively rebelling against the professor's recommended collection. "I can't believe how heavy this is," she said.

"It's the perfect murder weapon," suggested Lauren. "Don't you think Othello really ought to have murdered Desdemona with the collected works of William Shakespeare?"

"The perfect crime," Emily agreed. "But the Venetian Council would only have had to open the murder weapon to the inside front cover to discover that the murderer was Helena Dichter of Weld Hall. Take a look at this. Have you ever seen such artistic handwriting?" Lauren sat up to examine the delicate curls of the signature with which Helena had marked her Shakespeare. "If you ask me," Emily continued, "there's something a little psycho about writing your name so beautifully. Some kind of phenomenal self-obsession."

Lauren knew that this comment was intended as part of the ongoing debate. She put the question aloud. "Are we going to invite her to room with us?"

"I just don't know. I think she really wants to be asked.

She mentioned the latest letter from Augustine Wedgwood again and how much she wants to let you and me have a glimpse of it." Emily had fallen almost automatically into an exact imitation of Helena's soft, reverent references to Wedgwood's letters. And then she caught herself. "I'm being a bitch, aren't I?" said Emily. "Come on, let's do the scene."

"You can be Othello," said Lauren. "The caftan is perfect."

Lauren pulled Emily's blanket up to her neck, opened the enormous Shakespeare before her, and found her place. She looked up at Emily and said, " 'Will you come to bed, my lord?' "

" 'Have you prayed tonight, Desdemona?' "

It was frightening how suddenly Emily had transformed herself into Othello. Her expression was so dark, so intent upon death, that Lauren could barely bring out the reply " 'Aye my lord.' "

" 'If you bethink yourself of any crime,' " continued Emily, " 'unreconciled as yet to heaven and grace, solicit for it straight.' "

" 'Alack, my lord, what may you mean by that?' "

" 'Well, do it, and be brief. I will walk by. I would not kill thy unprepared spirit. No, heavens forfend, I would not kill thy soul.' " Emily stood at the foot of the bed before the erotic Hindu trio, which now took on a sinister air.

" 'Talk you of killing?' " recited Lauren, and she shivered.

" 'Aye, I do,' " proclaimed Emily. Then she lifted her finger to her lips and emerged from the part. She pointed silently to the door of the room, on which was posted a big photograph of Jean-Louis Barrault—Emily's favorite mime— in *Children of Paradise*, and Lauren's eyes and ears followed Emily's gesture. Lauren caught just the faintest hint of someone breathing on the other side of the narrow door, and in a moment she, too, was certain that someone was standing there, listening to the Shakespearean dialogue.

It was by no means the first case of snooping among Emily and her four ill-assorted freshman roommates. They all collected little bits of information about each other.

Emily herself, for instance, had stopped keeping a journal after the cozy afternoon in December when she and Helena and Debbie and the Princess had sat in the communal living room, drinking cocoa and reading aloud from Cookie's diary, a hysterically funny catalog of shopping expeditions and dates with Davids. The five girls lived in five adjoining rooms opening on to the same corridor, which led to the shared living room. Doors within the suite had no locks.

Now both Emily and Lauren stared at Jean-Louis Barrault and wondered who was on the other side of the door. Emily's eyes lit up with inspiration. "'Down, strumpet!'" she cried out, approaching Lauren but aiming her voice at the door.

Lauren immediately took the cue and jumped to the end of the scene. "'Kill me tomorrow,'" she cried, "'let me live tonight.'" She, too, was performing for the unseen audience.

They finished the scene by scuffling noisily with Emily's pillow, attempting to suggest the smothering of Desdemona. This gave way to a dramatic silence, the silence of death, during which both girls strained to hear the breathing on the other side of the door. "Whoever she was, she's gone," whispered Emily. "There's no one there now. I hope we scared the hell out of her. I hope she has nightmares about being murdered in bed." There was an opening and closing of doors in the corridor, and then, even as Lauren was staring at Jean-Louis Barrault, a sharp knock from the other side. Lauren caught her breath.

"Who's there?" called Emily from the bed, still preserving a trace of Othello in her voice.

"Cookie." The name itself, let alone the voice, was reassuringly comical. Then the door opened, and Cookie walked right in. "Hi, guys." She was wearing a transparent pink nightie that descended almost far enough to cover the matching pink panties. In one hand she carried *Cosmopolitan,* her own kind of Renaissance reading. "I heard a lot of yelling and noise coming from in here."

"We were acting out a scene from a Shakespeare play," said Emily.

"Shakespeare. Hmm." Cookie was trying to place the name. She succeeded. "Did he write *Romeo and Juliet*?"

"Among other things," said Emily, keeping a straight face.

"I went to see the movie with my high school English class," explained Cookie. "God, we all cried. And my best girlfriend, whose name was Juliet Moscowitz, she lost her virginity that week. Can you believe it?"

Emily gave Lauren a glance that meant: Can you believe *her*? And how can we possibly consider rooming with her? But Emily said only, "So what's new, Cookie?"

Cookie sat down on the bed with Lauren and Emily, settling her diaphanous nightie around her. "Well, guys," she said, very obviously about to make an announcement, "tonight's the night." Lauren and Emily waited with bated breath. "Tonight's the night I decide whether it's going to be David or David. They both really want me to choose. And I have so much work in chemistry and physics this semester that I just don't seem to have the time to keep both of them happy, so I've decided that this is it." Lauren could now see the cover of Cookie's *Cosmopolitan*. Next to Brooke Shields, who was photographed radiant and ready for spring, were the article titles set forth to lure the reader onward and inward. At the very top, right next to Brooke's big red hoop earring, was the title "Your Sexual Satisfaction—What Really Matters." Cookie was studying up for the big decision.

"How will you ever decide?" asked Emily, leading Cookie on.

"I'm going to give them each one more chance. David's coming tonight at midnight, and then David's coming at one, and after that I'm going to make myself decide, and then I'll call them both up to let them know who wins, and then I hope I'll still have an hour to study for my chemistry midterm tomorrow."

Lauren and Emily were both dazed. Finally, Emily managed to say something. "May the best man win."

"That's just what I said to them this afternoon!" exclaimed Cookie. And then she added irrelevantly, "Emily, you know, all those creases in your new robe . . ."

"I know," said Emily sharply. "It was folded up in its box longer than necessary."

"But Emily," Cookie continued, "if you just hang it up in the bathroom overnight, the steam from the shower will take out the creases."

"That's not a bad idea."

"Here, give it to me," said Cookie, tugging at the sleeve. "I'll hang it up for you—I'm on my way to the bathroom, anyway."

Emily had taken off the caftan from over her clothes and passed it to Cookie, who was already moving to the door. "I've gotta hurry," she was saying. "It's almost midnight, and David's going to get here any minute."

"Good luck with your decision," said Lauren.

"Good luck with chemistry," said Emily. "Thanks for hanging that up for me."

"'Bye, guys," said Cookie, but at Emily's door she paused before the photograph of Jean-Louis Barrault. "Boy, this guy really needs a nose job." And on that note Cookie made her exit.

Then there were doors opening and closing, movements in the corridor, the muffled sound of voices. "Methinks yon David arriveth," whispered Emily. "He hath but one short hour to show his stuff."

The next knock on Emily's door was Helena Dichter. She wore a long white Queen Anne's lace nightgown—a striking contrast to Emily, who was now in her usual mime's black. Helena's hair, with all its lovely lights, fell over her shoulders, and she paused in the doorway as if aware that the frame was becoming to her. She did not actually enter the room and sit down on the bed until Emily had insisted a second time. Hesitancy to intrude mingled perhaps a little too obviously with readiness to be importuned.

In Helena's hand was the letter that had arrived that morning from Cornwall. She sat between Lauren and Emily with the hallowed sheet of paper still folded in thirds in her lacy lap. "I hope that He wouldn't mind my showing it to you," said Helena, her tone suggesting the capitalized pronoun for the Poet. She looked from Lauren to Emily with an expression calculated to convey anguished delicacy.

It was really no more than a note, and Helena read it aloud in a hushed tone while Lauren and Emily looked over her shoulders at the shaky, spidery handwriting of the eighty-year-old poet.

> My dear Helena,
> Thank you for sending me your poem "To a Poet." It is a truly fine piece of work.
> I can not accept your flattering suggestion that the subject of the poem is myself. The poet you apostrophize is the poet you yourself will one day be. I can see that your talent is developing very rapidly indeed.
> I am glad to hear that you are happy at Harvard. If, as you say, there is a chance that you will be in England this summer, I hope you will come to call on me in Cornwall.
> Affectueusement,
Augustine Wedgwood

Quickly Helena folded her letter again, as if afraid that exposure to the dormitory air would make the precious characters fade. "Isn't it beautiful?" she whispered.

"Beautiful," Emily agreed a little shortly.

"*Are* you going to England this summer?" asked Lauren.

"I hope so. There's a special program in English literature at Oxford during the summer, and I really think that being in England would help me to feel closer to the English poets."

"And to one in particular," suggested Emily, and Helena responded with a lovely blush.

Changing the subject, Helena stared at the folded letter in her lap and asked, "Have you been thinking about next year?" It was not necessary to be more specific than that. Lauren and Emily understood precisely what she meant.

"The only thing we've definitely decided," said Emily, "is that the two of us will room together." Which implied:

we haven't decided about third, fourth, or fifth persons. "How about you?" asked Emily. "Are you going to be rooming with Debbie?" Which implied: if you are, then you should forget about rooming with us, because I can't stand Debbie.

Helena said nothing.

"I really don't think Debbie likes me," said Emily tactfully, and then tried to change the subject. "Thanks for lending me your Shakespeare." She handed over the heavy volume.

"Debbie thinks *you* don't like *her*," Helena insisted, taking the book. There was an embarrassing silence. "I should go to sleep." Helena rose from between them. "His letters make me so happy," she declared from the door, indifferent to Jean-Louis Barrault. "Even if I died tonight, I think I would die happy, knowing that He thinks I'm a real poet." Exit.

"If she died tonight," remarked Emily to Lauren a moment later, "we wouldn't have to worry about whether or not we want to room with her."

"If you put it that way," replied Lauren, "it does sort of sound like we've come to a decision."

"Yes and no. Deciding not to room with her probably means having to *tell* her that we've decided not to room with her, and I'm not sure I'm coldhearted enough to do that easily. If she died tonight, happily thinking that He thinks she's a poet, then we wouldn't have to tell her and make her unhappy." Emily paused. "Hey, what do you think of that invitation to go visit Wedgwood in Cornwall? Isn't that a kink?"

"Is it? Isn't Augustine Wedgwood only interested in little boys?"

"Oh, no!" Emily exclaimed. "It's little girls for Augustine Wedgwood! All those wives of his—he married them when they were sixteen or so. And back in the early fifties there was some sort of terrible scandal about him and a little girl who was quite a bit younger than that. I think somebody once told me that Nabokov wrote *Lolita* with Augustine Wedgwood in mind."

"Emily, you always know everything worth knowing.
But surely Helena is no Lolita?"

"No, she's not. But Augustine Wedgwood isn't getting
any younger himself."

"My God," said Lauren. "Do you think that Helena is
actually going to end up becoming Augustine Wedgwood's
lover? What a notch on the bedpost that would be."

"The bedpost of twentieth-century literature."

"The nitty-gritty doesn't sound too appetizing, but what
a way to think of yourself when it's all over: Augustine
Wedgwood's Lover."

"Knowing Helena," said Emily, "I don't think it's all that
unlikely she'd write a poem about the experience. What I
don't understand is why Augustine Wedgwood's lover would
want to be Debbie Doyle's roommate."

"Is Helena the only one in the suite with Debbie's
friends now?" asked Lauren.

"The only one," Emily replied. "For some reason Debbie's
never been horrible to Helena. Debbie and I can't stand
each other, and it's been that way since September. Cookie hates Debbie even more than I do now, even though
there was a time when they were friends. They used to
talk about diets together all the time, and Cookie firmly
committed herself to the public position that Debbie
doesn't need a nose job, just a really professional make-
over. I must say it would have to be some make-over. How
much powder and paint does it take to hide a sour soul?"

"Does Cookie know that afterwards Debbie used to
steal her diary and read it aloud in the living room?"

"What do you mean afterwards? That was when they
were still friends. Cookie never found out about it, though,
because none of us can comfortably tell. Helena, Her
Royal Highness, and I were listening and laughing. I think
that makes us accessories."

"Real roommates," commented Lauren, disturbed and
fascinated.

"Yes, I suppose we do deserve each other," said Emily,
responding to what Lauren had left unsaid. "Though I
wonder whether we really deserve Debbie. Sometimes I
feel as if she makes us the way we are, as if she brings out

bad things in us. Have I ever told you the story about Debbie and the wrong number?"

"Tell me," said Lauren, settling back on the bed, knowing that Emily was a great raconteuse. Her stories about her roommates were her masterpieces.

"It happened in January during exam period," Emily began. "We were all in the worst possible moods and particularly hostile to each other. One night, very late, the phone rang, and it happened that all five of us were at home, studying in bed. I remember the exact moment that I heard the phone ring, because for some reason— exam-period tension, you know—it terrified me. I suddenly had this awful fear I used to have years ago when I was a child—the fear that one night the phone would ring in our house, my mother would answer, and it would turn out that my father had been assassinated. You know, everyone was being assassinated back then, and diplomats were being taken hostage, and I knew my father had been friends with Robert Kennedy, and I became a little obsessed with the whole thing. Well, for some reason, it came back to me that night a few months ago when I was studying for my Chinese Civilization exam.

"Anyway, when I heard the phone, I went to the door of my room and stepped out into the corridor, and at the same moment Helena and Cookie and Her Royal Highness opened their doors and came out, too. And we could all look down the corridor and see Debbie standing by the phone in the living room—it was as if she'd been waiting there, as if she knew there was going to be a call. She let it ring three more times while we stood there and watched her—it might have been done to annoy us, but it almost looked like a sort of superstition. Then she picked up the phone, listened for a moment, and—by then I was certain that my father was dead—she said, 'You have a wrong number,' and hung up.

"Probably it really was a wrong number, but Debbie, being Debbie, managed to say, 'You have a wrong number,' in a tone that suggested that she was lying, that someone had asked to talk to one of us and Debbie was being nasty and refusing to pass on the call. I remember being enraged because I had been sure the call was for me—but at the same time I was a tiny bit amused, because, after all, the call might have been for Cookie or Helena or Her Royal Highness. And I remember being absolutely certain that the three of them were feeling exactly the same way, furious at Debbie but a little bit titillated by the consummate nastiness of the scene, by the way Debbie had managed to make something so emotionally explosive out of a wrong number. We all turned back into our rooms without saying a word. But the next morning I just casually checked the front page of the *New York Times* to make sure that nothing had happened to my father.

"So I've been analyzing that incident, because I think it contains all sorts of hidden clues about how the five of us work together as such a disastrous rooming combination. One of the things I've been thinking is that perhaps Debbie Doyle doesn't really exist at all. Perhaps her personality—the distilled essence of disagreeableness—is somehow created by the alchemy of all the little hostilities among the rest of us, the product of our combined accumulation of contempt, irritation, and selfishness. It might even be metaphysically connected to Debbie's diet, the way she stops eating so her hips will slim down and instead her breasts disappear. My theory is that if we all tried to control our bad thoughts, then Debbie would disappear. What do you think?"

Just at that moment, almost as if Debbie had been listening to Emily's monologue, the lovely muffled notes of the harp came to them through the wall, reminding them that the fifth roommate was not only the essence of disagreeableness but also an artist.

Lauren and Emily lay on the bed in silence, listening. It had never been questioned among the five roommates that Debbie, much as they may have disliked her, was welcome to play on her harp at any hour of the night. Far from keeping them awake, it inspired a wonderful drowsiness and filled the suite with an unaccustomed spirit of harmony. When Debbie sat at her harp, she herself was

hidden away in her room, and it was as if her unpleasantness had simply been turned off by the music.

Lauren began to feel contentedly sleepy. From the wall
came magical music and from the window the no less
potent magic of the spring night air. Lauren was thinking
about how happy she was to be at Harvard, about the
trees in Harvard Yard, about sitting on the grass that
afternoon, surrounded by the old brick buildings that
were so essentially Harvardian. New Jersey, she thought,
had been no fun at all, but now it was behind her forever.
She thought about how wonderful it was to have a friend
as extraordinary as Emily: Emily as a brilliant mime,
Emily as Othello, Emily with her impossible roommates
and her infatuation with a certain distinguished professor
of American history. Lauren also thought about her other
best friend, Michael, who was in his way every bit as
extraordinary. And perhaps it was just as well that Emily
and Michael were a little wary of each other, since that
way Lauren could luxuriate in two distinctly separate
friendships, two enchanted spheres. It left her feeling all
the more abundantly content. Even Machiavelli seemed
charming.

Lauren and Emily realized at the same moment that
there were now other sounds competing with those of
Debbie's harp, and the new notes were coming from an
immediately identifiable instrument and a well-practiced
artist. Turning away from the harp music, Lauren and
Emily watched the other wall, stifling their laughter. On
the other side was Cookie Fink and somebody else, and
Cookie was noisily letting him know how happy he was
making her. Back in the fall, *Cosmo* had run a special
feature entitled "How *He* Feels About How *You* Feel" in
which a number of men had candidly discussed with a
Cosmopolitan reporter the kinds of female responsiveness
that made them feel most successfully masculine. That
month Cookie had studied the article as carefully as she
studied her chemistry text; *Cosmopolitan* could indeed
provide information that one would never be able to learn
from *Seventeen*. Cookie had applied her new noises to
making both Davids feel ever so successfully masculine,

and now it was little wonder that she could no longer manage to decide which one she actually preferred.

Lauren looked at the clock and saw that it was just after one. Either the midnight David was staying late, or the one o'clock David was early and eager. What would happen, she wondered, if the two Davids were actually to meet in Cookie's room? Wasn't Cookie playing a dangerous game? What if one of the Davids ended up smashing that wonder of twentieth-century technology, Cookie's nose? The nose, Lauren supposed, could always be refixed, but some acts of violence could not be undone.

It was late. Lauren knew that she should be getting back to her own dorm, but then the music of the harp began to predominate again as Cookie subsided, and Lauren was overcome by an even more powerful wave of delicious sleepiness. Emily was already dozing. Lauren watched her sleeping friend for a moment, thinking how beautiful, how strikingly beautiful, Emily was. And then, a moment later, Lauren herself was dozing off to sleep, fully dressed, in Emily's narrow, uncomfortable bed.

Lauren slept with the notes of the harp weaving in and out of her dreams. She dreamed that she was waking up, putting on her shoes, that she was almost flying across Harvard Yard to return to her own room. She knew she had to escape from something very frightening in Emily's room—was it the assassination of Emily's father? Was it the Indian sculpture coming to life?—but when she finally managed to get back to her own room in Thayer Hall, she realized that she had ended up back in her parents' house in New Jersey. She woke up at that point and knew where she was by the harp music, which still came through the wall. Was Debbie going to play all night long? The music put Lauren right back to sleep again until morning.

Not until the next day did Lauren learn that Debbie Doyle had been murdered during the night.

3
Hell and the Freshman Union

■

After they had finished eating and all the other entertainment usual at such banquets was done with, Oliverotto artfully started to touch on subjects of grave importance.

Machiavelli

The following evening at dinnertime Lauren arrived at the Freshman Union, feeling that she was on the edge of some sort of emotional collapse. She had spent the entire afternoon, an endless and grueling afternoon, in the police station, being interrogated, then waiting, being interrogated again, then waiting some more. She had been asked to answer so many questions about the details of the night before that she could almost believe that what had happened had truly happened—but still, wasn't it too bizarre, too terrifying? Could it possibly be true?—that last night, while Lauren slept, someone had been murdered in the next room.

She stood on the front steps of the Union, and hundreds of students passed around her on their way in for dinner and on their way out after having eaten. She overheard fragments of conversation—about teams, about courses, about roommates—but she heard no one saying anything about the murder. And yet surely rumors were already circulating about a murder in the freshman class; surely by tomorrow it would be in the *Crimson* and everyone would know. Lauren nodded to some of the people going by, and they nodded back, but no one stopped to talk to her. Was it possible that she was somehow marked by the murder, that people could tell from her face that she had been sleeping in the next room, had spent the day being interrogated? Or was it simply that she looked the way she felt—looked like hell—and people were instinctively disinclined to engage her in friendly conversation? But no matter, for Lauren only wanted to talk to one person, and she was waiting for him now. Lauren knew that only Michael, her very best friend at Harvard, could reassure her now, could make her feel human again, could help her understand and resolve her gnawing, confusing, frightening feelings about the murder.

And then, there he was. Lauren felt a rush of relief at the sight of that intimately familiar, dearly beloved face. "Lauren darling," Michael was saying, "*what* is the matter? You look like the tormented heretics in the Sixth Circle of Dante's Inferno." Lauren, who had, after all, gone to a public high school in New Jersey, not to the Phillips Academy at Exeter, had no idea what precisely went on in the Sixth Circle, but it sounded vaguely appropriate to her present psychological state. "I leave you alone for forty-eight hours," Michael was saying, "and you go completely to pieces. Have you been taking care of your skin? It looks to me like you should go to sleep for the next fourteen hours and then spend all day tomorrow with me at Elizabeth Arden's in Boston, getting the full treatment." He paused to catch his breath. "And *where* were you last night? I knocked on your door at ten o'clock, I knocked on your door at eleven o'clock, I knocked on your door at midnight, I knocked at one, and I knocked at two, and then I went to bed like a decent young man. Your roommate, I presume, was spending the night with that incredibly unattractively oversized shot-putter. But where were *you*? And who was *he*, you bad girl? Did he beat you, or did he just keep you awake all night, you poor haggard thing? You know, they say sex is good for one's skin, but I never really believed it, and now I know I was right."

"Wait a minute; calm down," said Lauren, aware that Michael was really quite calm, that he was merely chattering, and that it was herself she was trying to calm. "I wasn't sleeping with anyone last night."

"No?" He seemed rather disappointed.

"I was sleeping with Emily."

Michael raised his eyebrows.

"I mean, I spent the night in Emily's room. And while I was there, during the night, one of Emily's roommates— the one who plays the harp, Debbie Doyle—" Lauren broke off and then made herself finish. "She was murdered. She was knocked unconscious and then strangled with one of her own harp strings."

Michael lived right upstairs from Lauren in Thayer Hall, so it had taken them no time at all to discover each other in September. Lauren, when she had packed up to leave New Jersey forever, had somehow forgotten to take along her Dramatically Different Moisturizing Lotion by Clinique. It was not an inconsequential oversight, and on her second day at Harvard Lauren found herself setting out to explore Harvard Square in search of moisturizer. She got no farther than the front steps of Thayer, however, where she came upon a pretty blond boy apparently immersed in *Lady Windermere's Fan*. Lauren introduced herself in proper freshman fashion, and no sooner had she explained her intended errand than Michael had his first opportunity to prove himself an angel. He had just the little Clinique bottle that she wanted up in his room, and he was delighted to give it to her, since he used quite a different moisturizer in autumn, anyway. This inaugurated both an ongoing symposium on skin care and a beautiful friendship. That very same day they had moved on from skin cream to ice cream and delightedly established their common interest in Henry James, chocolate marzipan, and boys.

Now they passed together through the cafeteria line of the Freshman Union, holding depressingly familiar red plastic trays. In front of Lauren were two steaming pans, Scylla and Charybdis—"Chinese Chicken," with celery and pineapple, and the famous Harvard "Beef Stew," with no readily identifiable ingredients. Facing Lauren from behind these two alluring pans, but separated from her by a curtain of mingling stewish odors, stood a fat woman in a white smock wielding two big serving spoons. Each student who passed by with a plastic tray was presented with a plateful of his or her choice, the Chinese Chicken or the Beef Stew.

"Stew or chicken," barked the fat woman at Lauren, waving her serving spoons menacingly to emphasize the grim alternatives. Lauren shook her head to both and passed on quickly, feeling as if she were about to faint. Michael, right behind her, also declined both stew and chicken, and the fat woman modulated her voice from a bark to an admonishing cluck. "Gotta eat to stay healthy, deary." No comment.

Farther down the line Michael took two little plastic dishes, each of which contained three little purple plums, stewed and sugared. "Only one dessert!" screamed another cafeteria lady, crankily insisting on a rarely enforced rule. "You have to come back if you want more." Michael decided he really didn't want any plums at all, and he and Lauren each ended up with a small serving of cottage cheese and a cup of the famously vile Union coffee. Really, in passing through the cafeteria line, they were both just going through the motions. In their hearts they knew they would end up taking themselves out for dinner at a restaurant. It had happened so many times before.

But now they emerged from the cafeteria and moved out into the great dining hall where more than a thousand of their fellow freshmen were feeding on Chinese Chicken and Beef Stew, creating a tremendous uproar of conversation. Again, Lauren felt faint. The Union was always raucous on nights when the food was particularly vile. Some of the boys—including, no doubt, several brilliant mathematicians or classicists and any number of future congressmen—had begun to throw plums at each other. Lauren lacked the energy to be either amused or contemptuous. Enormous portraits of distinguished alumni—university presidents and Supreme Court justices—looked down from the walls, concealing behind their somber expressions the memories of the times when they, too, had thrown plums at each other in days of yore.

Lauren and Michael found places in the far back corner, outside the center of the Union clamor, and finally faced each other across two plastic trays.

"With a harp string," said Michael, just loud enough to be heard over the din, and he raised his hands protectively, nervously, to his throat.

"Yes," said Lauren. "Horrible." And she couldn't help copying Michael's gesture. All afternoon she had been trying to resist the impulse to caress her own neck, and all afternoon she had been giving in.

"Horrible," Michael agreed, "but also beautiful, even elegant. An elegant way to murder someone. And an elegant way to die."

Lauren knew what he meant, but right now she was unable to accept it. "No, just horrible," she insisted. Michael, after all, had not been there last night, sleeping in the room next door to the murdered victim. And Michael had not spent the day being interrogated by the police.

Tactfully, Michael said no more about elegance. "The harpist," he said thoughtfully, "the harpist is the roommate Cookie hates—hated, I suppose. Something to do with chemistry. Cookie is passionately intense about getting an A in her chemistry course."

Surely one of the most outstanding social eccentricities in this year's freshman class was that Michael Hunt and Cookie Fink enjoyed an extremely improbable friendship. They had been friends, in fact, long before Lauren and Emily, dating from that autumn day when Cookie had approached Michael in Harvard Yard to inform him that she had decided, after careful comparative study, that he had the best male nose in the freshman class. She wanted his permission to examine it up close for a minute. Michael, of course, had immediately appreciated that Cookie was a completely unique character, but he was also always tremendously vain about his nose and was pleased to be approached on its account. He could not resist explaining to Cookie that his was the archetypal Boston Brahmin nose, and from that day they had carried on a friendship of sorts, though their conversation tended to be limited to one subject: Michael's nose. Apparently, at least on one occasion, they had also discussed Cookie's roommates.

"Yes," said Lauren. She remembered Cookie the night of the fire alarm. "Debbie had held on to some chemistry papers, something Cookie needed to prepare for her midterm." Just as she had held onto the caftan from Emily's father. It was as if Debbie studied her roommates to figure out just what really mattered to them, just where they were most vulnerable . . . and then she attacked. It was not difficult to imagine someone—any of her roommates, for instance—wanting to murder Debbie. But . . . but . . . what was it Debbie had done to make someone go from wanting to murder her . . . to doing it.

"Do you think . . ." asked Lauren, and before she could finish the sentence, before she even knew how exactly she was going to finish it, she had already realized its fateful significance. Almost automatically she had begun to investigate.

Two seconds before, Lauren would have sworn that she wanted nothing in the world so much as to forget about the murder that had happened last night in Weld Hall and never to think about it again. But now she was aware of some deep, hidden impulse, buried beneath her exhaustion, that wanted to figure out exactly what had happened and who had done it.

"Well, well, well," said Michael, who could not be fooled, who knew Lauren too well to misunderstand the implications of that unfinished question. "Well, well, well, well, well. But let's not kid ourselves about what it means to be going into these matters."

Lauren nodded to indicate that she understood. "I

think I see why Cookie hated Debbie," she said, "but why . . ."

"Why did Debbie hate Cookie?" Michael finished for her.

"Exactly." Lauren found herself perversely distracted, discussing Emily's roommates as if they were all still alive, trying to puzzle out their feelings toward each other.

"I have a feeling," said Michael, "that Cookie was always giving Debbie advice she wasn't really grateful for. For instance, I think Cookie was very proud of realizing just what was going wrong with Debbie's diet—and I think she told Debbie."

"Because Cookie hated her?"

"Oh, no, no, no, no." Michael was amused. "This was *before*, when they were still *friends!*" Had Cookie known, Lauren wondered, that Debbie was reading aloud from Cookie's diary? "Cookie meant it all in a friendly way," Michael continued. "You know, for Cookie that's what life is all about—diet problems, makeup options, plastic surgery. She's a walking women's magazine." Obviously Michael and Cookie *had* managed to talk about other things besides Michael's nose. Apparently even Cookie, oblivious Cookie, couldn't help being interested in her roommates and couldn't help talking about them. "Actually, as I recall," Michael was saying, "Debbie was the one roommate who really didn't need any plastic surgery at all according to Cookie. Cookie thought what Debbie really needed was a good make-over, but Debbie declined because she had too many inhibitions."

"Inhibitions about make-overs?"

"Yes, that was the word Cookie used, inhibitions. Cookie's own special interpretation of psychoanalysis—she is an amazing creature, completely inhuman. But she knows a good nose when she sees one." Michael stroked his fondly.

"No wonder Debbie ended up hating her, though. It can't have been any fun to have a friend who pointed out diet problems and pushed make-overs, even if Debbie was excused from plastic surgery."

"Ahh." Michael had thought of something. "Now *this* is interesting. Do you know what Cookie told me about Debbie after she found out about those chemistry notes?"

Suddenly Lauren was frightened. "That she wanted to kill her?"

"That she wanted to smash her face in and reset it so it would be the ugliest face in the world."

Michael repeated the line with a certain relish, and Lauren had to look away. She looked over Michael's shoulder, and before her was the whole freshman class eating dinner. Debbie Doyle was murdered last night, but everything else was just as before. Her classmates were throwing plums at each other. Boys were still boys.

Lauren looked higher and observed that the Union was also still the Union. She was sometimes a little dizzy when she looked up at the high, high ceiling of the Freshman Union, and this evening she had been shaky to begin with. The chandeliers were made out of grotesque configurations of antlers, and they gave very little light. Could they possibly be real antlers? Had somebody once told her that they were Theodore Roosevelt's antlers? No, surely not. Perhaps Theodore Roosevelt's hunting trophies—he, too, had once been a Harvard freshman. If the freshman class was now forty percent female, why did the Union still feel so oppressively male? How could Radcliffe have been so completely swallowed up by the Harvard Freshman Union? High ceilings, dark wood walls, gruesome portraits, and no light. And the hall was big enough to hold almost the entire freshman class. It was monstrous. How could everyone be so lively in such a creepy building on such a creepy evening? Well, boys were boys. And the Union was the Union. And Harvard was Harvard, and it would just go on being Harvard, century after century, with or without Debbie Doyle. Lauren's gaze returned to Michael's preppie collar and then focused on his perfect Brahmin nose.

"Lauren darling," Michael was saying. "Are you listening? Are you all right?"

"Sure, fine," said Lauren unconvincingly.

"You look as if you're about to swoon."

"It's been a strange day," pleaded Lauren. "I'm sorry I'm so distracted. Tell me what you were saying."

"Nothing really, I was just saying that Cookie thought Debbie was interested in one of Cookie's two identical boyfriends. She once saw Debbie whispering with him when he was supposedly coming to pick up Cookie. Not that Cookie was seriously worried about losing a man to Debbie. . . ." Michael's voice trailed off. He, too, seemed a little dizzy. "With a harp string," he said, and once again lifted his hands to his neck.

"A harp string and a blunt object," said Lauren. "Don't forget the traditional blunt object. You know, from the inside of Debbie's room—I've been inside once—a harp string couldn't have helped seeming like the obvious murder weapon. She was always retuning the harp, and there were old strings lying around the room the way the girls on my floor leave dental floss in the bathroom."

"A disgusting habit," commented Michael, "but nothing at all, I assure you, compared to the mess that the football players on my floor—pigs every one of them—leave in our bathroom. Unfortunately, they don't leave anything with which I could murder them. I mean, what kind of murder weapon could you make out of empty aerosol cans and semen-stained copies of *Playboy* magazine?"

Lauren, however, was thinking about harp strings. "I wish I could picture the scene—the scene of the crime, you know."

"I can't even picture the victim," said Michael. "I can't remember whether I've ever actually met her."

"I'm sure you've seen her a hundred times," said Lauren. "That was sort of the point about Debbie Doyle—she could never have made any sort of impression on a stranger. She was so plain, so deeply spiritually plain, so uninteresting to look at, that you would never have noticed her. Last night Emily said—" Lauren hesitated.

"Go on," said Michael encouragingly. "I understand it isn't a nice subject, but one can't help being just a little bit interested in what Emily said about Debbie last night of all nights."

"Yes, I know," said Lauren grudgingly. "Let me try to remember. Emily said—it was one of her grotesque metaphysical hypotheses—that Debbie didn't really exist, that she was only the product of all the bad feelings between the other four roommates, and that was why she was so unnaturally unpleasant."

"And now, of course, she really and truly doesn't exist, and we move from the realm of speculative gibberish to the world of facts and corpses. But really, Debbie Doyle couldn't have been that absolutely and irredeemably unpleasant if she was also a genuinely good harpist. Playing the harp is quite a picturesque thing to do. I knew a very pretty little boy at Exeter who played the harp so nicely— he was madly in love with me." Somehow everything ended up reminding Michael of people who had once been in love with him at Exeter. He had referred to so many admirers in conversation that Lauren was forced to conclude that either Exeter was an immensely big prep school or the student body and faculty consisted entirely of aspirants to Michael's favors.

"Michael," said Lauren, "I'm going to tell you a secret."

"How delightful!"

"No, be serious. It's a very serious sort of secret. I promised the police I wouldn't tell anyone at all. In fact, the officer wasn't supposed to have told me, and he got reprimanded for telling, but by then it was too late, and the secret had slipped out."

"You'd better tell me right this very minute," Michael insisted, "or I will simply collapse from not knowing. My constitution is too delicate to endure those long introductions that traditionally precede mysterious revelations."

"But you have to promise not to tell anyone at all, Michael, and you have to keep your promise better than I'm keeping mine."

"Promises to the police don't count. Just tell me quickly before I faint."

"You won't tell a soul?"

"Not a soul."

"No matter how pretty a soul and no matter how much it may have been in love with you at Exeter?"

"On my honor as an Anglican choirboy."

Lauren relented and revealed her secret. "Debbie was strangled with a loose harp string. But all the strings that were still on the harp had been cut."

"Say that again."

"Whoever murdered Debbie Doyle also cut the strings on her harp."

"Good heavens!" Michael was overwhelmed by the image. "How incredibly dreadful. Permit me to retract anything admiring I may have said about the style of the murderer."

"Actually I was hoping you would."

"Murdering a harpist with a harp string is horrible but not without a certain criminal elegance. But going so far as to vandalize the instrument is an aesthetic crime against the angels. We must bring this murderer to justice."

"Yes, I think so, too." That was the conclusion that Lauren, tantalized but reluctant, had been flirting with for the last hour. It was springtime, and she had so many other things to think about: romance, roommates, Machiavelli. However, she was unfortunately not blessed with any particular romantic obsession at the moment, and somehow she felt that she should come to terms with this bizarre outbreak of violence involving Emily's freshman roommates before reaching any definite decisions about roommates for next year. And as for her courses, well, Lauren reminded herself that according to the campus cliché, the Harvard experience was not supposed to be narrowly academic. She ate a bit of cottage cheese on the tip of her spoon and admitted to herself that she was not going to be able to keep this murder mystery out of her mind.

"Tell me," Michael was saying, "how did you happen to learn about the cut harp strings, and why is it supposed to be such a big secret?"

Lauren had been at the police station that afternoon, dutifully submitting to interrogation, trying to remember everything that had happened the night before. She told the police about how she and Emily had been acting out the final scene of *Othello* while somebody was listening at the door. She described Cookie's and Helena's appearances in Emily's room but disappointed the police by insisting that she had not seen Debbie or the Princess or Cookie's callers during the course of the evening. The next morning, Lauren had made her way out of the room in rumpled clothing to grab a cup of coffee at the Union before heading on to her International Relations lecture. She had left Emily still sleeping on the bed. In the corridor of the suite Lauren had encountered only a row of closed doors. She would never have imagined that behind one of them Debbie Doyle was dead.

The police had been especially interested in hearing about the harp music that had come through the wall from Debbie's room. Lauren thought that Debbie must have started playing around one, since she remembered looking at the clock soon after that when competing sounds began to come through the other wall from Cookie's side. Lauren did not tell the police what she had heard coming from Cookie's room; that was none of their business. She did, however, tell them that she thought she remembered waking up for a few moments in the middle of the night— she had no idea what time it was—and hearing the harp even then. She couldn't swear to it, though, since by the next morning it was hard to decide whether she had actually been awake or only dreaming.

"Not very helpful," commented Michael.

"I did my best," said Lauren, "and that's when one of the two cops suggested to the other one that maybe somebody cut the strings and killed her because she was blowing on the harp in the middle of the night."

"Blowing?"

"Yes, blowing—isn't that too much? This policeman didn't seem to know quite what a harp was or how it worked. I think he had it mixed up with a horn—you know, some angels play harps, and some angels play horns, and all celestial music sounds alike."

"Precious," said Michael. "Simply precious. What happened next?"

Lauren had politely pretended not to notice the officer's musical misconception, but she could not help asking what he had meant about cutting the strings. Then the other policeman had furiously reprimanded the first one for mentioning the strings in front of Lauren, but there was no way not to let her in on it now. The murderer, they explained, had cut the strings of the harp. It was being kept secret in the hope that he might carelessly reveal under interrogation that he knew about the cut strings and thus betray that he had been on the scene of the crime. The police always used the masculine pronoun in referring to the mysterious murderer.

"The murderer would have to be pretty careless to slip up over something like that," remarked Michael pessimistically.

"I know. It doesn't sound like a very promising trap, but on the other hand, the police have already been careless enough to tell me, so why shouldn't the murderer be careless enough to tell the police. Anyway, I promised them that I wouldn't tell a soul."

"And here you are, as good as your word."

"Michael, I had to tell you. I need your help or I won't have any chance at all of figuring out who the murderer is."

"Sounds to me like the police need both of us, my dear. I don't think they've made a very clever start of it. Once they've gathered together all the relevant information, they'll probably just sit around and blow on it. Meanwhile, the chief suspects are all Harvard students. Isn't it up to you and me to lend our Ivy League flair to the cause of justice?"

Justice, Lauren thought to herself, does it really have anything to do with justice? Somehow solving the mystery seemed to have more to do with gossip than with justice. It was connected to her passionate curiosity about people, especially about her fellow Harvard students and especially about Emily's roommates.

Meanwhile, Michael was sympathizing aloud, and Lauren

was only half listening. He thought it must have been unspeakably awful to spend the whole afternoon with those dreadful police officers. He didn't think that he would have been able to bear it, and besides, he had noticed that policemen tended to stare at him in the streets with rather more interest than the mere enforcement of the law would seem to require. He certainly would not want to be interrogated by two burly ones in an office in the police station. Poor Lauren, if only they had never found out about her staying the night in Weld Hall. Michael was almost indignant, and his indignation was reinforced by mixed feelings about Emily. Why had Emily had to tell the police that Lauren was there that night?

"Can't you guess?" said Lauren.

Michael reflected for a moment, and then his eyes opened wide with fascination as he realized the answer to his own question. "You're her alibi," said Michael, and he gave an appreciative whistle. "And she's yours. If you spent the whole night in the same little bed, then neither of you could have killed Debbie Doyle. Lucky Emily." He paused, then added, "Lucky Senator Ravello."

It was true that the position of Emily's father, with his presidential ambitions, had made it all the more imperative that Emily not be implicated in the murder. Apparently Emily and Helena and Cookie and the Princess had been found and summoned to the police station as soon as the murder was discovered—Lauren had no idea how the discovery had been made—and Emily had told the police that there was someone who could account for her actions during the night. When Lauren had returned to Thayer after International Relations, she had found a policeman waiting for her, and she, too, had been hustled off to the station and questioned alone. Though she had only been able to wave to Emily for a moment across an ugly waiting room, she quickly realized, from the questions that were being put to her, the significance of her presence in Emily's room the night before. Lauren was the alibi of the senator's daughter. And vice versa.

"Lucky Emily," said Michael again.

"Be nice, Michael," said Lauren. "I know you don't really like her."

"It's not that I don't like her, darling. It's just that those imitations she does make me a little uncomfortable. There's something diabolical about being able to mimic people so precisely." Lauren recalled that Emily had once done a devastating imitation of Michael looking at himself in the mirror. She had perfectly captured the vain little Michael Lauren knew and loved, but Lauren doubted that Michael, had he seen the performance, would have been entirely willing to laugh at himself wholeheartedly. "Also," Michael continued, "don't you get the impression that Emily's suppressing some sort of volcanic tension about her famous father, that she might someday explode?"

"Last night," said Lauren, "she told me about how frightened she sometimes is that her father will be assassinated."

"I'm sure she is," said Michael. "But if he actually is ever elected president—and I hope he isn't; he wears such tacky suits—then I think Emily's just as likely as anyone else to be the one who assassinates him. In fact, if he ever is assassinated, she'll be my very first suspect—unless, of course, she turned out to have spent the time in question in bed with an alibi. Heavens, what did the police think of *that*?"

The police had obviously thought a great deal about that, though no one had dared to say anything frank to Lauren. One officer had asked her meaningfully whether she and Emily were "very, very close friends." And Lauren had looked him straight in the eye and said yes. He had pursued the issue no further. Lauren did allow herself to wonder whether such suspicions of Emily might not be just as damaging to Senator Ravello as her possible implication in the murder.

Anyway, Lauren and Emily both seemed to be in the clear. Michael listed possible suspects on a napkin: Cookie, Helena, the Princess, David the prelaw, David the premed. They had all been in the suite that night, and presumably the police had already questioned them. Lauren and Michael would have to find out everything the police had learned—and then some. Lauren also wondered about J.B., who definitely had a key to the suite and went in and out at will, but Michael hesitated to list him formally on the napkin for fear that Lauren would then spend all her investigative energies and charms on one suspect. And Lauren remembered that there had once been a sixth roommate from the Midwest who had been driven out of the suite, but they decided not to list her, since they had no idea who she was.

"You know," said Michael, "yesterday Cookie told me she was going to do her spring shopping today at the Cambridge Shop."

"Whoopee," said Lauren.

"But she couldn't have gone shopping today. She must have spent the day in the police station like you. And that means she'll go shopping tomorrow. Because when Cookie decides to go shopping, nothing short of violent death— her own, I mean—is likely to stop her."

"I see," said Lauren. "So if we hang around outside the Cambridge Shop tomorrow morning, you think we'd have a good chance of accidentally running into Cookie and perhaps beginning our investigation."

That night Lauren was very tired; she fell asleep almost as soon as she had curled up in her own little bed in Thayer Hall. During the last few drowsy moments of wakefulness, however, she lay in her bed and tried to think back on those moments the night before when she thought she had awakened and heard Debbie playing her harp in the middle of the night, probably unaware that she was soon to die. Lauren still could not decide whether she had been awake or dreaming, and after another night's sleep she knew she would become even less certain. She would probably never know for sure. And now she admitted to herself what she had not told to either Michael or the police. Really, it was too nebulous a thing to tell, but now it made Lauren shiver and pull her blanket up around her neck. During those few moments when she might have been awake the night before, she did not think that she had either moved or opened her eyes. But she had heard Debbie's harp. And the harp music had enabled Lauren to realize that she was in Emily's room, not her own. And in those few dreamy moments before falling back to sleep to the notes of the harp, she had somehow received the impression that Emily was not sleeping alongside her in the bed.

4

Cookie Goes Shopping

◾

*The wish to acquire more is admittedly a very
natural and common thing, and when men succeed
in this they are always praised rather than condemned.*
Machiavelli

"I found the dead body," exclaimed Cookie Fink in the
middle of the Cambridge Shop. "That was really bad, like,
gag me with a spoon." The dippy salesgirl seemed somewhat taken aback, and Lauren and Michael, who had been
questioning Cookie casually while trying on ladies' scarves,
were instantly jolted to attention. They drew closer to
Cookie, unwinding and trailing scarves behind them. That
morning they had cut their classes to hang around the
entrance to the Cambridge Shop and wait for Cookie, and
sure enough, she had appeared ("Hi, guys!"), and they all
ended up shopping together. But who could have predicted
that such valuable information would pop out so quickly
and so publicly? "Yup, there she was, dead in bed, nothing to do about it," Cookie was saying, and she blew a big
pink bubble, which popped with a bang as if to emphasize
the finality of Debbie's demise.

Cookie was standing in front of the mirror, critically

considering a pair of pink pants. She did not seem to feel
compelled to dwell on thoughts of the dead body while
faced with the more pressing matter of dressing a live one.
The salesgirl, having recovered from Cookie's alarming
outburst, noted professionally that pink pants would be
appropriate for both formal and casual occasions and could
be worn in all seasons. Lauren thought Cookie was a treat
in pink pants, but she was most concerned with redirecting
Cookie's attention back to the body of Debbie Doyle.
"How did you happen to find the body?" asked Lauren,
and Cookie, still examining herself in the mirror, began to
tell the story.

Yesterday morning she had returned from her chemistry
midterm in a bad mood. She had not really had enough
time to study or to sleep the night before. Cookie might
be dumb about Shakespeare, but she was usually an ace
science student. Harvard had accepted her on the strength
of her Math SAT, not her long legs, blonde hair, and
carefully restructured nose—though Cookie herself was
the first to admit that those attributes had made their
impression on the "old geezer" who had interviewed her
in Los Angeles. Once settled at Harvard, Cookie had
worked ferociously hard and gotten A's in all her science
courses fall semester. She was determined to go to the
best possible medical school and become the best possible
plastic surgeon.

"I did lousy on the chemistry midterm," said Cookie
bitterly. "Really lousy, I don't even want to know the
grade." She was more than bitter, and Lauren remembered how furious Cookie had been the night of the fire
alarm because Debbie had withheld those papers Cookie
needed to study for the midterm, the ones that had been
left for Cookie by her smitten section leader. Was that why
Cookie thought she had done lousy? Lauren couldn't help
guessing that Cookie still blamed Debbie, even though
Debbie was dead, and that Cookie would never forgive
her.

So after her midterm, Cookie had returned to her room,
feeling tired and irritable. She had settled on her bed to
take comfort in working on her fingernails, and then—as if

her mood were not already bad enough—she discovered that her favorite little manicure scissors were missing. She gave up on her nails and selected a back issue of *Cosmo* to soothe her spirits. "Do you guys remember that article a few months ago about what you can tell about a man's personality from looking at the shape of his ass?" Lauren looked blank—she had missed that issue—but Michael nodded to indicate that he remembered.

While Cookie was reading, the telephone began to ring in the living room. Cookie had never been slow to respond to a ringing telephone, but her reflexes had become even quicker ever since Debbie had enacted that maddening scene with the wrong number. Actually, Cookie had enough suitors, and sufficiently persistent ones, so that she could afford to lose a call now and then without any traumatic effect on her social schedule. She was not, however, a natural beauty. She labored over her hair and skin and had spent no small sum of money on her nose. She was determined to reap the full harvest of her efforts: to receive every last phone call, consider every possible date, and add to what was already a not unimpressive collection of marriage proposals for a college freshman. She dropped *Cosmo* and dashed into the living room—but the race was uncontested. All the other doors in the suite remained closed. Cookie found herself alone in the living room with the ringing phone, thinking that it was somehow luxurious to have the entire suite to herself but also feeling inexplicably frightened by the solitude. She picked up the receiver, certain that the call would be for her.

But it was for Debbie, a boy calling for Debbie. This in itself was so irritating that Cookie almost hung up on the spot. But the voice on the other end of the line sounded vaguely familiar, and Cookie was curious. If she just walked five steps over to Debbie's door and knocked to make sure there was no one in the room, she could then return to the phone and offer to take a message in order to identify that familiar voice. She banged on the door and called out Debbie's name, knowing perfectly well that no one would answer: if Debbie had been in, she would have appeared at the door to see if the call was for her.

Carelessly, Cookie swung open the door and was startled to see that Debbie was asleep in bed with the covers up over her head. Cookie had not had enough sleep the night before, and the sight of Debbie fast asleep at half past ten was cause for new irritation. At least, Cookie thought, she would have the satisfaction of waking Debbie up. So it was that Cookie, announcing the phone call, approached her roommate's bed and threw back the cover. When she saw the face . . . and the neck . . . and the harp string . . . she was silent for a moment. And then she began to scream.

Cookie had run out of the suite, still screaming, and she was quickly surrounded by the boys and girls of Weld Hall. The phone call was forgotten. Soon the police arrived, and Cookie spent the rest of the morning and all of the afternoon at the station.

"What a drag!" said the dippy salesgirl. And then, professionally, she asked, "What were you wearing?"

Lauren and Michael exchanged glances, but Cookie did not seem to find the question out of place. "My red pants," she replied automatically, immediately distracted from the less interesting subject of Debbie Doyle's death. "And my pink blouse with the bow at the neck—I saw it in *Seventeen* last year."

"Pink pants with a red blouse looks really cute, too," said the salesgirl, hinting.

"Maybe cuter," said Cookie reflectively.

Cookie had come to Harvard with a vast wardrobe. Her arrival in September had been followed by that of one trunk after another, air freighted from Los Angeles. She was rumored to have over a hundred sweaters—and sweaters, after all, presumably constituted a proportionally lesser part of the wardrobe of someone who had lived her whole life in Southern California. Her father was rich—bathroom tiles—and Cookie simply shopped and shopped and shopped.

Oddly enough, Cookie had no interest in real fashion and little natural sartorial sensibility. She just tried to buy things that looked like what she saw in magazines and sometimes items that had been acclaimed as cute by her friends. Blissful acquisitiveness had run up against a basic constraint at Harvard, however, since Cookie's little room was not conceivably capable of holding all her clothes. She had, therefore, lost no time in befriending one of the janitors and persuading him to let her put her out-of-season outfits in storage. Now that winter was over, Cookie had just exiled most of her hundred sweaters, sending them off to join her autumn plaids in the basement of the dormitory. Her spring blouses seemed much less bulky by comparison, and Cookie was feeling ready and eager to make up the volume with some fresh purchases.

She indicated to the salesgirl that she would take the pink pants. Cookie's attention was already moving on to other things. "I really want some tops to wear with my minis," she was saying.

But before the salesgirl could explode into bright little suggestions, Lauren asked Cookie, "Were the police nice to you at least? They weren't so nice to me."

No, the police had not treated Cookie so pleasantly, either—or at least not at first. Cookie had screamed for a full five minutes after finding Debbie's corpse and had only just subsided into tears when the police appeared on the scene. They had refused to respect her desire to be left alone and had insisted on taking her away with them for questioning without even allowing her ten minutes to redo her face, let alone twenty to change her pink blouse with the bow for something more suitable. After such brutality it was little wonder that Cookie was still crying when she was finally installed in an office for interrogation. "I mean, my makeup was ruined anyway—I figured I might as well have a good cry and get everything out of my system."

The police, however, wanted other things out of Cookie. First of all, they insisted on an excruciatingly detailed account of what had transpired from the moment she had entered her suite that morning to the moment she had pulled the covers back to reveal the lifeless body. Two clumsy officers—perhaps the same ones who later badgered Lauren—managed to make clear to Cookie that they suspected her of murdering her roommate herself and then pretending to discover the crime. What had Cookie been doing in Debbie's room, anyway? Why was she poking around under Debbie's blanket? And what had made Cookie think she was alone in the suite? Had she checked into the other rooms, as well? It was not possible to explain to such ignorant and unworldly policemen that when the telephone rang in that particular suite, only death could conceivably prevent anyone present from making her presence known. The police seemed to find Cookie's account of herself highly suspicious. "Like these guys were really geeks," said Cookie.

Fortunately, they were not permitted to go on persecuting her. Her crying and general uncooperativeness—punctuated by contemptuous glaring at their correctable noses—eventually made them aware that they were getting nowhere. So when a new and important piece of evidence was brought over from the scene of the crime, the investigation of Cookie Fink was turned over to the police detective in charge of the whole case. Finally, Cookie stopped crying. Finally, she was permitted to retreat to a bathroom with a mirror where, armed only with the bare essentials that she carried in her bag, she was able to reapply her shadows and glosses. She returned to be examined, looking like a new Cookie—or rather, like the old Cookie. The detective was unexpectedly handsome, and Cookie, in her red pants and pink blouse with the bow at the neck, was now ready to be interrogated. "Almost a perfect face," she reflected in the Cambridge Shop. "Michael, I swear, his nose is almost as good as yours." Michael looked dubious. "And freckles! I think freckles are really cute. Just seeing this guy made me feel a lot better, like I knew the day wasn't going to be a complete waste; you know what I mean?"

Lauren did not think freckles were particularly cute, but Michael and the salesgirl seemed to be hanging on Cookie's every word.

"Is he tall?" Michael asked.

"Uh-huh," said Cookie contentedly. "Six-two, taller than I am."

"Is he young?" asked Michael.

"Yup. In his thirties, I guess."

"Oh." Michael seemed to lose interest.

The salesgirl, who held in her hands another pair of pants for Cookie's inspection, looked as if she, too, were on the point of asking a question pertinent to the attractiveness of the detective. But Cookie had already resumed her narrative and was explaining about the new piece of evidence.

Little manicure scissors. The handsome detective wanted to know if Cookie had ever seen them before. But he didn't even have time to formulate his question before Cookie grabbed them out of his hand. It was just the pair of scissors that had been missing from her manicure set that morning when she had returned from her chemistry midterm. The appearance of the detective and the reappearance of her manicure scissors were almost enough to transform a horrible day—a chemistry test, a murder—into a somewhat sunnier one. She realized too late that she might have done better to disown her scissors and buy a whole new set. They had been found in Debbie's room, alongside Debbie's dead body. What had Cookie's scissors been doing in Debbie's room? And why hadn't Cookie noticed them when she discovered the body? She could only suppose that the first sight of the strangled face—after which she had run screaming from the room—had distracted her attention. Oh, if she had only seen the scissors and snatched them on her way out of the room; then she wouldn't have been asked to explain about them later at the police station. Besides, the police ended up keeping the scissors as evidence, and Cookie would have to go buy a new pair now, anyway.

"I don't get it," said the salesgirl, who seemed even more interested in following the story than in showing the tops. "Why were the police so excited about your manicure scissors? I mean, I can't imagine how anyone could possibly be murdered with manicure scissors, anyway." She paused and made a face. "Well, maybe I can imagine it, but it's really disgusting. I suppose someone could have tried."

"No," said Cookie good-naturedly. "She wasn't murdered

with the scissors. The police think the scissors were used to cut Debbie's—"

She paused and looked confused. Lauren and Michael both held their breath, having realized at the same instant what the manicure scissors must have been used to cut. Cookie, too, must have been told about the harp strings. Was she now about to blab the whole thing out in the middle of the Cambridge Shop at the top of her lungs?

"Toenails," Cookie concluded after some fast thinking. "They were used to cut Debbie's toenails." Obviously the police had made her, like Lauren, swear to secrecy in the hope of trapping the murderer—and Cookie did not want to violate her oath. She was perhaps particularly unwilling to offend a particular police detective. She had caught herself just in time, but only by telling a completely absurd lie. Fortunately, both Lauren and Michael were already in on the secret and were not about to press for explanations.

The salesgirl, however, was puzzled. "I don't get it. Why do the police care about your roommate cutting her toenails with your manicure scissors? What does that have to do with her being murdered?"

"They think maybe she wasn't the one who did it," said Cookie, confused by her own lie, making the story more and more ridiculous.

"You mean somebody else cut your roommate's toenails with your scissors?"

"Well, maybe," said Cookie lamely.

"Oh-my-god!" the salesgirl exclaimed. "Maybe it was the murderer who cut her toenails!"

"Maybe," Cookie agreed, looking as if she would really prefer to hear about another pair of pants—or some tops, maybe.

But the salesgirl's imagination had been sparked, and now there was no stopping her. "I used to have a boyfriend who always wanted to cut my toenails, and God I really thought that was weird, but he was really cute. So I used to let him sometimes. I mean, I had boyfriends who wanted weirder things than that. But the thing with the toenails was like really a fetish, and maybe your roommate had a boyfriend who cut her toenails and then murdered her so no one else would ever cut them—that's so romantic!" She paused, and her eyes brightened as a new thought occurred to her. "Or maybe he murdered her first and then cut her toenails afterwards!"

Lauren and Michael exchanged a glance of amazement; this young woman was one of the dippiest dips either of them had ever encountered.

Even Cookie seemed to sense that there was something not quite right about her and made a point of addressing her next comment only to Lauren and Michael. "Debbie must have stolen the scissors, that little bitch," said Cookie indignantly; she seemed to feel no qualms about speaking ill of the dead. Debbie, by dying in the same room with those manicure scissors, had managed to aggravate Cookie once more and for the very last time. Cookie and Debbie had been unpleasant to each other for months— though they had once been friends—and now the manner of Debbie's death guaranteed that an unsentimental Cookie would always remember her with hatred. Still, when the detective had put the question to Cookie the day before—what was Debbie doing with your scissors?—Cookie had been less frank. Instead of accusing Debbie of having stolen them, she insisted that she had lent them to her roommate.

Cookie's powerful instincts for seduction and for self-protection had combined to produce this uncharacteristically charitable lie. First, she did not want an attractive detective to think that she was a spiteful girl. Second, she did not want him to think she was a murderess. She knew that the police were suspicious of her simply because she had been the one to find the body, and she knew that the discovery of her manicure scissors in Debbie's room had magnified those suspicions. The last thing she wanted was for the police to suspect how much she had disliked Debbie, how much Debbie had disliked her. To let on that the scissors had been stolen from the set—it was just the sort of sneaky little thing Debbie would have done—would have set the police on the trail of all those past animosities. The fiction of the loan, on the other hand, suggested amiable relations. Cookie had done her very best to seem regretful about Debbie's death, though, of course, she had stopped short of new tears. She could not afford to ruin her face again. "I mean, what was I supposed to do? Tell him about how that little creep didn't give me those chemistry papers I was counting on to study for the midterm? He probably would have put me right into the electric chair." Cookie ran a hand defensively over her artificially straight, artificially blonde, hair. Though decidedly ignorant about judicial procedure, she seemed to possess an instinctive certainty that a fatal dose of electricity would have disastrous effects on her hair.

"So I just figured I should let him think that Debbie and I had been friends—I mean, that doesn't do anyone any harm now, does it? And I guess we were sort of friends, anyway, except that we hated each other. And he believed my story about lending her the scissors—like why shouldn't he?—and then he asked me to tell him everything that had happened the night before, and I told him everything, or just about. And when I was finished, he saw that I couldn't possibly have murdered her."

"But how do you know he believed you?" asked Michael.

"Because he asked me out to dinner for next weekend," replied Cookie confidently. "I don't think he would have done that if he thought I had murdered someone. That would be like unprofessional behavior. But after I told him the whole story, he saw that I just couldn't have done it. Hey, you'll never guess what his name is!"

"Hercule Poirot," suggested Michael.

"I think I can guess," said Lauren.

"It's David!" exclaimed Cookie. "Now that's what I call a funny coincidence."

Naturally Lauren wanted nothing so much as the license to tie Cookie down with a few sturdy scarves in the middle of the Cambridge Shop and make her explain immediately just why David-the-detective had so readily agreed that she couldn't possibly have committed murder. The salesgirl, however, might have been alarmed by such procedures, and so Lauren had to swallow her impatience and bide her time while Cookie surrendered to a sudden and all-consuming impulse to examine the leotards. One whole corner of the Cambridge Shop was devoted to tight, bright dance accessories, which were, of course, rarely purchased by dancers. In no time at all, Cookie was examining necklines and sorting through colors, remarking over and over on how perfect these leotards would be to wear with her minis. The big basket of ballet slippers was of no interest to her whatsoever. The salesgirl was chanting with an air of ritual sincerity that leotards looked good on everyone (really?) and that they were appropriate for formal and casual occasions (really?) and that they could be worn in all seasons.

"Winter?" asked Michael, whimsically perplexed.

"You could wear it under a sweater," suggested the salesgirl.

"Of course, under a sweater. I should have thought of that myself."

The salesgirl could not help picking up on Michael's expression of interest, and she let him know that a lot of men she knew wore leotards, too, especially the ones who were dancers. Michael insisted that, alas, he was no dancer, but then it turned out that the salesgirl also knew a lot of men who weren't dancers who wore leotards. That provided quite enough of a provocation for Lauren to approach her best friend, a leotard in hand, to tease him into trying it on. So it was that a few minutes later, Cookie, Lauren, and Michael all disappeared into the changing cubicles to wriggle into their dance costumes.

Lauren, behind the curtain, unbuttoned her blouse while thinking very carefully about Cookie. Only the thinnest partition separated the two girls, who were changing into their leotards in adjoining cubicles, but Lauren found herself absolutely incapable of imagining what Cookie might be thinking about.

There was something alien and unfathomable about Cookie, and Lauren couldn't help wondering whether plastic surgery had somehow touched her soul, as if she were a robot recreated on the operating table with decidedly off-key emotional reactions to the world. And then

there was her air of extraordinary stupidity, which made
her such an unlikely Harvard freshman. There were plen-
ty of Harvard students who were stupid, of course, but
Cookie actually seemed to cultivate an image of dazzling,
impossible stupidity—while apparently remaining entirely
unaware of the impression she was making. Lauren no
longer had the slightest doubt that buried underneath was
a ferocious shrewdness, and Cookie's science grades testi-
fied to an utterly incongruous academic talent. With grades
like those, Cookie might confidently believe in her own
intelligence—if it mattered to her—just as she considered
the reconstructed perfection of her face a verifiable fact.
What was one to make of such a creature?

Lauren almost jumped when she looked down and saw a
piece of paper sliding into her stall from under the partition.
It was coming not from Cookie's side but from Michael's.
Michael loved passing notes, and the adjoining booths
were apparently too much of a temptation to resist. Michael,
it turned out, had been thinking along exactly the same
lines as Lauren. The note read:

She has the eyes of a dead lizard.
She could be beautiful if somebody blinded her.

Lauren shuddered and stuffed the note into the back
pocket of her jeans. She was uncomfortable just holding it
in her hand. What if Cookie—a tall girl, after all—were to
suddenly peer over the partition in search of something to
read. True, Cookie had never been seen reading anything
but science texts, *Seventeen*, and *Cosmopolitan*, but
still . . . Damn, Cookie really did have the eyes of a dead
lizard, and Lauren was almost angry at Michael for fixing
the horrible image in her mind.

Lauren was quite certain that Cookie was capable of
pulling a harp string tight around Debbie Doyle's neck
and that those dead-lizard eyes could have looked down at
their victim without seeming to see a thing. There's
definitely something wrong with Cookie, Emily had said
the night of the fire alarm, like she's a cheerleader without
a soul.

Why didn't the police think that Cookie could possibly have committed the murder? What had Cookie told the police to make them think that? She had lied to them about lending her manicure scissors. What other lies had she told? And what lies was she telling now in recounting to Lauren and Michael what she claimed to have told the police? Lauren did not doubt for a moment that Cookie could lie all day long. Certainly her eyes, set in the perfect mask of her surgically recreated face, would never give her away.

In a few minutes three Harvard freshmen were admiring each other's leotards, and an ecstatic salesgirl didn't know whose to admire first. Cookie's shiny scarlet was just the thing for her black mini, and she looked at herself in the mirror with a self-absorption intense enough to screen out the chirping of the salesgirl: "Goes with everything... formal or casual... all kinds of weather."

Michael was wearing a scoop neck, shocking pink, with his preppie khakis; the effect was unusual and definitely unpreppie. "Wrong pants," he commented, shrugging his shocking-pink shoulders.

But it turned out that the salesgirl had lots of friends who wore pink leotards with khakis. "Formal or casual," she was saying—but then Michael suggested another problem.

"I don't have any muscles," he remarked, looking in the mirror, "and in this little tutu one can hardly help noticing. I'm not sure I like that."

"You *could* lift weights," suggested Lauren wickedly, knowing that that was only somewhat more likely than the possibility that Michael would elope with the salesgirl.

"I couldn't!" Michael insisted. "I'm told—by people who know about these things—that once you begin exercising and start growing muscles, you can never stop or else the new muscles turn right to fat. I just can't take that chance." The salesgirl's face fell, and Michael reassured her. "I might buy the leotard, anyway, you know. I confess, it makes me feel rather like a delicious public scandal. I'd like to think I could recreate that feeling any time I wanted to in the privacy of my room."

Lauren's leotard was a lovely plum, but her mind was on other things. "Cookie," she said at last, surrendering to impatience but trying to mask the intensity of her curiosity. "What did you tell the police about what happened the night Debbie was murdered? How did you convince them that you were innocent?"

"I just said that I wasn't there, that I wasn't in the suite," said Cookie.

"What?" Lauren was confused. Hadn't Cookie knocked on Emily's door that night right after the murder of Desdemona? "I don't get it," Lauren said, and Cookie, in her shiny scarlet leotard, began to retell the story to her audience in plum and shocking pink.

Cookie had set herself a strenuous schedule for the night of Debbie's murder. She had decided to see David at midnight, then David at one o'clock, then decide between them, and finally study chemistry for one last hour before going to sleep. It was a pity to have to do this the night before the midterm, but David the premed was going to help her with a last-minute chemistry question, so she thought she might as well see them both and finally make a decision. When she had knocked on Emily's door, she had already slipped into her transparent pink nightie with the matching pink panties, and she was awaiting the midnight David. She was determined to decide once and for all whether *that* really mattered.

The first David had arrived and had his opportunity. Cookie had found herself bored, had found her mind wandering through the chemical elements on the periodic table. She had read enough *Cosmo* articles to know that that was not the kind of chemistry you were supposed to be thinking about while your boyfriend was making love to you. By twelve-thirty she had decided that perhaps *that* really did matter, after all, and she broke the news to David that their romance was, alas, over. She did it just as *Cosmo* prescribed. She told him he was a very attractive man and a very special person, that they had had some glorious moments together, and that she hoped they would always be friends.

"Well, at least you didn't tell him the real reason," said

Michael cheerfully. But Cookie remained ominously silent, and Michael's jaw dropped. "Oh Cookie, please say that you didn't." Michael suddenly seemed to feel an improbable sense of solidarity with this poor David. Even if they did belong to different species, they were both biologically male and therefore, Lauren supposed, bound to share certain common sensitivities.

"He asked," said Cookie. "He asked me what the other David had that he didn't have, and so I just told him. Besides, I really wanted him to leave before the other David got there, and this way I got him to go away quick. I think he was pretty angry, though." She thought for a moment. "He'll get over it. I mean it's not like I didn't remember to tell him that he was a very attractive man and a very special person."

"Did you describe all this to the police detective?" asked Lauren.

"No, of course not," said Cookie. "I just said that this guy I was dating came over, and that I told him I didn't want to go out with him anymore. I mean, I wouldn't want to embarrass anyone."

The second David arrived around one, and Cookie gave herself to him, thinking that when it was over, when she was lying in his arms, then she would tell him that his rival and namesake had been vanquished. Unfortunately, it was over before it began. That night David had a problem, and not even *Cosmopolitan*'s most recommended methods for overcoming this problem were of any use. Cookie became frustrated and irritated, and she began to think that perhaps she ought to have spent the whole evening studying chemistry instead of evaluating the Davids. She could not help feeling that his impotence was certainly no tribute to her, no proper recognition of the time and money and effort and magazine articles that had gone into making her as sexy as she knew she was. So it was that for the second time in the same night Cookie found herself telling a Harvard student named David that he was a very attractive man and a very special person, that they had had some glorious moments together, and that she hoped they would always be friends. And then she kicked him out, and he didn't even have to ask why. He left her room in an ugly mood.

Cookie really didn't doubt that she had only to whistle to get either one of them back again. "I was just afraid that they'd come back too soon. They both seemed so upset when they left—men just get upset so easily, you know—that I was afraid they might even come back to Weld that same night and make a big scene and beg me to take them back again. They might even have come at the same time, and that would have been pretty embarrassing for me, and they would have been really angry and unreasonable, and I would never have been able to get any studying done or get any sleep before my midterm. So I decided I'd just leave my room and spend the night someplace else so if one of the Davids came back, he wouldn't find me."

"What do you mean?" asked Lauren, beginning to sense what this was all leading up to.

"I decided to go spend the night in a hotel."

It was extremely uncommon for an undergraduate to decide to spend the night in a hotel instead of in the dormitory, but in this case the decision seemed to have a certain plausibility. Besides, Cookie was very rich; the prices of any two of her hundred sweaters would have covered a night in the fanciest hotel in Cambridge. She had telephoned the Sheraton on Garden Street, made a reservation, gotten dressed, and packed a bag with her chemistry text and a change of clothes: the red pants and the pink blouse with the bow at the neck. She had then departed from the little room that had witnessed such disappointing sex over the past two hours. On the way out she had heard Debbie playing the harp.

In other words, Debbie had been alive when Cookie left the suite for the night. Lauren herself had awakened for a moment and heard Debbie playing in the middle of the night, and much more importantly, there was a Harvard night guard who had walked past Weld on his rounds, heard the harp, and looked at his digital watch to see that it was two thirty-two. His testimony meant that Debbie was definitely alive at two-thirty, and just as definitely, at two o'clock Cookie had checked into the Sheraton, making a great impression on all the bellhops and desk clerks. They were able to describe her arrival to the police the next day. Cookie had spent a quiet hour reviewing her chemistry and then slept the night through on the fifth floor of the Sheraton. The next morning she had room service bring her breakfast in bed while she reviewed her notes one last time, and there was a waiter who could testify that Cookie was there in the morning. At a quarter to nine she had checked out, paying the bill with her father's American Express card, and at nine o'clock she was in the Science Center, starting her midterm exam. She finally returned to Weld Hall only after the test was over, and it was then that she had discovered Debbie's body. Medical evidence, however, suggested that Debbie had been killed during the night, and therefore Cookie was innocent. "So this weekend I can go out with David, my detective, and I really think he's cuter than those other two Davids, those washouts, even if we did have some glorious moments together." The memory of those glorious moments was certainly not enough to keep Cookie's attention from wandering back to the racks of leotards in search of other colors and necklines.

"And you know what?" said Cookie, giving one last thought to Debbie's murder. "David and David both came back to Weld Hall that night—like I predicted—but not at the same time. But some kids on the first floor saw them coming in and told the police about it the next day. So the police are pretty suspicious—especially since both Davids were behaving like they were angry and maybe drunk when they came back to Weld—but I don't think the police know why they were so upset. I mean, I didn't tell, and I bet the Davids didn't tell, either. It would have been pretty embarrassing for them." Cookie chuckled. "I'm sure glad I wasn't there when they came back. I've got to remember to ask them to give me back the keys I gave them. Wasn't there an article in *Cosmo* a few months ago about how to ask your ex-lover to give back your keys?"

She could have sneaked out of the hotel in the middle of the night, Lauren was thinking, and then sneaked back again in time to order breakfast from room service. Probably someone would have seen her and recognized her, but maybe not. One thing for sure: if she's dating David-the-detective, the police aren't going to pay a lot of attention to possible loopholes in her alibi. Especially not with those two Davids in and out of the dorm—angry, drunk, perfect suspects. Why did Lauren feel so unsatisfied about seeing Cookie so easily cleared?

Cookie was telling Michael for the hundredth time how much she admired his nose. Michael was trying on different scarves over the shocking-pink scoop neck. Lauren was thinking that she and Emily should certainly not consider rooming with Cookie next year. Cookie was unquestionably a scream, but Lauren found herself less and less eager to have such a scream at such close quarters. No, Lauren would room with Emily—perhaps Helena, too, perhaps the Princess. Oh, if only Michael could room with them too! But Lauren knew deep in her heart that the murder mystery would have to be solved before she could settle her rooming combination.

Now Lauren and Michael and Cookie were all gathered around one very happy salesgirl at the cash register. Michael and Lauren were each buying one leotard, and Cookie was buying ten. Nor had the salesgirl forgotten about the pink pants. "Formal or casual, winter or summer," the salesgirl was singing as she tried to figure out how to ring things up on the cash register. The three Harvard freshmen were feeling content after a good day's shopping. Lauren almost jumped when a male voice over her shoulder called out, "Hey."

They all turned around, startled, to see the tall young man in the Harvard athletic jacket who had slipped into the Cambridge Shop while their backs were turned. He looked very grim, and perhaps a little confused, and though his features were completely unremarkable, Lauren found them familiar. In fact, she knew his name even before Cookie greeted him.

"Hi, David," said Cookie coolly. "What are you doing here?" It was either David the prelaw or David the premed, and perhaps not even Cookie was quite sure which. And which was this one's sexual inadequacy? Did Cookie remember that? Did it matter?

"I saw you through the window," he said to Cookie. "There's something I want to tell you."

"Wait a minute," said Cookie, who seemed to have realized something while he was speaking. "It was you who called yesterday morning to talk to Debbie, right before I found her body. I thought it was a familiar voice, but I never thought of you. But it was you, wasn't it? What did you have to say to her? What was going on?" Cookie was apparently indignant, even though Debbie was now dead, even though David—whichever David this was—had been jilted.

"Yeah, that was me," said David, looking Cookie straight in her dead-lizard eyes, over the heads of Michael and Lauren. "That was me on the phone, and that's sort of what I wanted to tell you about. Debbie didn't want me to tell you this—I'm not really sure why—but I think I should tell you now." He paused, and Lauren held her breath, awaiting his revelation. "Debbie Doyle was my sister."

5
Diplomatic Relations

∎

We find that princes who have thought more of their
pleasures than of arms have lost their states.

Machiavelli

Lauren and Michael sat in the last row of a huge lecture
hall, looking down on some two hundred students arranged in ascending arcs around a small and funny-looking—
but very famous—professor of International Relations. There
had been a time when he had had a strong say in the
making of American foreign policy in Washington, and
Lauren happened to know for a fact that he was now in
close contact with Emily's father, advising him on foreign-
policy issues; if Senator Ravello were ever to become
President, then Professor Hopper was not unlikely to
become Secretary of State or perhaps National Security
Adviser. Students who had seen him lecture almost always
found themselves referring to him as Professor Grasshopper.

At the beginning of the semester Lauren and Michael
had persuaded themselves and each other that it would be
interesting and important to learn about international
relations from such a famous professor. Emily, who had

met him a few times, had advised against taking the course, but Lauren and Michael—along with two hundred other students who had not had the benefit of Emily's warning—had nevertheless plunged into International Relations. Now, halfway through the semester, Lauren was already irritated by Professor Grasshopper's insistence on identifying three kinds of everything: three kinds of wars, three kinds of governments, three kinds of treaties, three kinds of diplomacies, and so on, from lecture to lecture. This, Lauren supposed, was political science. Michael claimed to be even more irritated by Professor Grasshopper's predilection for labeling anything whatsoever a paradox, even when there was nothing even faintly paradoxical about it. Neither Lauren nor Michael had made great progress with the reading list. Lauren always carried Machiavelli around with her because it was slim enough to fit into her handbag. Michael, however, rarely carried a handbag.

Michael and Lauren usually sat in the last row, because they were usually late for lecture. For reasons connected to the nature of political science, the lectures had begun with the Cuban missile crisis and were now going backward in history, while the readings began with Machiavelli and were proceeding toward Robert Kennedy's *Thirteen Days*. The course, needless to say, was always a mess, and today Lauren and Michael had little attention to spare for Professor Grasshopper's remarks on the paradoxical origins of World War I.

Lauren wrote a note and passed it to Michael: *If he's her brother, does that mean he's more likely to have killed her or less likely?* Since yesterday's shopping trip, with all its remarkable revelations, Lauren had thought of little besides the murder of Debbie Doyle. Her immediate reaction had been that a brother could not possibly have murdered his younger sister, and therefore this particular David was necessarily cleared. But that night, when she was trying to make herself fall asleep, it had come to her forcefully that in fact the family connection might itself imply all sorts of twisted motivations for murder.

Michael did not hesitate over his response. Whereas

Lauren's note had been written on a page torn from her spiral notebook—originally purchased for notes on Professor Grasshopper's lectures—Michael was a more dedicated passer of notes who always carried with him a little pink notepad especially for the purpose. Now he wrote, *Definitely more likely.*

But her brother! Lauren wrote on the bottom of Michael's pink note, passing it back to him. She knew her comment was ingenuous, but she wanted Michael to tell her so. It was easy to become entirely fanciful and imagine the most outrageously bizarre things when trying to focus on the murder. She wanted Michael to confirm that the hypothesis of sister murder—sororicide?—was not too extravagant.

Michael wrote out a new pink slip: *If I ever murder anyone, it might well turn out to be my sister.* Michael insisted that his younger sister had become altogether too loud, even vulgar, and that she was an embarrassment on family occasions. Lauren suspected that this actually meant she was insufficiently reverent toward her older brother. And surely Debbie Doyle, that most unpleasant of roommates, had been also a most unpleasant sister.

Meanwhile, Michael had passed another note, not even waiting for Lauren to reply to the last one. *What about* The Duchess of Malfi?

Michael was a great fan of *The Duchess of Malfi.* He had played the wicked Cardinal in a prep-school production at Exeter. He had learned all the Duchess's lines, as well, and he could not help cursing the fact that co-education had made it impossible for him to have the title role.

Lauren had read the play in the fall—at Michael's insistence—and had perversely enjoyed it with all its horrors. Just thinking about the murder of the poor Duchess reassured her now by reminding her that her own suspicions and hypotheses were not in the least preposterous in comparison with Webster's drama. For once, Michael's reference to the play was entirely relevant: Jacobean England must have been fascinated by the possibility of sororicide. And furthermore, Lauren remembered, the Duchess of

Malfi had been strangled with a cord—not like Desdemona, who had been smothered with a pillow. Lauren's thoughts were wandering back to that night in Emily's room. Suddenly frightened, she forced herself to pay attention to little Professor Grasshopper down below at the lectern.

She even tried to take a few notes on the lecture. There were, the professor dogmatically asserted, three kinds of alliances that made up the system of alliances at the outbreak of World War I. Lauren was not surprised. She soon found herself doodling in her notebook, while her thoughts collapsed into sleepy confusion. Suppose Debbie Doyle was the Austrian archduke assassinated at Sarajevo. Then Helena could be Austria's ally, Germany. And Emily, Cookie, and the Princess could be England, France, and Russia. Cookie, Lauren supposed, would have to be England, since foreign languages were out of the question. And the Princess was the most exotic roommate, so she could be Russia—though wouldn't the Ottoman Empire be more appropriate? And Emily . . . Lauren forced herself awake and drove all this drivel from her mind. At this rate she would never understand anything about the murder, much less about World War I.

On the other side of the lecture hall, toward the back, Lauren spotted the Princess. She, too, was taking International Relations, and unlike certain other students, she was taking notes on the lecture. It took a moment for Lauren to register that there was something different about the Princess's presence at today's lecture, something that Lauren found deeply interesting. She quickly scribbled a note to Michael: *Look who's with the Princess.* Lauren indicated the direction, and Michael's eyes followed.

In a moment he replied to her note: *Rather more interesting than World War I, I think.*

The Princess was sitting with J.B. This was worth noticing, not only because Lauren was always glad to notice him, but also because the Princess usually went to lectures alone. Surely his attendance now could only mean that Debbie Doyle's murder had inspired an increased concern for the safety of her roommate the Princess. Lauren wondered whether there was any more particular reason for such precautions. Or was it possible that the Princess was suspected of having murdered her roommate and J.B. was just making sure she didn't murder anyone else?

While the Princess was taking notes on World War I, J.B. was reading—Lauren stared fixedly to be sure—yes, he was reading a little book concealed in his lap. It endeared him to Lauren more than ever, since she herself, before coming to Harvard, had spent the previous decade reading hidden books in her lap during the impossibly tedious schooling provided by the state of New Jersey. Still, Lauren thought, if *she* were the Princess and *she* had a personal bodyguard, she would see to it that *he* took the notes so that *she* could read a book in her lap. Taking notes in college lectures was servants' work if anything was. Lauren stared at him and wondered what he was reading, and just then he looked up and seemed to stare right back at her. She did not drop her gaze, however, until Michael slipped her a new note.

Michael's note said, *I think he's looking at me!*

Lauren was indignant and unwilling to let this pass. She replied, *He's looking at* me! Michael made a face that let her know in no uncertain terms that he remained unconvinced.

Professor Grasshopper wrapped up his lecture with one final paradox and was rewarded with the rather unenthusiastic applause that followed every class. It was less a mark of appreciation than an expression of relief that the lecture was finally over. In this case, the applause quickly gave way to groans as the teaching assistants began to hand out the take-home midterm exam.

Lauren and Michael accepted their copies of the exam sheet with reluctance. They were instructed to write a ten-page essay on the relevance of Machiavellian principles of statecraft for understanding the Cold War. It was due in class in a week, next Wednesday. A ridiculous topic, thought Lauren with irritation; she hadn't finished

reading Machiavelli and hadn't taken notes at the lectures
on the Cold War. Where to begin?

Lauren and Michael left the lecture hall together,
surrounded by their classmates who were already talking
about Machiavelli and the Cold War. Lauren saw the
Princess and J.B. going up the other aisle toward the
exit, also surrounded by preoccupied students. But one
of the students, thought Lauren, could be a murderer—that's
why J.B. is sticking so close, to make sure that whoever
killed Debbie Doyle doesn't kill the Princess next.

Who's going to protect me? thought Lauren suddenly. If
I keep on trying to find out who killed Debbie Doyle,
eventually the murderer is going to come for me. Which
means either I give up on the mystery, or I figure it out as
fast as I can, before somebody figures me out. Lauren was
scared, and, looking around her, she could imagine that
any of these students could be concealing a horrible
secret—or a deadly weapon. Michael will protect me,
Lauren told herself, resting her frightened eyes on him.
But that reassurance was not enough to dispose of her
fear.

Later that afternoon, sitting beneath a tree in Harvard
Yard with Machiavelli, Lauren was conscious of the effects
of spring. Suddenly it seemed that everyone was walking
in couples, not yet holding hands perhaps, but that too
would come with a few more weeks of such lovely weather. Today the sun was marvelously warm, and Lauren went
so far as to roll up her sleeves for a little early tanning. On
the other side of the Yard, coming out of Weld, was
Helena Dichter, walking with someone who almost had his
arm around her. Lauren stared, and even at a distance she
could see that Helena's spring romance was a remarkably
ugly young man, a regular troll. And Helena was so
lovely. . . .

Coupling, Lauren was sharply reminded, could be a
gruesome business. But, she thought again, it could be
awfully sweet. She should be meeting more boys, she
knew. She might have to sort through a thousand losers to
come up with a presentable specimen, but that was a fact

of life: most men were simply out of the question. Nothing to be done for it—except to start sorting. It was wearying just to think about it, but the alternative was sitting alone in Harvard Yard with Machiavelli. She examined the bust of Machiavelli pictured on the cover of *The Prince:* wimpy expression, receding hairline, nice cheekbones though.

The problem, Lauren knew, was that she had such wonderful friends. She would never be eager to spend an hour getting to know a new man, a new turkey most probably, when she could spend that same hour with Emily or with Michael.

Michael, of course, was not the sort of friend whose friends could be considered potential boyfriends for Lauren. Michael was even a sort of obstacle to meeting new men, since most of Thayer Hall was convinced that Lauren and Michael were a romantic item. It was hard to believe that there were people who failed to recognize Michael's true colors, but the dorm contained all sorts of innocents from the Midwest. All they knew was that Lauren and Michael were always together in each other's rooms and that in winter they sometimes appeared in each other's pajamas. They were the same size. Michael loved Lauren's ski pajamas because they had tiger stripes, and Lauren loved Michael's because they had feet.

And Emily... Lauren rose from the grass, thinking about Emily. Lauren had hardly spoken to Emily since the night of the murder, and this three-day hiatus in their friendship was remarkable enough considering that during the previous weeks they had spent hours together almost every day. They had exchanged a few words at the police station, but neither had made any allusion to the new twist in their relationship. They had both been in the suite when Debbie was murdered. They were both under suspicion of murder, and it was by vouching for each other that they could ward off those suspicions. Lauren wondered whether their friendship was being somehow corrupted, or at least transformed, by the hard fact that they were now so necessary to each other. She had not wanted to compare notes with Emily on the course of their respective interrogations. No matter how lightheartedly they might try to do it, no matter how much they might laugh at the clumsiness of the investigators, it would be impossible not to feel as if they were somehow coordinating their stories. No matter how innocent they might actually be, almost any discussion between them on the subject would feel like guilty complicity. Lauren simply took for granted that she had been cleared by Emily's testimony, just as Emily had been by hers. Lauren had told the police that they had spent the entire night sleeping in the same bed, that Emily had remained in her own room the whole night long.

But if only, Lauren thought, if only I were absolutely sure of that. She remembered the moment when she might have been awake in the middle of the night, when she might have heard the harp, when Emily might not have been lying alongside her. It was that moment that made Lauren so especially nervous about calling up Emily on the phone or dropping by her room. But why, then, had Emily not telephoned Lauren or sought her out? Was Emily actually avoiding Lauren?

Now Lauren crossed Harvard Yard to Weld Hall. She looked up at the old red brick facade and couldn't help being pleased with the building's sturdy, academic air; it was austerely, even awesomely, Harvardian. What Lauren could not quite believe was that behind one of those plain rectangular windows on the third floor, Debbie Doyle had been strangled. That event seemed entirely inappropriate to the building's Ivy League aura. Lauren entered the dorm and began to climb the stairs. She was going to visit Emily, to break the disconcerting silence of the past few days. She did not know, however, whether she was going to raise with Emily the subject that had made her so uneasy: Debbie Doyle's murder and the question of who could have murdered her and why. Lauren had a feeling that Emily might be able to tell her something important, and that made her all the more nervous about asking.

Lauren stood before the door of the suite and thought: one of these four roommates must have murdered the fifth. It was the first time she had put it to herself so flatly.

Of course there was the possibility of the two Davids, but standing at the door of the suite, Lauren suddenly felt that the nastiness of the crime must have been nourished within, that its only plausible context was the web of animosities which had entangled the five roommates. Lauren remembered what Emily had said the night of the fire alarm: we bring out the worst in each other. Lauren remembered her own intuition that night, that something about the rooming combination was somehow very, very wrong. Now the same intuition told her that Debbie Doyle had been murdered by one of her roommates.

The murderer is standing on the other side of this door, thought Lauren suddenly, irrationally, absolutely terrified. But she steeled herself, took a deep breath, and knocked. And then she waited, still terrified... but the door remained closed, the knock unanswered.

Lauren could not help feeling relieved, and without exactly thinking about what she was doing, she began to wander farther up the stairs to the upper floors of Weld Hall. On each floor were the doors to four or five suites and one bathroom. The walls themselves were dark brick, like the outer facades, and the banister, along which Lauren idly ran her hand, was smooth light wood. Each floor was either male or female, and on the fourth floor Lauren had only to sniff to know that it was male. She looked down over the banister to Emily's floor, still deserted. She looked up to the fifth and final floor, equally silent. Weld Hall felt strangely empty, even oppressively so: as if all those Harvard bricks were enclosing just one person, Lauren herself. Surely there was someone else in the dorm either studying or napping, but in midafternoon most students were likely to be in the libraries, prowling around Cambridge, attending late classes and discussion sections, or else just enjoying the sun after a long winter.

Lauren ascended to the fifth floor and found herself emerging from the dim oppressiveness of dark brick and low ceilings into a sort of solarium. The fifth floor rose to a high rectangular cupola with big windows on all sides. The sunlight through the windows reminded Lauren of what a glorious day it was outside, but the windows were way up over her head in the cupola. She could not look out.

Or perhaps she could. Before her was a white metal ladder, a sort of fire-escape ladder that had been lowered so that it reached down from the windows of the cupola to Lauren's knees. Drawn to the light, feeling very brave, she climbed the ladder. Her low heels, she knew, were still too high for this sort of climbing, but by stepping carefully, she was able to rise rung by rung to the top.

She was rewarded by a tremendous view in the clearest daylight. Before her lay Harvard with its brick buildings and white towers, beyond that Cambridge and the curves of the Charles River separating Cambridge from Boston. Lauren's delight was spiced with an element of fear. She knew that she was dangerously high above the fifth floor of Weld, and she dared not look down for fear of dizziness. It was with both fascination and relief that she realized that the tall rectangular window before her was actually a glass door leading out onto the roof of Weld Hall. Cautiously, feeling like Alice in Wonderland about to slip from one peculiar world into another, she pushed open the glass door and stepped from the top rung of the white ladder onto the roof in the open air. It was not until she felt both heels planted firmly on the gravelly roof that she permitted herself at last to look down. In doing so, she very nearly lost the balance she had been striving to preserve, because almost at her feet, lying on a big electric-blue towel spread out on the roof of the dormitory, was a sleeping young man in the nude.

He was lying faceup, quite completely exposed, arms and legs spread lightly, palms open. Lauren, her heels two feet from his head, looked him over without the least timidity. Obviously the first thing that had struck her about him was his nakedness beneath the blue sky. It had only taken her another split second, however, to note that he was also pretty. This happy combination of prettiness and nudity made him all the more worthy of inspection. His hair was long, much longer than that of most Harvard men, and came down to his shoulders. It was not exactly curly, but there were more than a few artless ringlets, and

the color was a not too shiny, very evidently clean, blond—
set off by the electric blue of the towel. The sleeping face
was not exactly handsome but almost elfin. A small mouth
with thin lips was parted far enough to reveal two rather
small top front teeth; the eyelashes were almost disturbingly
long.

His body was pleasingly slender—and still pale despite
such purposeful sunning. His chest was barely defined,
gracefully unmuscular, though his waist tapered neatly and
the stomach was perfectly flat. His belly button was turned
out, which Lauren found somehow alluring. There was
rather little, very blond pubic hair, the scantness contrasting
with the extravagance of the hair on his head. He was,
Lauren noticed not without interest, uncircumcised—a
detail that enhanced the peculiar air of classical mythology
that made the circumstances into that much more of an
adventure: the unexpected discovery of a sleeping, naked,
long-haired youth on a high rooftop beneath the open sky.
And most suggestive of all was the absence of any evidence of undressing—there was no little mound of clothes.
Lauren couldn't imagine what he would wear if he were
clothed—if he ever was clothed—and neither could she
imagine how he had gotten where he was. Did he wander
around Harvard wrapped in a towel? Or had he perhaps
descended from the clouds?

I would like to see his eyes, thought Lauren, feeling
more and more like Alice in Wonderland with every
passing moment, and her wish was immediately granted.
The sleeping figure opened its eyes—which were bright
and blue—and looked up at Lauren with a suggestion of
surprise but no hint of alarm. "Hello," he said in a hoarse
voice—Lauren had been expecting something more high-
pitched. And then, barely nonplussed, cheerfully ironic,
he said, "How do you do?"

"Hello," replied Lauren. "Very well, thank you. And
you?"

"Likewise," said he. "I think I was having a very strange
dream—I was somehow deeply involved with a starfish, or
perhaps a seahorse—but when I woke up and saw you, I

seem to have forgotten all the details. I was surprised to see you, you know."

"Who were you expecting?"

His face darkened for a moment, and Lauren wondered whether perhaps he actually *had* been expecting someone. But then he replied, "A seahorse, I suppose, or a starfish."

"I hope you're not too disappointed."

"Not at all," he said sweetly. "I'm not really sure what etiquette prescribes, but I have a feeling that until we are better acquainted, it would be more modest of me to lie on my tummy." He turned over, revealing adorable buns. "Have to tan that side, too, you know."

"I know, I know," said Lauren, finding him more and more charming, thinking what a prize of a spring romance *this* would be—and what a story! Michael would die!

"What are you doing up here?" inquired the object of these reflections. He had propped himself up on his elbows, and his hair fell down past his shoulders.

"I was going to read a book," said Lauren, who had climbed up to the roof for no good reason at all, just impulsive adventurousness. And now she was having an adventure.

"What book?" he inquired politely.

Lauren, of course, was carrying only one book in her little bag. "Machiavelli," she said. *"The Prince."*

Her new friend's eyes lit up with considerable interest. "Are you in International Relations?" he asked.

"Alas," said Lauren. "Are you? I'm sure I've never seen you there."

"I hardly ever go," he said. "And when I do go, I'm usually dressed, so you might not recognize me."

"What do you wear?"

"Greek sandals," he replied, "and a rhinestone tiara."

"I'm surprised I haven't noticed," said Lauren. "All the other boys wear G-strings and feather boas. Harvard students are so trendy."

"No G-strings for me," he said.

"I noticed that," said Lauren. "How did you get here, anyway? Where did you leave your tiara and your sandals?"

"I live right here on the fifth floor of Weld," he said, "so

I can just pop out of my room and zip up the ladder. We Weldies have all been expressly forbidden by our dorm proctors to ever play on the roof under any circumstances. So I usually have it to myself. You're not from Weld, are you?"

"No, but a friend of mine lives on the third floor, Emily Ravello. I was here in Weld to see her, but she wasn't home, so I just wandered up here." She paused. "In search of adventure."

He smiled. "I've seen you with Emily."

"Really?" Lauren was delighted to learn that this mysterious stranger had already noticed her in the past. Being noticed was so gratifying to one's vanity.

"I saw you together the night of the fire alarm. That was you, wasn't it?"

"Yes, that was me."

"Well, then, this is only almost our first acquaintance. Let me introduce myself, since I have a feeling it isn't proper for us to be up here like this, unintroduced as well as unchaperoned. I'm Ted."

"Don't you think first names are a little too casual considering the formality of the circumstances?" Lauren was still standing on the roof, and he was still resting on his elbows, looking up at her.

"Ted Roosevelt," he said. "How about you?"

"My name is Mary," said Lauren.

"Don't forget the formality of the circumstances."

"Mary Todd Lincoln," said Lauren.

"A fine name."

"So tell me, Theodore Roosevelt—"

"Ted, please," he interrupted.

"So tell me, Ted. Are you a friend of Emily's?" Lauren didn't think she had ever heard Emily refer to this charming creature.

"Not really, but we're very old acquaintances. My parents were living in Bangkok—my father was there for business—when Emily's father was the ambassador, and so Emily and I—we were both children—went to the same English school. We were the only Americans in the class, and we were also the smartest and the worst behaved."

"Were you always taking off your clothes in class?"

"I was worse than that. But Emily was worse than I was. And so you'd think we would have been friends, or at least allies, but it turned out neither of us liked the idea of being only tied for smartest and worst behaved."

"Especially worst behaved?"

"Most especially. And then ten years later we were both living in Washington, and I was going to St. Andrew's and she was going to National Cathedral, and so we used to see each other at very preppie dances."

"I can just imagine you wearing your tiara."

"Exactly. And imagine Emily in black and white, very unpreppie colors. She and I were the unpreppiest people in our respective prep schools, and somehow we still never quite ended up dancing with each other. It's sort of infuriating actually that life keeps throwing us back together again. But let's talk about you, Mary Todd Lincoln." He obviously meant to change the subject, and Lauren, always pleased to be asked about herself, could not resist.

"Me?" she said. "There's nothing to tell. I'm vain and frivolous and extremely curious. Tell me about you."

"I'm extremely idle, a veritable black sheep, a disgrace to the family name." It was only then that Lauren suddenly realized that he hadn't been joking about the name, that he really was named Theodore Roosevelt. She thought she remembered people saying there was a Roosevelt, a direct descendant, in the freshman class. Lauren was profoundly titillated.

"Well," said Lauren, "put idleness behind you. I hate to be the bearer of bad news, but today Professor Grasshopper handed out the take-home midterm."

Ted's face fell. "I don't suppose you have any notes on the lectures?" he inquired hopefully.

"Sorry," said Lauren. "I do usually go to the lectures, but I have to draw the line somewhere." He looked very glum indeed, and Lauren resolved to cheer him up. "We'll think of something—we can collaborate. Between the two of us we should be able to manage." Lauren's tone had become more suggestive than academic. Still, in the back of her mind, she was thinking that in preparing this midterm, she should try to avoid any direct three-way collaboration that would bring Ted and Michael together.

"Thank you," said Ted. "Do you think we know each other well enough now so that I could sit up—even at the risk of being immodest—and invite you up to sit down on the other half of the towel. We could even read aloud to each other from Machiavelli."

Lauren smiled, Ted sat up, and as Lauren sat down next to him, she said, "Would you mind if I slipped off my shoes?"

6
Biography

■

*Men nearly always follow the tracks made by others
and proceed in their affairs by imitation, even though
they can not entirely keep to the tracks of others or
emulate the prowess of their models. So a prudent
man should always follow in the footsteps of great
men and imitate those who have been outstanding. If
his own prowess fails to compare with theirs, at least
it has an air of greatness about it.*

Machiavelli

Lauren stepped into the Harvard Book Store to escape
from the spring drizzle. Really, it was much more purposeful* than that. She had spent most of the morning in
Lamont Library, trying to make her way through the
reserve readings on the Cold War, trying to imagine
herself constructing a midterm essay on the Cold War and
Machiavelli. It was slow going, however, because Franklin
Delano Roosevelt was a much less appealing subject for
reflection than his great-great-nephew, with whom Lauren
had dallied on the roof the day before. And the mystery
surrounding the death of Debbie Doyle was so much more
intriguing than the Soviet power struggle that followed the

death of Stalin. At last Lauren had left the library for a breath of fresh air, and when she found that it was raining, instead of dutifully reentering the library, she dashed across Mass. Ave. to take refuge in the Harvard Book Store. After the dusty library covers and photocopied reserve articles in Lamont, the bookstore's glossy new paperbacks reminded Lauren of how much she used to love to read before she came to Harvard.

She checked out current paperback best-sellers and then made her way to the long wall of general fiction, where she spent the next hour browsing alphabetically from Louisa May Alcott and Jane Austen to P. G. Wodehouse and Virginia Woolf. The bookstore was filled with Cambridge graduate-student types, lots of beards, lots of corduroy jackets—people with nothing to do but browse in bookstores all day while they tried to overcome the diverse neuroses that prevented them from ever finishing their Ph.D. dissertations. Lauren turned into the center aisle to stand alone before the murder mysteries, and there she felt herself rooted to the spot. No question about it—murder was on her mind. And detection. She began picking up Agatha Christie mysteries and flipping through the pages, trying to recall the plots and solutions—she had read them all several times during the course of her childhood, scaring herself to death every time and loving it—trying to decide whether any of them had any insights to offer into the murder of Debbie Doyle. Eventually she gave up—what did Agatha Christie know about Radcliffe roommates?—but Lauren, just remembering, had managed to recreate enough of her old childhood terror, so that when she stepped back and bumped into someone behind her, she started with fear.

"Excuse me," said Lauren, quickly regaining control of herself, and a voice behind her, immediately familiar, said, "Excuse me."

Lauren turned to see not a bearded graduate student but Helena Dichter, who had herself just turned around from examining the literary and poetry journals. "Oh, hi," said Lauren, thinking, while Helena greeted her in return: What a coincidence, just when I was thinking about the roommates and the murder. And then suddenly, watching Helena, she wondered: Was it a complete coincidence? Or had Helena been aware that she was standing back to back with Lauren, that Lauren was flipping through the murder mysteries?

"I'm glad I bumped into you," said Helena. Her voice was soft and almost musical—but somehow a little nervous. And Lauren wondered further: Did she follow me into the store? But then she made herself dismiss such silly thoughts from her mind. "I really wanted to talk to you about—" Helena broke off and seemed to be waiting for Lauren to finish the sentence.

"About Debbie," said Lauren, suddenly sure that that was what was on Helena's mind. But she was wrong.

"Oh, no, no. Not that." Helena was flustered, perhaps embarrassed. "About rooming," she said. "I wanted to talk to you about next year." And then she seemed to become shy, to regret having mentioned the subject at all, and she quickly handed Lauren an open copy of the *Paris Review* and said, "What do you think of this poem?"

Lauren read the poem quickly, aware that Helena was watching her with a certain intensity, as if awaiting Lauren's judgment. The poem was called "Night Thoughts on Lake Lucerne," and as far as Lauren could tell, it was a prose description of a lake, randomly broken up into poetic lines. Lauren recited two lines to herself but was unable to detect any meter at all. Apparently just being on Lake Lucerne at night and thinking night thoughts was poetic enough. "It's very pretty," said Lauren tentatively, not wanting to offend Helena.

But Helena was disappointed. "Do you really think so? It doesn't have any meter at all." Two points for me, thought Lauren. "I know I shouldn't say this, but really, I think a lot of my poems are better than this one, and the *Paris Review* just rejected two of mine without even a comment, just a printed form." Suddenly Lauren found herself liking Helena more—this sort of egotism Lauren could identify with much more easily than with artistic poses.

"Don't even think about it," said Lauren, ready with good-natured consolation. "They say that the only way to get your stuff published in these journals is to be one of the editors or else to be sleeping with one of the editors." Helena turned almost red, and Lauren thought, *is* she sleeping with one of the editors? Surely Helena couldn't be so embarrassed by the mere mention of sex. After all, she carried herself as if she were a French movie star, and she presented herself as an aspiring artist—she could hardly be an innocent, blushing virgin. Still, Lauren tried to change the subject, grasping for the first thing that came to mind. "Maybe you could ask Augustine Wedgwood to send your poems to the *Paris Review* with an accompanying note. They wouldn't dare send *him* a printed form."

Helena smiled. A reference to Augustine Wedgwood seemed enough to remind her that she was not without a certain poetic standing, that someone at least, someone very important, recognized her talent. But she gently rejected Lauren's suggestion. "I couldn't ask him to do that," said Helena. "It would be—" She searched for the right word. "Presuming."

Lauren was touched. The connection to Wedgwood was obviously of tremendous psychological importance to Helena, a crucial part of the way she saw herself and the way she wanted other people to see her, but she was not actually interested in exploiting the connection to further her career as a poet. "He probably wouldn't mind at all," said Lauren. "He wrote that letter of recommendation for you when you were applying to Harvard, didn't he?"

"That's true," said Helena. "But he was the one who suggested it. I would never have dreamed of asking him. You see—" But then she interrupted herself, apparently not quite sure of what she was about to explain. "Come over here," she said, touching Lauren's arm and leading her away from the magazines and journals so quickly that Lauren barely had a second to place the *Paris Review* on top of a stack of *Good Housekeeping*. Lauren followed, finding herself half hypnotized by the swaying of Helena's marvelous hair, with its magical lights, and oddly disconcerted by Helena's way of interrupting her own sentences, as if they were either too precious, or somehow too dangerous, to complete. When would Helena return to the subject of rooming, which she had so tentatively raised, and what exactly did she intend to say?

Now they stood before the row of handsome trade paperback biographies, which began on one end with John Quincy Adams and Alexander the Great and proceeded right through to Queen Victoria, Richard Wagner, George Washington, and—Helena had already picked up a copy—Augustine Wedgwood. In hastily taking the book from the shelf, she had carelessly knocked its neighbor—the Duke of Wellington—to the floor. "I wanted to show you," Helena was saying, "since you're so interested in Augustine Wedgwood—" (Oh, so *I'm* the one who's so interested in Augustine Wedgwood, thought Lauren, amused, bending to retrieve the Duke of Wellington.) "And this has just come to the bookstores; it just got here yesterday. I've been watching for it. You see, it was published in England five years ago, and it's only now being published in America. My father was working in London back then—his law firm has an office there—and I went to visit him for a week, and he bought the book for me because even then I just worshiped Augustine Wedgwood. I thought he was the greatest living poet. And I read it when I got back home, and that gave me the idea of writing to him and sending him some of my poems, and so this book was the beginning of"—she sighed—"the most important thing in my life." Reverently, she handed the book to Lauren.

The cover photograph was, of course, the face of Wedgwood himself, looking young and attractive, with brilliant eyes. Lauren turned to the back cover and read that the photograph was from 1929. She skimmed the quoted British reviews: "At last a biography that does justice to one of our most important poets . . ." "Wedgwood's story is the intellectual history of England in the twentieth century . . ." "A great poet and a fascinating personality." At the bottom was the price: $12.95. For a paperback. If I want to find out more about Wedgwood, thought Lauren, I'll borrow Helena's copy.

But Helena was watching now, as if expecting some sort of reaction, so Lauren opened the book and glanced at the chapter titles in the Table of Contents: "An Edwardian Childhood," "Encounters with Bloomsbury," "The Spanish Civil War," and so on. Instinctively, Lauren sought out the pictures in the center of the book: Wedgwood with T. S. Eliot, with Rebecca West, with W. H. Auden. Then a photograph of a poem in manuscript, in Wedgwood's handwriting; Helena reached over and turned the page, impatient to move on to the next set of photographs. Wedgwood with his first wife in London in 1926, with his second wife in Paris in 1935, with his third wife in Sicily in 1949, with his fourth wife in Cornwall in 1962. Wedgwood got older and older; his wives got younger and younger. And Helena was definitely his type—there was a decided resemblance to number two, who actually was a French actress. Lauren turned back to that photograph for a second and wondered whether Helena was consciously modeling herself, her hair and her carriage, on this obscure French beauty of the thirties? It didn't seem unlikely, but there was really no polite way to ask. Helena might even be doing it without being aware of what she was doing.

"It looks very interesting," said Lauren, handing the book back to Helena, "and I'd love to buy it and read it right away, but you know, I'm frantically busy with my International Relations take-home midterm this weekend." So frantic, thought Lauren, I can't even concentrate on Machiavelli for five minutes at a time.

"There's something else I can tell you," said Helena, leaning closer, her voice lowered to a confidential whisper. "He's in New York." For a moment Lauren thought she meant Machiavelli and couldn't help looking perplexed, but then she realized that Helena was talking about Wedgwood. "There's a symposium on Auden at Columbia, and he and Auden were so close. He wrote to me two months ago and told me he might be coming and asked me to keep it secret, but today there was a little article in the

Boston Globe about the symposium, mentioning that Wedgwood was there, so I think it's all right for me to tell you."

If it was mentioned in the *Globe*, thought Lauren, then you don't even have to whisper. But she said, "Are you going to go down to New York to see him?"

Helena replied with just one word: "Midterms." And her features formed an expression of poetic agony.

Lauren nodded sympathetically. "Believe me, I understand."

"I'm dying to go, but I just don't think I can." Helena's face brightened. "But I'm going to see him this summer in England, I talked to my father last night on the phone, and he's almost definitely willing to pay for the summer at Oxford, and he's going to be flying to London himself a few times during the summer on business. Do you think I should introduce my father to Augustine Wedgwood?"

"Why not?"

"Well, he doesn't care at all about poetry or anything like that. He's only a lawyer." And then in a voice Lauren could barely hear, Helena said, "He's vulgar; he's . . ." Her voice had become almost bitter, had lost its beauty, and now she seemed unwilling to finish.

Lauren, though not uninterested in Helena's attitude toward her father, was willing to change the subject. She really should be getting back to Lamont if she wanted to have any time at all to study before dinner, and she was not going to leave Helena without raising again the subject Helena herself seemed ready to defer indefinitely. "What did you want to say to me about rooming?" asked Lauren.

Helena put her hero's biography back on the shelf and then carefully rearranged the half-dozen copies in such a prominent display that both George Washington and the Duke of Wellington were now completely out of sight. "I was going to room with Debbie," said Helena, staring at the cover of the biography, Wedgwood in 1929.

She was going to room with Debbie, thought Lauren, and now she is not going to room with Debbie, and the reason is because somebody strangled Debbie with one of her own harp strings. It was too extraordinary, too impossible to comprehend. But Lauren could not help asking, "Why?"

And Helena knew exactly what Lauren meant. "I know there were a lot of people who didn't like her, and I don't know if I'd even say that she and I were friends—but, well, we understood each other." Lauren told herself again, Debbie is dead, and was surprised to find herself on the edge of tears. "What do you mean?"

"Well, for one thing, we both thought that art was the most important thing in the world and that nothing else really mattered."

"She was very talented, wasn't she?" said Lauren, strangely overcome with sadness in the middle of the Harvard Book Store. A talented eighteen-year-old girl. Dead. Lauren picked up the biography of Queen Victoria and absentmindedly shuffled through the pages with her thumb. Hadn't Queen Victoria come to the throne of England at the age of eighteen? And she lived to be very, very old.

"Very talented," murmured Helena. "A true artist, a dedicated artist."

"You know, I was in the suite the night she died," said Lauren. "Remember, you lent us your Shakespeare that evening, and you showed us the letter you'd just received—"

"I remember."

"And later that night Debbie was playing the harp. Beautifully. I ended up falling asleep in Emily's room and staying all night, and I heard the music of the harp as I was falling asleep."

"I heard it, too," said Helena, "as I was going out." Going out? It took a moment for the words to register on Lauren's mind, to intrude upon the terrible memories of that night, the night of the murder, and by the time Lauren realized what Helena had said, Helena was already continuing. "And the other way that Debbie and I understood each other was connected to our families. You know, her parents are divorced, and my parents are divorced. Debbie may have seemed tough, but underneath she was very insecure. About being loved, I think. And that's why she ended up doing things that made people dislike her. Because if she knew they disliked her, she didn't have to worry about whether they liked her or not. I know that doesn't quite sound like it makes sense, but do you see what I mean?"

"Yes, I see," said Lauren, bursting with a question. But this was not the right moment to ask. Going out?

"And the other reason that Debbie and I understood each other was that none of our parents was ever really able to appreciate the importance of the things that really mattered to us, poetry for me, music for Debbie. Neither of us ever had family encouragement. Well, neither of us really had a family. Do your parents appreciate the things that are really important to you?"

"Yes and no," said Lauren meaninglessly. She was not quite sure herself what things were really important to her. Right now it seemed desperately important to learn why Helena had been going out the night of the murder. She tried to come up with a conversational transition, however implausible. "My parents called me last night from New Jersey, and I told them someone was murdered here, and they warned me over and over again to be careful about going out at night."

"My mother's like that," said Helena, "but worse—now she doesn't want me to go out at all at night. She read about the murder in the *Boston Globe*."

Odd, thought Lauren, that Helena had not told her mother that her roommate had been murdered—but there was not time to think about that now. "You went out, though, the night of the murder," said Lauren, speaking a little too loudly, excited about finally returning to that point. A bearded browser turned from the history cases to look at Lauren, then turned back again to the book in his hands. "Of course, that night no one knew Debbie had been murdered yet," Lauren continued more softly. "But did you see anything when you went out? Did you see anyone suspicious hanging around the dorm?"

Helena thought for a moment. "When I came out, I thought I saw someone standing alongside the front of the dorm—I couldn't swear to it, just a dark shape in the night really, and when I got closer, it was gone. You know, my imagination." Helena seemed rather proud of her imagination, a part of her poetic soul.

"How about when you came back? That must have been pretty late."

"I didn't come back that night," said Helena.

"No?" Lauren could barely contain her interest.

"No."

"Romance?" Lauren tried to sound lighthearted, but she suspected something much more sinister, though she couldn't have said what.

"Yes, actually. Romance."

"Who might that have been?" More false playfulness.

"His name is Frank Frosch, he lives in Matthews. He's a poet." Lauren was not surprised. "It was sort of embarrassing," Helena continued hesitantly. "You see, it was our first time together." Lauren nodded encouragingly, a little surprised that Helena was being so confiding. "And then the next day the police had to find him to check with him that I had spent the night in his room. Just the idea that I could have killed Debbie is, well, mad—but the police had to check on everyone who was in our suite, and this way they know for certain that I couldn't possibly have—"

"Because she was still alive when you left the suite; you heard her playing the harp."

"Yes, I went out around one o'clock. I remember the harp very clearly. It was as if she was playing especially beautifully that night. . . ."

The perfect alibi. The Harvard night guard had heard the harp at two thirty-two. And Helena hadn't been in the suite since one; she had been with someone else who could confirm that. Lauren was so disappointed she felt almost ready to start thinking about International Relations. She looked at her watch. She had been in the bookstore for two hours. "I've got to get back to Lamont," she said halfheartedly. "Glad we bumped into each other."

"But I haven't told you what I wanted to tell you,"

protested Helena, "about rooming." Somehow Lauren was no longer interested, but Helena was finally ready to speak out. "I don't have anyone to room with now, and I'd like to room with you and Emily."

And suddenly, for no reason at all, Lauren was certain that Debbie Doyle had somehow been coercing Helena Dichter, that she had had some kind of power over Helena, that Helena hadn't dared refuse to room with Debbie—and that Helena Dichter had murdered Debbie Doyle in order to liberate herself, in order to make herself free to room with Lauren and Emily.

Lauren darling, said Lauren to herself, imagining Michael's inflections, that is the most pre-*pos*-terous thing I have ever heard.

"Lauren darling, that is the *most* preposterous thing I have ever heard," said Michael. She hadn't imagined the emphasis quite right. They were standing in a long line at Steve's, waiting with every intention of buying themselves ice cream sundaes when they finally made it to the front of the line. "Granted that it would be utterly delightful to room with you and Emily—I would consider it myself were the university somewhat more enlightened about these things—but I hardly think that anyone would murder anyone else in order to obtain the privilege. Your vanity rivals even my own."

"You're right, you're right. I take it back. Pretend I never said anything," said Lauren. "There was just this one insane moment in the Harvard Book Store when it seemed wonderfully insightful and perfectly plausible. So I'm a fool; let's forget it."

"And besides," said Michael, unwilling to forget it, "an alibi is an alibi. Helena wasn't in Weld Hall the night of the murder; ergo, she is not the murderer."

"She was in Matthews," replied Lauren querulously. "That's right across the Yard from Weld. She could have just dashed across the Yard while what's his name was douching himself in the bathroom, or whatever it is that boys do in the bathroom after sex."

"We feel melancholy," said Michael, "like all other

animals. Didn't you say Helena's animal is a poet? He probably writes postcoital poems. And she probably does, too, instead of racing across Harvard Yard to strangle her roommate and then racing back again. I mean, Lauren, it's *too* preposterous. Besides, does Helena seem like a murderess? From what you've told me, it sounds like she's not up for anything more strenuous than taking care of her hair and boasting about her letters from Augustine Wedgwood."

"It's true; she doesn't come across as a ferocious murderess."

"What about what's his name, her poet and alibi? What *is* his name?"

"Frank," said Lauren.

"Not Frank Frosch?"

"Yes, as a matter of fact, I think that was the name. You know him?"

"Know him?" Michael was extremely amused. "He was madly in love with me for two whole years at Exeter." Lauren had her doubts about this, but she said nothing. "And he is the ugliest boy anyone ever knew. Frosch means frog in German, not freshman, and he is a frog among frogs."

"I saw Helena walking in the Yard yesterday with some-one who would have to be described as a hideous troll. Could that be our frog?"

"A froggish troll or a trollish frog," said Michael, "de-pending on the light. I suppose the lovely Helena sees through his repulsive exterior to his poetic spirit; but I must say I never dared to. I think he managed to get himself on the poetry editorial board of the *Harvard Advocate* in the fall. At Exeter he likewise reigned su-preme on the literary magazine when it came to poetry, which, I'm sorry to say, it often did."

Lauren remembered how Helena had blushed at the inadvertent reference to sleeping with the editors of the *Paris Review*. "Is he any good?" asked Lauren.

"Is he any good?" repeated Michael rhetorically. "He has the poetic sensibility of an electric eel. Don't you remember, I showed you one of his poems in the winter issue of the *Advocate*. Remember, I told you it was by someone who used to be in love with me at Exeter."

"I seem to recall there were poems and stories by three or four people who used to be in love with you at Exeter," said Lauren suspiciously.

"That's true," Michael admitted. "But this was the poem about wanting to commit suicide because the world is so unfair. You can't have forgotten—we laughed for fifteen minutes."

"So that was Frank Frosch."

"And speaking of giggling," said Michael, "I had a little chat this morning with my dear friend Cookie Fink, who was wearing her new pink pants and looking quite the flamingo." Michael rubbed his nose affectionately, just thinking about his conversation with Cookie. "I asked her about Debbie's brother, the fraternal David."

"What did she say?" The ice cream line was moving very slowly. This was what everyone else in Cambridge did while the graduate students were browsing in the bookstores. What flavor will I have, thought Lauren, chocolate, cinnamon, or malted vanilla?

"Well," Michael was saying, "you know how we were wondering how Cookie, even Cookie, could possibly have failed to notice that one of her Davids had the same last name as one of her roommates. Well, apparently that problem was bothering Cookie, too, and she even took the trouble to telephone the David in question—though I can't imagine how she remembered which one he was. And it turned out that Debbie's divorced mother remarried several years ago and took a new name. And Debbie changed her name, too, to match her mother's, but her brother wanted to keep his father's name. So he isn't David Doyle at all. He's David, um, something, I forget."

"Naturally."

"Cookie now says she should have guessed, anyway, because there was something about the noses and the chins."

Interesting, thought Lauren, but really the question of why Cookie didn't know was overshadowed by the question of why Debbie didn't tell. Why hadn't she wanted

Cookie to know? Clearly it had been in David's interest to follow his sister's injunction, since any connection to Debbie—let alone such a close connection—would certainly not have made him a more competitive candidate in the contest for Cookie. Debbie's own motivation was murkier but by no means out of character. She must have felt that she was somehow infiltrating Cookie's life by sneaking her brother into Cookie's bed, and although it was impossible to imagine just how Debbie had hoped to exploit these circumstances, it was easy to suppose that her intentions were not pleasant. "Was Debbie trying to use her brother to find out something embarrassing about Cookie, something she could maybe use against Cookie when the time came?" Now, of course, the time would never come.

"I can't imagine *what* she hoped to find out about Cookie," remarked Michael. "It seems to me that Cookie tells everyone everything, anyway. She certainly tells me everything. She hardly strikes me as a young lady with big secrets. At any rate, she isn't concealing a murder; she has an alibi. As does the lovely Helena."

They had reached the front of the line, and Lauren was being waited on by a fourteen-year-old boy with pink hair. "A small sundae, please. Malted vanilla ice cream, hot fudge, whipped cream, and fresh strawberries." He turned to fill her order.

"Did you see the way that little boy was looking at me?" whispered Michael.

"No." One of the occupational hazards of going out for ice cream with Michael (for Lauren it was virtually an occupation—she did it almost daily) was his special obsession with the boys who work behind ice cream counters. He always suspected that they thought of nothing but ravishing him on a bed of chocolate sprinkles.

"Chocolate ice cream with hot butterscotch topping and whipped cream," said Michael to a thirteen-year-old girl who was working behind the counter on roller skates.

"There are two things I don't understand," said Lauren, waiting for her sundae. "Why would someone as beautiful as Helena be sleeping with your frog? And why, if she was going to sleep with him in his room in Matthews the night of the murder, why was she wearing a nightgown when she came in to Emily's room to show us the letter from Augustine Wedgwood."

"She's sleeping with your troll because there is no accounting for taste, and she was wearing her nightgown because she's more comfortable lying around her room in a nightgown—I feel that way myself. And the only reason you find all this so disturbing is because, for some reason, you are instinctively intent upon making this into a murder mystery among roommates. But Cookie was at the Sheraton, and Helena was in Matthews, and Emily was with you—and if the Princess turns out to have an alibi, you're going to have to give up on your Radcliffe roommates solution. It was only an intuition to begin with, a brilliant intuition I admit, but not necessarily a correct one. Lauren darling, we've got to face the facts and accept the evidence. And we've got to find the murderer before someone else is killed. You know what they say about someone who has murdered once."

Lauren knew. And she also knew that she and Michael with all their undergraduate inquisitiveness were obvious candidates for the next murder. If they were going to find the killer, they couldn't afford to waste time.

"We have to start looking into those two Davids," said Michael, "at least find out which is which. You know, they did both return to Weld that night. Both Davids were on the scene of the crime, furious, all their sexual dignity cut to the quick. Natural murderers. And you know, something occurred to me this morning—what if there are more than just two Davids? What if there are several and not even Cookie can tell because they're interchangeable? What a complication *that* would be for the murder mystery!"

Michael darling, thought Lauren, now *that* is the most preposterous thing I have ever heard. But instead she just said, "Michael, tell me one thing."

"What shall I tell you?"

"Tell me how you're doing with Machiavelli."

"Fabulously!" exclaimed Michael, producing the little paperback from a pocket of his khakis. He opened to the tassled bookmark. "I've reached Chapter Four, 'Why The Kingdom of Darius Conquered by Alexander Did Not Rebel Against His Successors After His Death.' Top that."

Lauren produced her copy from her bag. "Chapter Eight," she announced, "'Those Who Come to Power by Crime.'"

"You win," Michael conceded. "I pay for the ice cream sundaes." His eyes brightened. "And here they are at last!"

7
Ladies of the Harem

■

But if once the Turk has been vanquished and broken in battle so that he can not reform his armies, there is nothing to worry about except the ruler's family. When that has been wiped out there is no one left to fear.

Machiavelli

Once again, Lauren ascended the little ladder, up to the high window that opened on to the roof of Weld Hall. She had not made an appointment with Ted to meet him there—it would be somehow wrong, Lauren thought, to meet on that magical roof by formal appointment—but she had high hopes of finding him there waiting for her, just by chance. The casualness of her appearance as she climbed did not give away the shameless premeditation and delicious anticipation with which she had looked toward this ascent ever since the last one two days before. She wore her new plum leotard (very sexy, really) with old Levi's (freshly laundered), low-heeled sandals (suitable for climbing), hardly any makeup (the roof, after all, was the great outdoors), hair just shampooed and dried, completely free down her back (it would blow romantically in the roof breezes).

The most damning evidence of premeditation was invisible. Under her Levi's, Lauren was wearing her diaphragm—which, unfortunately, she had not been wearing two days before, and so she and Ted had been able to amuse themselves only up to a certain point. Lauren had no interest, for the moment, in conceiving Theodore Roosevelt's great-great-great-grandchild. Today, however—if Ted was up there waiting for her—that would not be an, ahem, issue. Lauren had gone right past the door of Ted's fifth-floor suite to get to the ladder, and she would pass it again on the way down—but she had no intention of knocking. Either he would be waiting for her naked on the roof, or he wouldn't be. And if he's on the roof, Lauren idly reflected as she reached the final rungs of the ladder, either he will be lying faceup or facedown. She flipped an imaginary coin, and then let it fall to the floor far below her so that whichever way it turned out, it would be a surprise. Then she raised herself to peer through the glass door and was very much surprised indeed.

Ted was nowhere to be seen, dressed or undressed, faceup or facedown, but neither was the roof deserted. On the far side, standing near the edge and looking out intently at Harvard and Cambridge in the clear spring sunlight, was a man, immediately recognizable from behind, in a fine dark suit. The shocking contrast between the expected nudity of Ted and the overdressed formality of J.B. was enough to make Lauren feel dizzily insecure on the high ladder. Either she should descend immediately, or she should go out onto the roof—and it took her only a moment to decide. This is my lucky roof, she thought, opening the glass door as silently as she could and then closing it behind her. For a moment, high up in the open air, she was frightened, alone on the roof with this somewhat sinister figure who had not yet noticed her presence. Then she thought of her diaphragm in place and smiled to herself, thinking, I have all the protection I want.

Feeling brazen, she struck a sultry pose, leaning against the door behind her, arms pressed behind her back, plum leotard thrust slightly forward, hips pivoting at an angle. Lauren Bacall, she thought to herself, not Lauren Adler—if only there were fog instead of sunshine. But now she was ready to make her presence known, and drawing her lips into a circle as if to teach Humphrey Bogart how to whistle, she spoke just loud enough to carry her voice across the roof, spoke just one word. "Boo."

And then he moved so quickly that she almost didn't see him move. In a split second he had turned and was holding a pistol in his hand, aimed at her—could he have drawn it so quickly, or had he been holding it in his hand as he looked down at Harvard from the roof? In that first moment Lauren thought, He's about to kill me. And it was only in the second moment, when she realized that he had not killed her yet, that she also became aware of how terrified she had been in that first moment. She was standing in the bright, warm sunshine, and her body felt ice-cold with fear. She was unable to move, remained frozen in the sultry Hollywood pose she had struck two seconds before. Then her eyes met his, and she heard her own voice—or was it the voice of Lauren Bacall?—speaking hoarse and cool. "Pretty fancy footwork."

"What are you doing up here?" The gun was gone. He had put it away with such a quick motion of the hand that she didn't even see where he had put it.

"What are *you* doing up here?" If I were Emily, thought Lauren, I would repeat his question back to him in his own British accent. If I were Emily... No time to think about that now; he was walking toward her.

She didn't move a muscle but stared him in the eye as he approached until he stood two feet from her. She could almost see her reflection in those eyes, very dark blue, almost black, devastating. She reminded herself that her eyes, a remarkable green, were not without impact of their own. It was the corners of his eyes, however, the tiny, barely visible creases there, that reminded Lauren that she was not looking into the eyes of a fellow Harvard student. Aside from the differences in style between J.B. and the average American college student, there was also the fundamental difference in age. This very attractive

man, thought Lauren, is significantly older than I am.
Thirty? Thirty-five? Even forty was not out of the
question.

He was almost a foot taller than she was, and so, gazing
upward, it took her a moment to realize that he was
holding something in his hand at waist level. Bracing
herself, she looked down, and masked her relief at seeing
not the gun but only a gold cigarette case, open, and
shining in the sun. On the inside of the cover she could
actually read the tiny mark of 14k. If there was a more
personal inscription on the outside of the cover, she could
not see. But somehow she doubted it—this was a man of
mystery.

Alongside the rectangular gold of the cigarette case was
a small circle of gold, a cuff link, also brilliant in the sun.
But neither case nor cuff link could distract Lauren's
attention from the overpoweringly, fascinatingly masculine
wrist. She glanced over at the other wrist that hung at his
side and thought, His wrists are even more hypnotic than
his eyes. She lusted after his wrists.

"No, thank you," she finally said, declining the ciga-
rettes. Let's fuck. Had she actually said that or merely
thought it? She looked up again into his eyes, which
registered nothing—apparently she had not spoken aloud,
and just as well.

He was bringing a lighted cigarette to his lips, a cigarette she had not seen him light. Sleight of hand was
clearly a part of his professional repertoire.

Finally, Lauren moved. Without speaking, indeed without thinking, she stepped around him and walked over to
the other side of the roof, escaping not only from his
overpowering proximity but also from her own lust. But,
she realized as she moved, her intention was more purposeful than mere escape. She was heading for the spot at
the edge of the roof where he had been standing before,
and reaching her goal, she peered over the edge to see
what he had seen. In Harvard Yard, far below, near where
Lauren and Emily had been sitting a week ago, Emily was
now sitting with the Princess. Fascinating, disturbing, a
much more marked appearance of friendship than Lauren

had ever noted before. But there was no time to think about that now.

She turned and looked back at him, and he, obviously aware that they had now changed places, said, "Boo."

"Tell me," said Lauren, calling across the roof, "do you think that someone will try to murder the Princess next?" She had not forgotten his appearance in International Relations on Wednesday.

"Next?" Once again he walked toward her, until they both stood at the edge.

"Yes, do you think that whoever murdered Debbie will murder the Princess next?" Or me, she mentally added, will the murderer try to murder me?

"I don't know who murdered Miss Doyle," he said.

"I didn't say that you did."

He hesitated. Lauren knew that he was thinking not about her question—clearly he had given that sufficient thought already—but about whether he should answer. And then he did. "Frankly, I don't think it's impossible that whoever murdered Miss Doyle might try to murder Princess Yazmin."

Lauren looked down at Emily and the Princess again and said, "If someone tried to murder the Princess while you were up here, could you pick off the murderer with a bullet?"

"Perhaps."

"And that's why you're up on the roof?"

He hesitated again. "The roof also interests me for other reasons."

Me, too, thought Lauren; in fact, it interests me more and more. We have something in common. But she just said, "Oh?"

"You seem to be extremely interested in the murder of Miss Doyle," he remarked.

"Not extremely," said Lauren, lying, aware that he knew she was lying.

"Then you can give me a disinterested opinion," he said with irony. "You seem to know your way around this roof. Do you think it would be possible to climb down from the roof and into one of the windows on the second floor?"

"What an interesting suggestion." Does he think, wondered Lauren, that *I* climbed down the side of Weld Hall and murdered Debbie Doyle? Who does he think I am? Batman?

"I don't mean to suggest that you ever did such a thing, Miss Adler. I happen to know that on the night that Miss Doyle was murdered, it would not have been necessary for you to climb into the suite through a window."

You've been looking into things, thought Lauren. I think that *you* seem extremely interested in the murder yourself. But she said, "Please don't stand on ceremony. You can call me Lauren, even if we haven't been properly introduced." And then, out of curiosity, she asked, "What's your name?"

"You can call me whatever you'd like," he said, smiling.

"We do," said Lauren, smiling.

"I know."

Impertinently, flirtatiously, Lauren began, "We call you—"

He interrupted her. "I know what you call me, and I'm really very flattered." His smile became broader, even more handsome. He, too, was flirting. "Besides, I understand that my profession might seem rather cinematic."

"Then you don't mind if I call you—"

"Not in the least." The cigarette case appeared again, and Lauren declined a second time, said she didn't smoke. And he lit another cigarette.

"Well, then, J.B.," said Lauren, "why would a person who wanted to murder Debbie Doyle want to murder the Princess next? What possible reason could there be for one to imply the other?"

"No reason," said J.B. "No reason at all. Unless that person didn't actually want to kill Miss Doyle in the first place."

"But Debbie is dead," said Lauren, confused. "I don't understand what you're talking about. Somebody must have wanted to murder her."

"Unless . . . " he said encouragingly.

"Unless?"

"Unless the wrong person was murdered."

They sat on the edge of the roof, their legs hanging over the edge, her faded blue jeans alongside his dark navy trousers, and together they examined the old newspaper photograph he had been carrying in his wallet. Lauren had no trouble recognizing the facade of Weld Hall, and he didn't have to say anything to direct her attention to the windows of the second floor. And there was the Princess herself, unmistakable, sitting in the window, smoking a cigarette, looking out. Lauren was familiar with the aloof expression, but here it was mixed with an element of sadness, even loneliness, that she had never seen in the Princess's face. Lauren looked at the newspaper date above the photograph—September 29, last fall, the very beginning of freshman year. Lauren remembered that she, too, had sometimes felt sad and lonely back in the beginning, even though the predominant emotion was joy at having escaped from New Jersey. Going away to college, perhaps especially to Harvard, was undeniably intimidating to one extent or another, and the photograph of the many windows of Weld Hall, with only one person to be seen, vividly dramatized the lonely fears of September.

But there was something else that bothered Lauren about this photograph, and she didn't know what it was. She looked up at J.B. and saw that he was watching her, waiting for her to figure out what was wrong. Lauren looked down below at the Princess, who was still sitting in Harvard Yard in the flesh with Emily, then at the photograph where the Princess sat alone in her window six months before. Lauren looked at the other windows, but they were empty and held no clue to what was wrong with the picture. There, at the corner of the building, was Helena's window, blinds down. Perhaps Helena was behind, within, writing a lonely poem about coming to Harvard. And next was Cookie's window, blind up but nothing to be seen inside—Cookie was probably not lonely, since, according to Michael, by the end of September she was already dated up for every Saturday night through the beginning of December. And third was Emily's window, blind down, and it was in that room that Lauren had slept almost a week ago on the night of the murder, when Debbie was strangled with a harp string in the adjoining room. And there—there was the Princess! *That* was what was wrong with the photograph, and now it seemed almost terrifying.

"The Princess is sitting in Debbie's window," said Lauren aloud. "I don't understand. Why is the Princess sitting in Debbie's window? Were they good friends in the beginning?" But Lauren didn't believe it even as she asked. The Princess was definitely at home, at ease, in that window. She was not a guest.

"Very good, very observant. That was Princess Yazmin's room originally, and they switched rooms during the first week of October."

"Right after this picture was taken."

"Exactly, and that, as it happens, is not a coincidence."

"Why did they switch rooms?"

"Somebody, some bastard—I do not know who—took this photograph of Princess Yazmin and sold it to a British scandal sheet. She is of no interest to the American public—in fact, happily, she is virtually unknown in this country—but in England, unfortunately, her picture has appeared before in such papers. I would go so far as to say that she has managed to acquire a certain notoriety in England."

"How did she manage to do that?"

"Before coming to Harvard, Princess Yazmin was a student at a very fine school in London. And there her name came to be linked with that of a certain member of the British royal family. And there were photographs, and there were rumors and—"

"Was there actually something going on?" asked Lauren, who had never been able to keep those princes straight and didn't care which one it was—just as well, since J.B. was not going to tell her.

"That depends on what you mean by 'going on'." He seemed to find the phrase amusing, and Lauren opened her mouth to tell him precisely what she meant, but he spoke first. "I think I'd rather not know just what you mean. Whatever was going on, it was enough for Queen Elizabeth to consult with the emir, and they decided together that it would be better if Princess Yazmin were to go to Harvard University instead of to Oxford or Cambridge, where the other members of her family have traditionally gone."

"What a scream," commented Lauren irreverently.

"I don't think it's so funny. For me it means exile among the American barbarians."

"Poor, poor J.B.," said Lauren, too amused to be offended, daring to put a hand on his shoulder in mock consolation. "If you think we're barbarians here at Harvard, you must let me take you to visit New Jersey sometime." Mommy, Daddy, she thought, this is James Bond. He'll be staying in my room.

He neither accepted nor declined. "Anyway, that's why this picture was such a prize back in September. This rag"—he gestured at the piece of newspaper in Lauren's hand—"must have sent a photographer. Or else offered a lot of money to some bloody shit of a Harvard student to get the picture for them. Princess Yazmin was furious, and I was disturbed."

"Tell me," said Lauren. "Is that why the Princess needs you? To keep away the photographers? Or are you supposed to protect her from the American barbarians?"

He laughed. "Neither, believe me. You may think I'm just a cinematic property, but it happens that during the last ten years, fourteen members of Princess Yazmin's extended family have been murdered. Granted, it's quite a large family, but the statistic is nevertheless a significant one."

"Who murders them? Do they have a lot of enemies?"

He laughed again. "They murder each other—or, I should say, they arrange to have each other murdered. It's not a very cozy family."

"Why do they murder each other?"

"It's connected to the succession to the throne of the emirate, and that, in turn, is connected to the control of billions and billions and billions of dollars worth of oil assets. Do you know anything about harem politics?"

"Teach me," said Lauren sluttishly.

"In the previous generation, the emir and each of his brothers and each of his male cousins had a harem of several wives and therefore several families. The rivalries among the brothers and cousins were complicated by the rivalries among each of their respective wives, and those rivalries have bequeathed to this generation tensions furious enough to result in constant assassinations."

"The ladies of the harem," reflected Lauren, "sound worse than Radcliffe roommates."

"What was that?"

"Just an idle observation. Tell me, how does the Princess fit in?"

"Princess Yazmin is right in the center of it all. She was eventually supposed to marry her cousin, the heir, and thus conciliate two branches of the family, but he was assassinated in Paris six months ago—around the time that this photograph was published. Now they will probably want her to marry a different cousin, the new heir—if they both live long enough. As a rule, it's the males who are killed, but two of the fourteen have been princesses. I might add that the young man she is supposed to marry makes the princes of the English royal family appear as paupers by comparison. In Buckingham Palace and on the Gulf they were equally concerned to obliterate that embarrassing entanglement."

But Lauren was less interested than ever in the English royal family. She now understood. "You think that whoever murdered Debbie was actually sent to murder the Princess. That the murderer made a mistake."

"I think it's just barely possible. And if it's true, then it's very much my affair."

"And you think that the murderer might have killed the wrong person because of this photograph, because the window in the photograph that the Princess is sitting in has been Debbie's window since October, Debbie's room."

"I think that that, too, is just barely possible. Especially since it was precisely what I feared when I arranged for the rooms to be switched after I saw the photograph. I was afraid that someone might use this photograph to try to murder the Princess."

"What do you mean, you arranged..."

"It seemed like a reasonable precaution—even if the odds were only one in a million that anything would ever happen because of the photograph...."

"How did you arrange the switch?"

"Quite simple, really. Harvard itself takes no interest in, doesn't even keep any record of, which rooms the students live in *within* each suite. So on my own I just looked into which of Princess Yazmin's four roommates would be most susceptible to a financial proposition. And then I made a quite considerable offer."

It was true—Cookie and Helena and Emily were all obviously wealthy, in varying degrees. Debbie was not. "So she accepted your offer. Did you tell her you were afraid of a murderer coming through the window?"

"I told her I was worried about photographers."

"In other words, you set her up to be murdered."

"The danger was only one chance in a million."

"You thought those odds justified switching the rooms."

"That was my job."

He did not really care to defend himself against Lauren's imputations. He accepted no responsibility—or perhaps didn't even care whether he was responsible or not. I've been looking for Debbie's murderer, she thought, and perhaps, in a sense, he is sitting next to me on the roof. She stole a glance at his wrists. They now looked almost menacing, though undeniably sexy.

Lauren looked back at the picture, and something else occurred to her; she wondered if it had also occurred to J.B. Debbie had accepted the money that was offered her to switch rooms. Was it possible that she would have also been willing to take a candid photograph of her royal roommate if the price was right? And if it somehow came out, would J.B.'s employers in the Persian Gulf have commissioned him to kill the photographer? Would the Princess herself have murdered Debbie if she found out? The Princess was furious, J.B. had said about the photograph, and he was disturbed. If the Princess had murdered Debbie Doyle, obviously it would be J.B.'s job to cover it up.

"Were you around the night of the murder?"

His reply was prompt and precise, as if he had been expecting the question, as if he had answered it before. "I was in Princess Yazmin's room. And she was there, too."

"Oh?"

"I stopped by at half past one to check on her—I heard Miss Doyle playing the harp when I came in—and I read for a half hour in the chair in the corner while Princess Yazmin studied on the bed. And we both ended up falling asleep." A convenient alibi for both of them.

"Oh?"

"I believe something similar happened to you that night." His story, he seemed to be reminding her, was no more implausible than hers.

"What were you reading?" asked Lauren casually, wondering whether he would hesitate over the details of the story.

But he answered immediately, as if he had been asked before. "*Vile Bodies*. It's an Evelyn Waugh novel."

"I know," said Lauren. "I've read it, American barbarian though I may be. I love it."

"Then we have something else in common—beyond the fact that we both fell asleep next door to the room in which Miss Doyle was murdered." Another reminder.

"Where do you usually sleep?" asked Lauren out of genuine curiosity.

But she was asking more than he was willing to tell. "Somewhere around." He was being intentionally vague.

"You sleep around?" she said, keeping a straight face.

But he grinned. "Are you surprised?"

"Were you trying to surprise me?" Now she was being frankly flirtatious, and it was in that tone that she decided to make her next remark. "I'll tell you what surprises me a little—that you and I have become such confidantes about such matters." She gestured toward the newspaper photograph and then passed it back to him. "Tell me, J.B., why have you been telling me all this?"

She looked down at Harvard Yard for a moment, and when she looked back at him, the photograph had vanished. "Because I like you," he said, "and I have to talk about these things with someone if I want to see them clearly, and it would be very good for me to have, well, an ally—"

"An agent?"

"A friend—okay?—among the students, a friend who might mention it to me if she happened to learn about anything that seemed to fit together with the things I've been telling you."

"I see." She only half believed him.

"And of course I count on your discretion."

"You can count on me," said Lauren, wondering whether she could reach Michael quickly enough to be able to repeat this whole conversation verbatim. She smiled at J.B. and inquired, "Anything else I can do for you?"

"So, Lauren," her mother was saying over the phone from New Jersey, "remember you promised me you wouldn't go out alone after dark. Not until they find out who's been murdering the girls at Harvard. If only you went to Princeton like I wanted you to, we could just drive over in the evening to make sure you were okay—"

"Jackie honey, would you leave her alone," said Lauren's father on the upstairs extension. "It was one girl who was murdered, and Lauren's already promised you four times—"

"Herbert, thank you very much for the precise body count, I'm just trying to give our daughter a little bit of sensible advice so she won't be the next—"

"Mommy, Daddy," Lauren intervened, "do you have to call me up long distance to argue with each other?" And she thought, Thank God I didn't go to Princeton.

"All right, all right," her mother said, "just remember you promised. You see, Herbert, she wants you to stop arguing." And then, before he could reply, she said, "So, Lauren, what have you been doing?"

"I've been working on my International Relations midterm, Mommy." Sure.

"You know what I mean, Lauren Adler. Are you seeing anyone?"

This week, Mommy, I did everything but with Theodore Roosevelt's great-great-grandson up on the roof. "No one, Mommy. Are *you* seeing anyone?"

"Ha, ha, that's funny," said her father. "Tell me about your International Relations midterm."

"There really isn't much to tell, Daddy. I'm going to write an essay about Machiavelli and the Cold War." Lauren's father was tremendously interested in the details of what Lauren was doing in her classes—far more interested than Lauren herself, and for that reason she found his interest somewhat irritating. When her parents had come up to visit her at Harvard, he had attended all her lectures with her and taken embarrassingly extensive notes. Lauren tried to humor him, though, reminding herself that for the money he was paying in tuition, room, and board, he was entitled to attend Harvard vicariously along with her.

"Machiavelli and the Cold War," he was saying. "It sounds like a fascinating topic."

"Uh-huh." Then *you* write the essay. Of course she couldn't say that aloud, because he would be only too happy to take her up on it. Before she had started college, he had wanted her to become a doctor like him. Now he wanted to become a college student like her.

"Are you going to write about the electrocution of the Rosenbergs?" he asked, eager to be helpful.

"Well—"

"Herbert," Lauren's mother interrupted, "don't start on the electrocution of the Rosenbergs long-distance. Lauren, you know how he is when he gets started on the electrocution of the Rosenbergs."

"All right, Jackie honey, forget I mentioned it. Lauren, how are your other courses going?"

"Fine." My other courses? Lauren had almost forgotten about them. There was the required freshman expository writing—a joke. There was a required course on moral reasoning—a joke. And there was a course on Paris and London in the nineteenth century—that, at least, was fun, lots of slide shows. "My other courses are fine, Daddy."

"Well, we'll call you again soon," said Lauren's mother,

who had little interest in hearing about Lauren's courses and enjoyed cutting off her father's inquiries.

Finally, they hung up, and Lauren lay back on her bed, alone in her own little room in Thayer Hall. It was almost midnight. She looked up at the wall, at the two Klimt reproductions of striking women swimming in painted gold—they had been a Christmas present from Michael—and sleepily Lauren tried to imagine them as college roommates in fin-de-siècle Vienna. No, now she must concentrate. One of the redeeming features of telephone conversations with her parents was that they occupied only a part of Lauren's attention. Half her mind, at least half, had been left free to mull over all that she had learned up on the roof that afternoon with J.B.

But what was most fundamentally important? Lauren felt herself grappling with something, seeking some sort of mental summation of the situation. Was it the Princess's melodramatically dangerous position? And the odd way that the Princess was suddenly friends with Emily—was that somehow connected to Debbie's murder? Or was it connected to rooming for next year? I have to see Emily, thought Lauren. I have to talk to her. But about what? Does Emily know what J.B. told me. . . .

And do I really care? Ah, that was the key. Now Lauren saw what she was trying to formulate. The Princess and J.B. had been together in the same room while Debbie was murdered. (So he says.) Helena had been in Matthews with her poet. (Matthews is just across the Yard from Weld.) Cookie had been at the Sheraton. (Can I be sure that she was there the whole night?) And Emily was in bed with me. (Or was she?) Everyone, all the roommates, had alibis—suspect alibis, perhaps, but only to a suspicious mind. Therefore, in all probability Debbie was not murdered by one of her roommates—Michael was right. And in that case, does the mystery still interest me? Do I really care?

Perhaps not. A faceless, unknown character, a hired assassin commissioned by someone on the Persian Gulf, could have climbed through Debbie's window and murdered her by mistake. What about the forgotten sixth roommate?

thought Lauren. Had she already been driven out of the suite by the time the rooms were switched in October? Presumably. Lauren looked up again at her Klimt women, but they had nothing to tell her. She reached for Machiavelli, curled up on her side with the book, and opened to Chapter Eleven, "Ecclesiastical Principalities." Surely that couldn't possibly have anything to do with the Cold War. She flipped ahead to Chapter Twelve and began in on "Military Organization and Mercenary Troops."

8
Baroque

■

Nor I hope will it be considered presumptuous for a
man of low and humble status to dare discuss and
lay down the law about how princes should rule.
Machiavelli

By the next morning there were hundreds of announcements posted all over the university. But it was a Saturday,
and Lauren and Michael had both gotten out of bed very
late and then taken shamelessly long showers on their
respective floors of Thayer Hall—so they were probably
among the last to know. That, however, made them no less
intrigued when they finally descended to the ground floor
and caught sight of the announcements on the dormitory
bulletin board. A pale blue sheet of paper informed them
that on Sunday afternoon, the very next day, Senator
Anthony Ravello of Pennsylvania, just returned from a
visit to the Middle East, would speak at Harvard on "Oil
and Foreign Policy." And right alongside was a pale green
sheet announcing that on Tuesday afternoon there was to be
a poetry reading by Augustine Wedgwood.

"Too, too, too much," said Michael.

And Lauren said, "Michael, shall we say that you and I

have a date, two dates—Sunday afternoon and Tuesday afternoon?"

"I wouldn't miss Wedgwood—this is probably one's last chance; he's ancient. But *must* I put in an appearance at "Oil and Foreign Policy"? It will be like having International Relations on Sunday—and I can hardly bear it on Monday and Wednesday."

"You must."

"But I have to work on Machiavelli and the Cold War," said Michael slyly.

"Ha," Lauren replied. "I suppose you'll be working too hard to go see *Philadelphia Story* tonight for the two hundredth time."

"I really couldn't miss it," Michael admitted. "I've come to feel that Katharine Hepburn can't make it through the movie without me." He looked lovingly at the pale pink announcement of the movie, just above the pale green that heralded Augustine Wedgwood.

The other weekend movies on campus were also posted on the same bulletin board—*The Graduate*, *The Maltese Falcon*, *Bananas*, *A Night at the Opera*—all Harvard perennials that Lauren had seen before. And there was a glee club concert and a student production of *Fiddler on the Roof*. Lauren's gaze quickly returned to the two new announcements that must have been tacked up early this morning, the only two that interested her, the pale green alongside the pale blue. By now they were probably posted in every freshman dorm, in every upperclassmen's entry at the Harvard Houses, in the Freshman Union, in the Science Center, at Lamont, up at Radcliffe.

"You know," said Michael, "this is really very short notice for such famous people to be speaking at Harvard."

"Helena says that Wedgwood just came to New York this week and nobody really knew until the last minute that he was coming. So some venerable professor in the Harvard English Department—"

"Someone who used to sleep with someone who used to sleep with someone who used to sleep with Wedgwood back in the twenties—"

"Must have called him in New York this week and set

up the lecture at Harvard just in time before Wedgwood goes back to England. Good God, Helena is going to be ecstatic; she's going to have kittens."

"From what you've told me about the poetic Helena," said Michael, "I'm not sure I care to see her being ecstatic. I would, however, be ready to pay the price of an orchestra ticket at La Scala in order to see her having kittens. But what about *il senatore*? Why is he coming to speak on even shorter notice?"

"Well," said Lauren hesitantly, "after talking to J.B. on the roof yesterday, I can't help wondering whether perhaps it has something to do with—"

"Security?"

"Well, perhaps."

"Lauren, you are becoming increasingly morbid with each passing day. Now, try to tear yourself away from this bulletin board and help me decide where we should go for brunch."

They left the dorm and headed toward Harvard Square, thinking about Bloody Marys and Roquefort omelets. "Tell me more about this James Bond character," said Michael as they walked. "Cookie says he has a perfect chin."

"He does. Doesn't she approve of his nose?"

"She says it's a good nose," admitted Michael grudgingly, "but not quite perfect." He petted his own affectionately. "You know, if he was with the Princess that night, then there's really nothing left of your roommates hypothesis."

"I suppose not."

"And so you're losing interest in the whole mystery?"

"I'm afraid so."

"I wonder. If you were really losing interest, would you be so interested in tuning in to Anthony Ravello and Augustine Wedgwood?" But he didn't give her time to answer. "You know, if we want to get seats, we're going to have to go early—they'll both be mobbed. Wedgwood is Dante Alighieri compared to some of the poets the English Department invites for readings. And Ravello, they say, is going to be President someday soon. 'Oil and Foreign Policy'—Lord protect us. It's going to be simply fabulously boring."

*   *   *

Later that afternoon Lauren encountered the same two announcements, side by side, on the bulletin board that occupied one side of the covered outdoor porch of Weld Hall. She paused and read them both again, collecting her thoughts. She was going to call on Emily; she was finally going to talk to Emily. The announcement of Senator Ravello's lecture could be a sort of excuse for the visit, an opening for conversation. An excuse? An opening? How was it that in less than a week Lauren had come to feel that she needed an excuse and an opening in order to approach Emily?

She tried the door of Weld and found it unexpectedly locked. It was always locked at night but not usually during the day—was this a new security regulation after the murder? Lauren would have to wait until somebody opened the door to come out or until a Weld resident with a key returned to go in. She didn't have to wait long. After about a minute, Helena stepped out of the dorm, obviously distracted, even agitated, so much so that she almost didn't recognize Lauren, who took hold of the doorknob to keep the door open for herself.

"Helena, it's me, Lauren."

She was startled. "Oh, Lauren, you." Her instinctive reaction, of course, was to smooth her hair. "Excuse me, I didn't see you." Now she was in control of herself again, even posing. "I was in such a rush." She smiled.

"Helena, I saw the announcement that Augustine Wedgwood is coming to Harvard. You must be so surprised and so excited. I thought of you as soon as I saw it."

"Thank you," said Helena, as if she were accepting congratulations. "Excited, of course, but"—she spoke modestly but knowingly—"not completely surprised."

"You knew?"

"Well... Lauren, are you going to be there for the reading?"

"I wouldn't miss it."

Helena beamed, accepting more congratulations, and then her expression suddenly darkened. "I've really got to go get—" But she was overcome by distraction again and couldn't finish.

"Helena, are you all right?"

"I've got to get a new dress. I need something to wear. Lauren—" She lowered her voice to the same breathless, confidential whisper that Lauren remembered from the bookstore. "Lauren, I'm going to have dinner with him Tuesday evening after the reading." Now her lovely face expressed the poetic ecstasy that Michael had preferred not to observe.

But Lauren was more sympathetic. She, too, had had great crushes in her time. "Then you do need a new dress," she said. "I won't keep you any longer. Give me a call later; I'm dying to hear all about it."

"I will," Helena promised, and virtually flew off into Harvard Yard.

Lauren, who had held on to the doorknob, now entered Weld Hall. She started up the stairs, trying to put Helena's joyous news from her mind, trying to concentrate on Emily. Once before during the week Lauren had climbed these stairs, intending to confront Emily, but there had been no one in the suite, and Lauren had continued climbing until she discovered Ted on the roof. Then, yesterday, she had come to Weld again, hoping to find Ted on the roof, and instead she had come upon J.B. The acoustics of Weld, the sounds of her own footsteps on the dormitory stairs, were becoming eerily familiar. These stairs—to whom would they lead her today?

Today, at least, there was someone in the suite, because the door was ajar. Odd, even sinister, that the downstairs door to the dormitory should be locked for security but the door to the suite where the murder had taken place was left carelessly ajar. Lauren didn't knock. She entered as quietly as she could and crossed the empty communal living room, heading toward the corridor of private bedrooms. Already she could see that the door to Debbie's bedroom was open, and there were noises coming from within. In another moment Lauren was looking inside, and she found herself staring into the face of a woman she had never seen before, someone much too old to be a college student, someone completely out of place in Weld Hall. And this stranger was, not to put too fine a point on it, extremely fat.

It was the stranger who shattered the silence. "So what are you staring at, anyway? Haven't you ever seen a fat lady before? Are you one of those useless roommates who doesn't have any time to help me out with what I gotta do?" Lauren was unprepared for this direct assault and had no idea where to begin to respond. The tone was anything but Ivy League. But that was certainly not enough to tell Lauren who this woman was, let alone what she thought she had to do here in Debbie's room. The room, Lauren finally registered as she looked beyond and around the fat woman who stood in the center, the room was a shambles: clothes, books, sheet music, all in disorderly piles on the bed, the desk, the dresser, and the floor. Is it possible, Lauren wondered, that she's searching for something? In the corner stood the harp—no, just the frame of the harp; all of the strings were gone! And a rather unattractive brown dress hung on a hanger from the top of the frame, hung within the triangle of the harp. It was bizarrely disconcerting—especially since, at first glance, Lauren had taken the dress for a hanging body. This room, after all, had witnessed equally horrible, equally improbable happenings.

"Whatsa matter? Can't you talk? Or are you too snooty to talk to me?" Lauren was eager to have a closer look at the peculiarly disordered room, but first it was the woman within who demanded her attention.

"I don't live here," Lauren began, thinking as she spoke. "I just came to visit someone. But you said you needed some help with something—and I'd be glad to help you. My name is Lauren."

"A real Girl Scout," said the woman approvingly, giving much satisfaction to Lauren, who had been expelled from the Brownies ten years ago for insisting on reading a book during meetings. "I could really use some help, because, you see, I'm not a very organized person. And you can't visit anyone anyway now because there's no one left here to visit—I think I scared them all away. I'm Debbie's Aunt

Arlie, and I'm trying to pack up her stuff and get it out of here. You can call me Arlie; pleased to meet ya." She held out a plump hand.

"Pleased to meet you." Lauren stepped into the room and took the hand. Actually, she was beginning to like Arlie. The features, which Lauren now saw up close, were surprisingly strong, matching the voice and personality rather than the flabby hulk of a body. Sharp little eyes, heavily made up, a big mouth made bigger by the generous application of pink lipstick, and short, curly red hair. She wore black pants and a shiny blouse with a pattern of—now Lauren was close enough to identify it—a pattern of tiny, colorful fruits and vegetables.

"Listen, sweetheart," said Arlie, who apparently made friends—and enemies—quickly, "I'm making some progress with all this clothing, just stuffing it in this big camp trunk, so why don't you start throwing the books together into that big brown box I brought along. With two people this is gonna go lickety-split."

Lauren reached for Plato's *Republic* on the top shelf of the bookcase, then for Aristotle's *Metaphysics*, which stood right alongside. She flipped through them and saw that the pages were marked sloppily and thoroughly in blue ink; she placed them in the box. Debbie must have taken Introduction to Philosophy last semester, or perhaps she was taking it now, had been taking it until last week. Until last week Debbie had been taking courses like every other Harvard student, boring courses, silly courses, even perhaps—who knows?—fascinating courses, all of them fundamentally irrelevant to her life. And to her death?

"Boy, this is great, having someone to help me," announced Arlie, whose packing efforts were making the room into more and more of a mess. "The other two were just lazy, unfriendly snoots."

"The other two?" inquired Lauren.

"Sure, there was the tall one with the fake blonde hair." Cookie presumably. "She just stood there right outside the door and stared at me like I was some kind of sideshow, and finally—can you believe this?—she asked if she could see my profile. So I say to her, 'Listen, sweetie, I'm not

here to pose for my portrait; I'm trying to pack. How about some help?' And she says, 'Uh-uh, I'm not going in there again.' So I say, 'I'm not gonna ask you again . . . ' "
Lauren remembered Cookie's account of finding the body. No wonder she hadn't wanted to help pack up Debbie's things. Besides, she had hated Debbie.

"And then there was the fancy one. I'm sure she would have been happy to show anyone *her* profile any time of day." Helena, Lauren supposed. "She came in at least, and she sort of peeked around at Debbie's things, but real nervous, like she thought they were going to jump up and bite her. And when I say to her, 'How about giving a hand?' do you know what she does? She practically runs out of the room like a rabbit. . . . " And it must have been right after that that I ran into her downstairs, thought Lauren.

"Helena and Debbie were good friends," said Lauren, trying to explain.

"Hmmph. A fine friend." And with that Arlie plopped down on Debbie's bed and burst into tears. "They don't care about Debbie; nobody cared about Debbie except me. Nobody loved her except me. It's not fair; it's not fair somebody should go and kill her like that." Lauren sat down on the bed next to Arlie and reached an arm around her shoulder. With her other hand she reached into her bag and took out a Kleenex for Arlie. Then, Lauren suddenly realized that she herself was also crying. For Debbie, for Arlie. It was horribly unfair; there was no way to measure the unfairness. Poor unlovable Debbie, now dead; poor Arlie, sobbing on the bed where Debbie was murdered.

"My sister, Debbie's mother, got a letter from Harvard saying she could come get Debbie's stuff, and I said, 'Let me; I'll do it on Saturday.' Because I wanted to see the room where she lived and where she got killed. Who coulda done that? And I thought it would be, like, beautiful, just to pack up her stuff by myself, one last time. So I drove up from Long Island this morning, and as soon as I got into the room, I knew I just couldn't do it alone; it was too creepy. That's why I wanted someone to help me. Poor

Debbie, you know, she played on that harp like she was an angel."

"I know."

"You know, I bought her that harp. I saved up all my money and I bought it for her, and I paid for lessons, too. When I was little, I always wanted to play the piano. My sister doesn't really appreciate that sort of thing. And Debbie's father—that shit, thank god she hardly ever saw him—he wouldn't have known the difference between a musical instrument and a flat tire. But Debbie—" Arlie picked up pages of sheet music from the rumpled bed and held them in her lap. Lauren looked over her shoulder: Bach, Handel, Debussy.

"Put on that record, sweetheart," said Arlie, calmer now. "I was listening before, but I just couldn't take it, but as long as I've got a friend here with me now, I wanna keep listening. Go ahead, put it on. I won't cry." Lauren rose from the bed, crossed the little room to the stereo, and raised the arm. The turntable automatically began to turn, and Lauren placed the needle on the record, which was already in place. Beneath that record were four others that had already been played—Arlie must have been letting them drop one by one, listening to them all, until, as she said, she couldn't take it anymore. In a few seconds she heard the first notes of the harp, magically beautiful. And then a melodic phrase so delicate, so exquisite, that it filled her with a sort of inexplicable terror. She had to look away from the hypnotically turning black disk, and her eyes fell upon the boxed set alongside from which the five records had come: *Harp Music of the Baroque*. On the cover was a photograph of the instrument with all its strings in place, taut, ready to be played—unlike the empty, lifeless harp that stood in the corner of the room. The artist who played on the records was someone Lauren had never heard of—what did she know of the world's great harpists?—with a name she could not hope to pronounce. Greek? Rumanian? He played that phrase again, and Lauren closed her eyes. Behind her she heard Arlie sigh.

"I'll bring you a glass of water," said Lauren. "I'll just

step out and fill a glass in the second-floor bathroom. I'll
be back in a minute." Really, she wanted very much to get
out of Debbie's room for a moment, to escape from Debbie
and the shambles of her possessions, from Arlie, and from
that musical phrase. Lauren stepped to the door, which
was three-quarters closed. She pulled it open and saw the
form of a large man standing before her on the other side.
She opened her mouth to scream.

But then she saw that it was only David.

David looked past Lauren without seeming to recognize
her and just said, "Aunt Arlie, I got your message."

"Hello, David sweetheart." But there was no rush of
family feeling on either side, certainly no movement toward hugging or kissing. "I called and left that message
with your roommate so you could come help me out. But
Lauren here came along, and I think we've got things
under control." Lauren looked around her and thought, If
this is what she considers under control . . .

Now David was looking at Lauren uneasily. "You were
with Cookie the other day in the store, weren't you?"

"Yes." She wondered about his uneasiness. Was it something about the room in which his sister had died? Was it
something about being in the suite in which Cookie still
lived? He must really hate *her*, thought Lauren, remembering that the night of the murder was also the night of
the two Davids. Or did Lauren make him uneasy now
because he was ashamed of his aunt?

Without saying another word, David walked right over
to the stereo and removed the arm from the record, right
in the middle of that same phrase. And as if to put an end
to the harp music even more definitively, he silently began
to put the five records on the turntable back into their
envelopes and into the box.

Lauren thought that she should perhaps give aunt and
nephew a minute alone together, and she went out for the
glass of water for Arlie. In the bathroom she was detained
in front of the mirror by the need to remove from her
cheek some of Arlie's pink lipstick, which must have
rubbed off while Lauren was providing consolation and

Kleenex. Brothers do not kill their sisters, said Lauren to herself in the mirror, except in Michael's Duchess of Malfi fantasies. How peculiar—and yet how natural it seemed for Debbie—to have kept from Cookie that one of the two Davids was her brother. And Cookie had even seen them whispering together and suspected that—but wait. What if Debbie had been whispering with the *other* David? What if there was something being kept from Cookie there, too? And who would ever be able to figure out now which David was which?

When she returned to Debbie's room with the glass of water, Arlie and David seemed to be quarreling.

"But the cop told me," Arlie was saying, "that I should leave the harp for a while in case they wanted to look at it. So I said, 'Sure, buddy, whatever you say.' "

"But that's stupid. You shouldn't have to make another trip up to Boston for the harp, and you've got the U-Haul now. And the police won't know how to handle it, anyway; they'll damage it. And it's valuable, and you paid for it, so I think you're entitled to take it. Besides, they've had long enough to look at it." Long enough to blow on it, thought Lauren, recalling the men who had interrogated her. Why was David speaking so irritably to his aunt about this? And was he overeager to remove the harp from the scene of the crime? "I mean, look," he was saying, "they've already taken out all the strings. Why would they do a stupid thing like that?"

"I dunno," said Arlie. Of course *she* doesn't know, thought Lauren, but it's worth noting that he doesn't seem to know, either. That would confirm that he didn't cut the strings and didn't murder Debbie. Unless he's being *very* clever . . .

"I'll take it down to the U-Haul for you," said David, as if it were all settled. And since she didn't object any longer, perhaps it was. He removed the hanger with Debbie's brown dress and tossed it on the bed, then looked the harp over carefully, trying to decide how to carry it.

"Are you premed?" asked Lauren cheerfully. Really, it was a ridiculous question to ask out of the blue, but at

Harvard such questions were, in fact, acceptable casual conversation.

"Prelaw," mumbled David without looking away from the harp. Well, then, thought Lauren, the brother is the prelaw, and the other is the premed. Michael will be glad to have that straight. And as for the only other crucial distinguishing detail between the Davids, well, those kinds of questions do not constitute acceptable casual conversation, at least not at Harvard. Michael would have to find that out for himself if he really cared.

Arlie, on the bed, had taken out a pink plastic compact and was lavishly reapplying pink lipstick with the largest lipstick Lauren had ever seen in her life. Economy size? Lauren preferred to watch David watching the harp, occasionally shouldering it tentatively, then putting it down again. Debbie was a musician, of course, an artist, while he was only a prelaw, and those came a dime a dozen at Harvard. But neither of them had either personality or remarkable features. It was Arlie, though she was virtually grotesque, who had both personality and presence. Lauren remembered again what Emily had said about Debbie: that she didn't really exist, that she was only created by the intersecting tensions of the other four roommates. And David, though not as distinctively unpleasant as Debbie, was really nothing more than the essence of Davidness.

Finally he carried the harp out of the room, and Lauren found herself relieved to be left alone in the room with Arlie, glad to be rid of, for the moment, not only David but also the presence of the ghostly, stringless harp. She and Arlie returned to the business of packing, and by the time David returned fifteen minutes later, they really had made some substantial progress.

"One last book," called out Arlie, bending with a groan and picking up a hardcover from beside the bed. She dropped it on the neatly packed box of paperbacks from Debbie's courses that Lauren had gathered together.

"I think that's a library book," said Lauren, picking it up and opening the blank black cover. Inside was a penciled call number, the words Harvard College Library, and the

Harvard insignia shield with the motto *Veritas*. "I can return it," said Lauren. "It's no trouble."

And at that moment David spoke up abruptly. "My aunt and I can finish this by ourselves now. Thanks for helping her." It was definitely a dismissal.

Lauren looked from David to Arlie and back to David again, and then she graciously took her leave. "It was nothing," she said. And then to Arlie, she added, "Goodbye, it was nice meeting you."

"It was great meeting you, sweetheart. Thanks a million."

Impulsively, Lauren stepped over the big camp trunk and gave Arlie a parting hug, then accepted a kiss on the cheek—never mind the lipstick. For a second Lauren thought that they were both going to start crying again, but she turned and left the room quickly, closing the door firmly behind her.

She walked out into the living room, heading for the door, but she stopped short. In the living room, on the secondhand couch for which each roommate had chipped in twenty dollars back in September, Emily and the Princess were sitting side by side.

Lauren turned to face them, feeling the intensity of their four eyes upon her. She lifted a hand self-consciously to her cheek, which, she knew, must be covered with pink lipstick. Was there something wicked in those four eyes, or was it just curiosity? What, after all, had Lauren been doing in Debbie's room? For a moment she couldn't speak. And neither did they.

The Princess sat with one leg crossed over the other, gracefully, and she held her head at an angle. Emily's legs were identically crossed—Lauren knew Emily too well to suppose that this was a coincidence—and her eyes stared at Lauren from a face tilted at just the same angle. Uncanny. The striking difference was in the hair. Both had very long hair, and true black, but the Princess's was glassy and perfectly straight, while Emily's was impossibly curly.

"Emily," said Lauren finally, after five seconds that seemed like five minutes, "I came here to see you. I wanted to talk to you. Hello, Yazmin."

"I'd like to talk with you, too." Emily's voice was completely friendly, nothing wicked there or insincere. "We haven't talked in quite a while, and there are a lot of things to talk about."

"Well, yes," said Lauren, and gestured with both palms faceup, as if to say, Here I am at your disposal.

"But not now," said Emily, reading the gesture. Was it because of the Princess, Lauren wondered with a certain jealousy. "Because I have to go to the airport now," said Emily. "I'm going to meet my father. He's going to be here tonight and tomorrow."

"Right, of course; I saw he was giving a lecture. I'll be there."

"Good—I will, too," said Emily, "but we certainly won't be able to have our talk. What are you doing Monday?"

"Reading Machiavelli, of course—unless you can think of something more amusing for us to do."

"I think I can," said Emily. "Let's consider it a date, Monday evening."

"Lauren—" The Princess now spoke for the first time, an oddly musical British accent. "What about Sunday evening? Are you doing anything? My cousin is visiting me this weekend in Cambridge—he goes to school at the other Cambridge—and he's giving a little reception tomorrow in his suite at the Sheraton." Lauren did not interrupt to ask whether this was the cousin whom the Princess was supposed to marry, the heir to the emirate. Somehow Lauren just knew. "I was told last week that I should invite my four roommates, but one of my roommates has since become, well, as you know, unavailable. Can you come?"

"Yes, thank you." Unavailable? thought Lauren. What a word to choose! Impossible to imagine what the Princess thought about the murder. And how terrifying, how ghoulish, to be invited to the reception in Debbie's place! And yet how fascinating, how irresistible.

"Good, then you're coming," said the Princess. And then, "As long as *you* approve." But she no longer seemed to be talking to Lauren. Her tone had become distinctly ironical, and she was looking over Lauren's shoulder. "If there are no security objections."

Lauren turned around to see that J.B. was standing behind her, looking at the Princess. And he said, "I approve."

It was not until Lauren was walking home from Weld to Thayer that she realized she was still holding in her hand Debbie's library book. No matter, she could return it tomorrow. Idly, as she walked, she opened to the title page, and smiled to see that it was the very same biography of Augustine Wedgwood which Helena had showed her in the Harvard Book Store. Obviously Helena had urged the book upon Debbie as well, and Debbie, a better friend than Lauren, had taken the trouble to get the book out of the library. In fact, Lauren remembered, Debbie had been reading it the night of the fire alarm, had carried it out of the dorm with her. Now Lauren opened to the bookmark and was amused to see that Debbie had been looking at the pictures, just as Lauren had. There was the photograph of the Wedgwood poem in handwritten manuscript. Lauren turned and flipped through the pictures of the beautiful Wedgwood wives. To think that Helena was finally about to meet him—who knows, thought Lauren, perhaps she may still become number five.

That night, as Lauren was falling asleep in her bed, that phrase of Baroque harp music kept winding through her head. In fact, she couldn't banish it even if she tried. This obsession with the musical phrase was Proustian, she knew, had something to do with *Swann in Love*. Lauren had once read it for fun and romance, had not found it particularly funny or romantic, and now had a great deal of trouble remembering the details. Something about a musical phrase, once heard, never forgotten, coming back to haunt you. Had she ever heard that phrase before?

Suddenly she sat up in bed, completely awake, feverish with fear and excitement. Everything had come to her in a flash. She *had* heard that phrase before. She had heard

that phrase in Emily's room, in Emily's bed, the night of
the murder, during that dreamy moment when she had
awakened in the middle of the night, then fallen back
asleep again, and Debbie had still been playing the harp,
had been playing that phrase. But now it was all too
clear—Oh, how could I have been so stupid—that Debbie
had not been playing the harp, that it had been the stereo,
that five records of harp music had dropped one after
another through the night. And they had remained on the
turntable until this afternoon, the all-important clue
undetected.

Because all of the alibis depended on Debbie's being
alive and playing the harp. Playing until very late. At least
until two thirty-two, when the passing Harvard night
guard had looked at his digital watch. Cookie had heard
Debbie playing when she went out to the Sheraton.
Helena, too, going out to Matthews. And J.B. had heard
the music when he came into the suite to see the Princess.
Which had seemed to mean that Debbie was still alive,
that the others were all innocent, accounted for with the
most excellent alibis. But it meant nothing! Now the
mystery was wide open again. Up until a certain point
Debbie had been alive and playing the harp, and then she
was dead, and the records played instead. And obviously
there could be no doubt about it; it was the murderer who
had set up the five records after committing the crime so
that Debbie would seem to be still alive, so that there
would be time to establish an alibi for herself. Herself?
Oh, yes, it could not possibly be a coincidence that all the
alibis depended on that trick with the stereo, on the
continuing harp music. Terrified, Lauren forced herself to
think it through. She had suspected from the start, then
she had grudgingly had to admit that she might be wrong,
but now she was more certain than ever. As certain as she
could possibly be without knowing who or why. Debbie
Doyle had been murdered by one of her roommates.

9
International Affairs

■

Moreover, a prince can never make himself safe against a hostile people: there are too many of them.
                                        Machiavelli

Senator Ravello's lecture was to take place in the same hall in which International Relations met on Monday and Wednesday mornings. It was in the hideous, modern Science Center, whose lecture halls were often used for unscientific purposes. They were big and comfortable, and the amplification system usually worked—which was, alas, not the case with some of the older halls, designed for nineteenth-century professors whose oratorical training must have been dramatically superior to that of their twentieth-century counterparts. Outside the Science Center microphones had a tendency to whimper and die in the middle of lectures. At the Science Center there were also lots of blackboards that could be manipulated electronically with buttons at the lectern—Professor Grasshopper, for instance, was obviously childishly captivated by those buttons and moved the blackboards around on the slightest pretext during International Relations lectures. It was also possible to do all sorts of chemistry experiments at the lecterns in the Science Center, but Professor Grass-hopper had no excuse (and presumably no knowledge) for indulging. And it was unlikely that Senator Ravello actual-ly intended to refine crude Middle Eastern oil for the amusement of his audience.

"This is where they were showing *Philadelphia Story* last night," said Michael as he and Lauren took seats in the already crowded lecture hall. "How I wept at the end! Wouldn't it be delightful if it turned out that Senator Ravello had the measles and they had decided to show *Philadelphia Story* again in place of his lecture. How I would weep!"

"I weep, too," said Lauren, "whenever I think about walking you down the aisle in your wedding dress to give you away in holy matrimony to Cary Grant. I weep for Cary Grant. Listen, if you get bored during the lecture, I give you my permission to reflect upon how brilliant I was to figure that out about Debbie's stereo and how stupid I was not to think of it sooner."

"Cary Grant would be delighted," said Michael indignantly, "as would Jimmy Stewart, I assure you."

To this there was no possible reply; instead, Lauren made sure that her bag was comfortable on the seat alongside her. True, the hall was almost filled, but this was a bag that deserved a seat of its own, dark brown leather, Italian, imported, a gift from her parents. Some Harvard student could sit in the aisle.

"Excuse me, is that seat taken," said a male voice from the aisle, and Lauren was about to say yes—whoever he was, he could hardly be more worthy than an Italian leather bag—but then she looked up and saw who was speaking.

"Not at all," said Lauren sweetly, promptly moving the bag to her lap. "It's true, one almost fails to recognize you when you are wearing your clothes."

"Pardon, did I just hear what I thought I heard?" said Michael as Ted took the seat on the other side of Lauren.

"No," said Lauren quickly. "You must have been think-ing about *Philadelphia Story.*" She had not been especially eager for Michael and Ted to meet, but now there was nothing to be done about it. "Michael, this is Ted. Ted, Michael."

"*Enchanté*," said Michael, extending a hand across Lauren, which Ted politely shook instead of kissing.

A fine pair of escorts, thought Lauren of the two young men who sat on either side of her. Michael, as always, looked very preppie, granted a little more effete than that image ordinarily requires. Ted, of a surely no less illustrious family, wore army pants, a black T-shirt not tucked in, flip-flops, and a small stud earring that he had certainly not been wearing up on the roof—Lauren would have noticed. She was completely charmed by his attire. In his lap he, too, held a bag, an old army bag, and on the front pocket was pinned a shiny black metal button with the pink slogan "Commie-Fag."

"I hope you're not a Communist," said Michael conversationally, reminding Lauren of exactly why she had been reluctant to encourage this meeting.

"I don't think I'd know if I was," answered Ted idly.

And Michael followed up. "Would you know if you were a—"

But Lauren interrupted just in time. "Did you see the Harvard Young Spartacus League demonstrating outside the lecture hall?"

"Couldn't miss them," said Ted, "all ten of them, waving that big sheet with their mysterious message: 'Abolish U.S. Imperialism in the Middle East.' What do you suppose they mean?"

"How can America be imperialist when there isn't even an empress?" said Michael.

"Michael," said Lauren, "don't you remember Professor Grasshopper said there are three kinds of imperialism?"

"No, as a matter of fact. I think you just made that up."

"I did, as a matter of fact. But I'm sure he said it, anyway."

"What I find most interesting about the Harvard Young Sparticists," said Michael, "is that they confirm my hypothesis about the mutually causal connection between radical politics and bad skin."

"I never thought of that," said Ted. Lauren, of course, had heard the hypothesis before, several times.

"The Young Sparticists are simply ravaged," Michael continued. "It must be some sort of pox. I really don't see how they can hope to make a meaningful revolution until they learn something about skin care."

"Karl Marx," intoned Lauren solemnly, "Friedrich Engels, Lenin, Mao, and Elizabeth Arden. We will study their works."

"Not at Harvard you won't," said Ted, laughing, "but really, what if those ten out there are sincerely bananas? What if they decide that Senator Ravello is the very incarnation of American imperialism and they sit in the back row and assassinate him during the lecture?"

"Nonsense," said Michael, but Lauren couldn't help feeling suddenly queasy, reminding herself that she was looking for a murderer, that perhaps a murderer was even looking for her. "On the other hand," Michael was saying, "there is the possibility that they might kidnap somebody." When they had passed the demonstrating Sparticists at the entrance to the hall, Michael had managed to indicate to Lauren his horrified suspicion that they were looking at him lasciviously.

"Nonsense," said Lauren. And then she asked, "Ted, why are you spending a lovely Sunday afternoon at a lecture on 'Oil and Foreign Policy'?"

"I told you the other day," said Ted. "The Ravellos are old family friends, going back to Bangkok. I kind of like Senator Ravello—I'll go down and say hello to him after the lecture, and maybe he'll even report back to my father that I seem to be growing up into a fine young Commie-Fag. I think I'd like that, and my father will like it even more."

"I can just imagine," said Lauren. And then she asked, because it suddenly seemed important, "Do you see Emily anywhere in the audience?"

All three of them gazed around the lecture hall, looking for Emily. The hall was almost filled now, and Lauren found it difficult to pick out individuals. She guessed there were about five hundred people there—twice as many as were taking International Relations on Monday and Wednesday mornings—and so the hall seemed quite unfamiliar. At International Relations Lauren's Italian bag could always have a seat of its own. And what a din—all the little conversations that were going on in a crowd of five hundred. The hall was arranged in neat semicircular rows, each one considerably higher than the one before it so that there was never any trouble seeing the lecturer down below—or Katharine Hepburn, depending on the occasion. The sharp rise between rows, however, also meant that the last row was very high indeed and very far from the lectern. That was where Lauren and Michael (and Lauren's bag) usually sat for International Relations, but today, in order to mark the fact that this was *not* International Relations, they were sitting halfway down, on the side.

Lauren looked over her shoulder to that back row she knew so well, and there she saw J.B. and the Princess, talking very seriously. Oddly enough, it was a gesture of the Princess's that J.B. followed with his eyes, and then Lauren with hers, that finally enabled Lauren to locate Emily on the other side of the hall. She seemed to be alone, and next to her was one of the last remaining empty seats. As Lauren watched, someone spoke to Emily from the aisle, and after Emily responded, moved into the row to take the empty seat alongside her. It was only after the newcomer was seated that Lauren was able to identify her as Helena Dichter.

Just then the conversational roar subsided, and Lauren turned her attention to the lectern, where someone now stood. Not yet Senator Ravello—Lauren was amused to see that it was Professor Grasshopper, just where he stood on Monday and Wednesday mornings, now preparing to introduce the senator. With a great show of solicitousness, he established a glass of water alongside the lectern for the speaker, then moved it over a fraction of an inch and stepped back to admire his work. Lauren recalled that, according to Emily, Grasshopper was in close contact with her father, that if Senator Ravello were to become President of the United States, Professor Grasshopper might well be chosen as Secretary of State.

No surprise, then, that the introductory remarks were entirely flattering, though undercut by their unwarranted length and the speaker's characteristically unimpressive buggishness. "There are three kinds of politicians," he was saying, and of course Senator Anthony Ravello was the very best kind. Ted passed Lauren a scrap of paper on which he had written, *Who is this poor old fish?* And Lauren wrote back, *He teaches the International Relations course that you are taking.* Ted looked sweetly sheepish.

Senator Ravello was welcomed with applause, and Lauren thought that after watching Professor Grasshopper, it was pleasant to look upon a man who had shoulders. Definitely a handsome man, Emily's father, but not Lauren's type—too old, too senatorial. Before beginning to speak, he wet his throat with the glass of water that Professor Grasshopper had positioned with such ridiculous care. "This week, when I was on the airplane flying back home to America from the Middle East, there were a few very basic things about our foreign policy that I kept turning over in my mind." An informal beginning, and Lauren could see immediately that he was an excellent speaker. Professor Grasshopper had actually had to read the introduction, but Senator Ravello didn't even have any notes. He spoke directly to the audience of five hundred, bringing them all on board that airplane, inviting them to consider what he had been considering that day.

Lauren would not have minded paying attention to what he was saying were it not that she herself kept turning things over in her mind. She had been doing so ever since last night. It was a list really, and now she thought that if she could just jot it down in outline form on a piece of paper, she might be able to exorcise it from her mind.

Roommates	Possible Motives
Helena	To room with me and Emily
Emily	The caftan from her father
Cookie	The chemistry midterm
The Princess	The photograph

Lauren shielded the paper with her hand and looked over the list. All the motives seemed equally implausible. Obviously Helena couldn't have murdered Debbie in order to room with Lauren and Emily—Lauren only wrote it down because she couldn't think of anything else and she was determined to list all four roommates, for the sake of formal completeness. But it was really equally unlikely that Emily would have murdered Debbie because Debbie kept the caftan package in her room for two days before turning it over. Although, Lauren thought, what really bothered Emily about that was that the caftan was a present from her father. Lauren looked up at Senator Ravello—what if Debbie had done something else that touched on Emily's father? But what? And as for Cookie, certainly she was fiercely determined to succeed in her premed courses, and probably she was odd enough, inhuman enough, to consider killing someone who got in her way. And Debbie would not have hesitated to get in her way, just out of spite; but that still didn't explain what Debbie could have done that would have mattered *that much*. And Lauren had no real reason to believe that it was Debbie who had taken that photograph of the Princess and sold it to the scandal sheet. And even if she had—how would the Princess find out? Debbie might have told her, spitefully. But would the Princess care enough to kill her?

Lauren's list was suddenly covered by a folded piece of paper coming from Michael's side. She unfolded it and read: *Who is this Ted, and how does he look when he isn't wearing his clothes?* Lauren wrote at the bottom: *Delicious*. And then decided to append: *Hands off!* Michael read this and raised his eyebrows in a way that did not leave Lauren feeling entirely at ease.

But just then a note appeared from Ted's side, and Lauren was pleased, though not surprised, to read, *What are you doing this evening?* The reception at the Sheraton, the Princess's cousin. Lauren wrote her reply, shielding it from Michael's view: *All dated up. What are you doing tonight?* Oh, shameless one, she thought, admiring herself. In a moment she had Ted's reply: *Prowling!* And unhesitatingly she suggested: *Try the second floor of Thayer around midnight*.

She passed this back just in time to receive Michael's note: *Oh, shameless one!* Had he managed to peek while she was writing, or could her messages be read in her face? Pleased with herself, she looked straight down at Senator Ravello. Aware that both Michael and Ted were watching her, she tried to adopt the expression of a concerned citizen.

"Our foreign policy can not be based on our economic needs." The senator was now declaiming while gesturing broadly with an outstretched hand. "But neither can it remain completely aloof from those needs." Still listening, Lauren shifted her gaze to Emily and Helena on the other side of the hall, then focused on Emily. "Strategy and economy are necessarily inseparable." Emily wasn't even watching him. She was looking at her lap, apparently indifferent—just as if, Lauren thought, just as if he weren't really her father at all. An odd thought. Lauren tried to read Emily's face across the hall, but it was completely blank, the way it sometimes looked when Emily was about to plunge into an impersonation, effacing herself as she prepared to become someone else.

And then there was an explosive crash.

And instantly Emily was roused. Her face expressed not mere alarm but utter terror. The blank mask of indifference was so completely shattered that Lauren could barely remember it. It was all too clear that Emily's first thought was of assassination and equally clear that she had been dreading it all along. As if in trying not to think about it she had taken refuge in thinking about nothing. It was not until a second later, when Lauren saw the terror in that face give way to relief, that she herself was able to wrench her gaze from Emily to her father. And then Lauren saw what had happened.

With one of his gestures, Senator Ravello had knocked over the glass of water—poor Professor Grasshopper—which had fallen to the floor with a crash. And that crash had been picked up by the famous Science Center amplification system and transformed into a thunderous explosion.

"Well," said the senator, smiling, unruffled, "too bad. You know, after two weeks in the Middle East, with the members of my staff reminding me every ten minutes not to drink the water, I've come to feel that good old American tap water is one of our precious resources. And it tastes better than crude oil."

The audience laughed, and Lauren turned her gaze back again to see that Helena was smiling. But Emily was not amused.

All hotel rooms are tacky, as Lauren well knew. Someone responsible for this reception appreciated that axiom so completely that he or she had actually taken the trouble to transform the suite for the occasion. In the central room the supremely tacky beige hotel wall-to-wall carpeting had been covered with several large, overlapping, colorful Persian rugs. And covering most of one wall was the most splendid rug of all, a pattern of gold vines on a background of purple and blue. That must have been the wall on which the hotel painting of a sailboat had been hanging— Lauren later found the painting turned against the tiled wall in the bathroom of the suite, just where it belonged. The transformation of the room was simple, a few bold strokes, but absolute— and absolutely successful.

At the door, the Princess and her cousin were receiving guests, side by side, as if they were already formally affianced, or even married. There was, Lauren immediately saw, a problem with the matching: aside from the likelihood that he would die violently in the near future, he was at least six inches shorter than the Princess. And she, cruelly indifferent, was wearing silver lamé sandals with three-inch heels.

"Lauren," she said, "I'm glad you could come. Lauren Adler, my cousin Prince Hussein."

"You must be one of my cousin's roommates," he said. Lauren glanced at the Princess, who said nothing, so Lauren followed her cue and nodded to him, thinking, At last I am one of the roommates. "She tells everyone about

her roommates," he continued. "You are all famous through-
out the Middle East." His British English was even more
perfect than hers—not a trace of an exotic intonation.
Short, thought Lauren, but not without charm.

"Famous or notorious?" asked Lauren, as if it were a
joke, just silly conversation. "What does she tell everyone
about us?"

"Scandalous, scandalous things," said the prince, revealing
nothing.

"Oh, very scandalous," the Princess chimed in, and
then, stepping away from her cousin, she pointed across
the room. "Why don't you get a drink from the bar?" she
suggested to Lauren, and then, lowering her voice to a
whisper, she said, "I'd like to talk to you for a moment
later on." She stepped back to her cousin's side and turned
to greet a new guest.

Somehow Lauren was certain that the Princess wanted
to tell her something about Debbie's murder, but for now
all she could do was head across the crowded room for the
bar. When she arrived, she was considerably amused to
find a familiar pair of wrists mixing the drinks.

"A man of many, many talents," commented Lauren.

"More than you suspect," replied J.B. "What can I do
for you?"

"I thought you'd never ask." He grinned, and she, after
a long, deliberate, flirtatious pause, asked for a screwdriver.

"I'm sorry," said J.B., "but your host is a Moslem. No
alcohol. May I offer you a glass of orange juice?"

"Fantastic," said Lauren, slightly irritated. "If you think
I'm old enough."

"I think so," he said, pouring her a glass from a full
pitcher. As he handed the glass to her, he lowered his
voice and asked, "Have you learned anything that might be
of interest to me, I mean, connected to what we were
talking about the other day?"

"Perhaps," said Lauren, wondering whether she should
tell him about the stereo and confront him with the fact
that neither he nor the Princess had a real alibi. Lauren
looked back across the room, and through a gap in the
small crowd she caught sight of the Princess and her

cousin, greeting new guests. Some heads moved, the gap widened, and now Lauren could see that the new guests were Emily and her father.

"Perhaps," said Lauren to J.B., "we can chat some other time. This is a party"—she gestured around the room— "and I really should be mixing." She gestured at the bar before adding, "And so should you." An exchange of friendly but very intent smiles.

Lauren stepped away from the bar and took a sip of her orange juice. She took another sip to figure out why it tasted funny and then realized that she was drinking a screwdriver. A fine pitcher of orange juice, she thought. Well, when in Arabia . . .

"Lauren, we're over here!" An unmistakable voice. A waving hand with a gold charm bracelet. Lots of charms.

"Hi, Cookie." Lauren approached and saw that Helena was there, too. And forming a sort of circle around Cookie and Helena were five young Middle Eastern men. They wore expensive suits and conservative ties.

"These are the guys," said Cookie, waving her charm bracelet by way of introduction. Her dress was bright green, strapless, slit up to the very top of her right thigh and belted with a big black bow that made her look like somebody's birthday present. She was a sight to see.

"We will introduce ourselves," said one of the five young men, seeing that Cookie had no more to add. And they did. They all spoke perfect English. Two went to school at Cambridge with the prince, two at Oxford, and one was just up from Yale for the reception. They all declared themselves to be cousins of either Prince Hussein or Princess Yazmin, which, Lauren recalled, meant that they probably all had some sort of stake in either the assassination or the survival of the host. They were all drinking orange juice, just like Lauren, all good Moslems. Funny how the room had been transformed into the tent of the Ottoman sultan with those Persian rugs and all the guests were from Oxford and Cambridge. And Harvard and Yale.

Lauren introduced herself, keeping one eye on Emily and Senator Ravello, who were still talking with Prince

Hussein and Princess Yazmin. Clearly, the Princess's roommates (of whom I am now one, Lauren reminded herself—those famous roommates) had been invited to help balance the prince's traveling entourage of male Oxbridge cousins. But this particular group of seven was not quite working. The one young man who was tall enough to be of possible interest to Cookie was deep in conversation with Helena, talking about Augustine Wedgwood, whom he greatly admired, whom he had once talked to for two seconds at Oxford. Meanwhile, Cookie was telling the others about the rides at Disneyland and—Lauren guessed from three of their four noses—performing mental surgery. They were being extremely polite, inquiring about the speed of the different roller coasters, forming heaven knows what impression of Radcliffe women—no doubt unaware that they were on the operating table. If I were they, thought Lauren, I would be tempted to give a tug on Cookie's big black bow just to see if the whole dress sort of unwraps. But they were obviously much too well bred to think of such a thing.

"Guys, I've gotta talk to my girlfriend for a second," announced Cookie, and they nodded graciously as Cookie took Lauren aside.

"These guys," she whispered to Lauren with evident disappointment, "they're all Chicanos!" The Los Angeles perspective on Middle Eastern affairs. Too good to be true. "But they look really rich; what do you think?"

"I think they're really rich," whispered Lauren, remembering the senator's lecture that morning on "Oil and Foreign Policy."

"Oh, wow!" said Cookie, who was generous enough to give credit where credit was due. And then, regretfully, she said, "I wish policemen could be rich. David took me out to dinner last night."

"David the detective? Has he figured out who murdered Debbie?"

"Hasn't got a clue," said Cookie with an odd sort of satisfaction.

"Have you got a clue?" asked Lauren.

Cookie fixed her with those dead-lizard eyes before

answering. "No." And then, very purposefully, she changed the subject. "David has a perfect nose, maybe even more perfect than your friend Michael's. Don't tell him I said so."

"I won't," Lauren promised, thinking that she probably would, wondering if Cookie was concealing something about the murder. Cookie had been right here in this same hotel, Lauren recalled, on that other night.

"Gotta go fix my makeup," announced Cookie, and she left Lauren. The crowd of guests seemed to part for her, and all eyes were on her dress.

Lauren turned back toward the young men they had abandoned, and saw, with a start, that the Princess was standing at her shoulder. For how long?

"There's something I wanted to ask you about," said the Princess confidentially.

"I was going to come over to you and Emily," said Lauren, somehow suspecting that Emily could be included in this confidence.

"Emily and her father have left," said the Princess. "They could only stop in for ten minutes; they're going to the airport. Emily's father has to be on the last plane to Washington."

Lauren felt frustrated, as if she had once again failed to make contact with Emily. At any rate they had a firm date for tomorrow night. For now she should find out what was on the Princess's mind. "What did you want to ask me?" said Lauren.

The Princess raised her purse, which matched her sandals, silver lamé. She snapped it open, and Lauren was suddenly certain that she was going to take out the newspaper photograph of herself in the window, Debbie's window. A spooky picture, and Lauren braced herself nervously for the sight of it, so nervously that she had to laugh out loud when the Princess took out instead a copy of Machiavelli.

"What does all this have to do with the Cold War?" asked the Princess earnestly.

And Lauren was about to declare her own helplessness when they were both startled by a crashing noise behind them. A familiar crash, thought Lauren, this time muffled by a Persian rug. She turned to see that Helena, of all people, had dropped her glass of orange juice. All five young men murmured solicitous things, and Helena stared, stunned with embarrassment, down at the mess. A puddle of orange juice and shattered glass. And perhaps a little vodka.

10
Young Gentlemen

∎

*Fortune is a woman and . . . always, being a woman,
she favors young men, because they are less circum-
spect and more ardent, and because they command
her with greater audacity.*

Machiavelli

As Lauren dreamily emerged from sleep the next morning, she was not quite certain whether she was in Emily's
room or her own; it was an uncertainty that had been
coming over her often enough—falling asleep at night,
waking up in the morning, sometimes even in the middle
of the night—ever since the night of the murder. Involun-
tarily, she extended her arm to see if Emily was sleeping
alongside her or had mysteriously vanished, and Lauren's
arm came up against a body, a sleeping body, Emily's
body. Then I must be in Emily's room . . . and the
murder . . . Lauren forced herself to open her eyes, and
looking up, she encountered those two extraordinary Klimt
ladies in their respective seas of gold, and they were
looking down at Lauren with expressions of peculiar interest. Then I must be in my own room, after all, and this
must be—she extended her arm again and finally remem-

145

bered last night, just before turning over to confirm her memory—this must be young Theodore Roosevelt. What a relief—now Lauren turned over—and how lovely he looked.

He was asleep, just as he had been when Lauren had first set eyes on him up on the roof. Moreover, beneath Lauren's patchwork quilt, he was perfectly naked, just as he had been, et cetera, et cetera. Lauren reached a hand under the quilt and ran it caressingly down his abdomen just to satisfy herself that he was indeed as naked as she supposed. At which, not very much to Lauren's surprise, he smiled, then opened those fabulous blue eyes—Lauren remembered vividly the first time she had seen him open them up on the roof. As her hand dallied under the quilt, she felt him responding, and she said wickedly, "Good morning, Mr. Roosevelt."

He extended his own hand to return the caress and said, "Good morning, Mrs. Lincoln."

What did it really matter, thought Lauren vaguely, whether Ted's name and ancestry were genealogically true or a wild hoax? What if, what if this young man with the longish hair and the stud earring, this young man whose hands were stroking her now, what if he were a completely unrelated Roosevelt of no family distinction whatsoever? What if a quirky sense of humor had induced him to adopt the name itself? Really, what difference did it make? Anyway, he *was* a real Roosevelt, a true descendant. Silly speculation, inanely metaphysical all this, provoked by morning drowsiness combined with sexual arousal, and the vague feeling that in sex itself the names and identities of the bodies involved became somehow almost detachable, even irrelevant. Mr. Roosevelt. Mrs. Lincoln.

While Lauren's mind was engaged in such silliness, four hands beneath the quilt were moving beyond the bounds of mere playfulness. As he took her in his arms, Lauren heard herself saying, "Here we are, sir, writing a new chapter in American history."

One hour later they lay contentedly beneath the same quilt, on the same bed—it was, of course, one of those frustratingly narrow Harvard beds, but Ted, happily, was slender. Ted raised himself up on one elbow and looked at the clock on Lauren's desk. "International Relations is about to begin," he announced.

"Do you think you can afford to miss a lecture?" inquired Lauren, pulling him down again and snuggling up against his smooth chest. Michael, she thought, would probably come by after the lecture to find out why she was cutting. Probably he would already have guessed.

"I suppose," said Ted, "that International Relations are not the only kinds of relations worth studying."

"We'll go on Wednesday," said Lauren, "to turn in our midterms."

"A date with destiny. I'll write it on my calendar."

"If you prefer, I could mark it on your buttocks," suggested Lauren, wondering which shade of lipstick would look best.

"Hmm. It would be easier for me to check my calendar." Teasing her, he dangled a hand over the edge of the bed and reached into his army bag; he fished out not a calendar but a magazine. It was the literary magazine, the *Harvard Advocate*. "Just look what I have here," said Ted. "Have you ever had a lover who read you poems in bed in the morning?"

"Yes," said Lauren, remembering him with distaste. "Why are you carrying *that* around? You don't *read* it, do you?"

"God, no. One of my roommates gave me a copy—he did a drawing in this issue. Here it is. I think it's supposed to be an abstract depiction of existential anguish. My roommate is sort of an asshole."

Lauren glanced at the drawing and agreed. Then she saw that the poem on the facing page was by Frank Frosch, Helena's troll. "Bitter Almonds." Yet another poem about suicide—she and Michael had found the last one pretty hysterically funny. "I press the poison to my palm," she read aloud.

"What?"

"Nothing, just a brilliant poem about killing yourself with cyanide because all your fellow students at Harvard are so superficial."

"Let me see."

"No," said Lauren, throwing the *Advocate* across the room, tired of it already. "You can read it alone the next time you're sunning yourself up on the roof."

"Alone? Aren't you going to come sun yourself along with me sometimes?"

"Maybe. I was up there the other day—but you were not."

"If you had let me know . . . "

"That's okay," said Lauren, feeling mischievous. "I ran into, um, somebody else."

"Oh?"

Lauren was looking for a hint of jealousy, but from one word it was difficult to tell. Push a little further, then. "A handsome man in a dark suit."

"Oh, him." No jealousy at all. Amusement, perhaps. And familiarity!

"You know him?"

"He's Princess Yazmin's security guard."

"I mean, you know him as a visitor to the roof?" Of course he did. On some level she'd known it all along.

"Now Mary Todd Lincoln," he said, evading the question, "I do believe you're trying to make me jealous. But I assure you, I am not jealous."

"So I see," said Lauren, whose intuitions had been racing along. "Should *I* be jealous?"

"What do you mean?" His face revealed that he knew exactly what she meant, and perhaps it revealed a little more than that. She waited for him to continue. "Well, no, you shouldn't be."

"Why 'well, no'? Why not just no?"

"Well, because the time we met up there, he did, well, make his intentions clear."

"And did you make your intentions clear? Did you challenge him to a duel for insulting your masculinity?" Lauren rested an elbow on Ted's chest and looked right down into his eyes.

And his reply was endearingly sheepish. "I flirted."

Well, that was that. It explained a great deal about J.B. and no little bit about Ted. Fascinating, absolutely fascinating—Lauren could have gone on questioning him about that flirtation all morning. But as long as she had him pinioned with her elbow, as long as she had started him in on replying to questions of this nature, there was something else in the back of her mind. Rapidly, she brought it forward. "You and Emily are old friends, right?"

"Well, more like old enemies, I'd say, as I told you the other day." He was trying to wriggle out from under her, but she brought up another elbow to reinforce the first one, and she settled them both neatly, but firmly, on his nipples.

"Old enemies—exactly what I mean. Have you and Emily ever slept together?"

"I could turn that question around, too, couldn't I?" He was nervous, Lauren could see, but he was also enjoying the situation. And so was she. Really, they deserved each other.

"You answer first," said Lauren, pleased to have something to bargain with.

"Once," said Ted. More adorable sheepishness.

"On the roof?"

"Oh, no, not here at Harvard!"

"In Bangkok?"

"Emily and I were little children in Bangkok. I can not speak for Emily, but I myself was perfectly chaste until the age of fourteen. This happened in Washington, when we were both in high school, and . . . "

"And?"

"The setting was even better than the roof of Weld Hall, better than Bangkok. It was right at the foot of the Lincoln Memorial, in the middle of the night. Abraham Lincoln looking on, with malice toward none, you know. Anyway, Emily and I remained enemies during and after; we just don't get along." Now Ted really did look embarrassed. "I should go take a shower," he suggested, without even asking Lauren to fulfill her half of the bargain.

So she sent him upstairs, in her own bathrobe, to the boys' showers on the third floor, and she herself took advantage of his absence to search through his army bag. But she didn't find anything very interesting or revealing until she idly dipped into the pockets of his army pants. In the back left pocket she found the scrap of paper she had been doodling on the day before at Senator Ravello's lecture. On it were listed in two neat columns Debbie's four roommates and the four possible motives for murder.

Lauren stared with endless fascination at the young gentleman in the mirror, the green-eyed gentleman in the top hat and black tails, very grand, profoundly alluring. He was, of course, herself. And Emily was kneeling at her feet, adjusting the cuffs of the trousers over shiny black shoes.

Emily rose and stood alongside Lauren, dressed identically except that her spectacular hair was still down, curling around her lapels. Now, as Lauren watched in the mirror, she put it up on her head with two quick motions and an equal number of bobby pins. She brought her own top hat down over her brow, and the costuming was complete. Emily had chosen jackets just a little too big, so that, worn over ruffled white shirts, they very effectively camouflaged even generous female figures. Emily leaned an elbow on Lauren's shoulder in parody of gentlemanly camaraderie, the same leaning pose that Lauren had often seen her bring to bear upon imaginary lampposts; it was one of the fundamental tricks in any mime's repertoire. Now, however, following upon the utter transformation of their appearances, Emily's pose made Lauren feel as if she herself were some sort of imaginary lamppost, as if, in substance, Lauren Adler no longer existed.

"My dear Emil," said Lauren finally, "doesn't it seem to you that we are, dare I say it"—she lowered her voice to the male register—"in drag."

"Double drag," said Emily, stroking an imaginary goatee, "my dear Laurence."

"I'm closing," called the old man at the cash register on the other side of the store. "If you wanna buy all that stuff, you gotta buy it now." Lauren and Emily were surrounded by racks of secondhand evening clothes, piles of navy sailors' pants, shoeboxes filled with grotesque costume jewelry from the forties and fifties.

They approached the register, and the man looked them

over carefully from head to foot—not pruriently, however, since he was just calculating the cost of the various items they were wearing. Two hats, two black bow ties, two shirts, six ruby-glass buttonhole studs, four matching cuff links, tails, trousers, shoes. Emily had stuffed into her big shoulder bag the clothes they had been wearing when they came into the store as young ladies.

"I'll treat," said Emily to Lauren. "It was my idea." Emily had called that afternoon, suggested they go out for dinner and then go to a party, and mysteriously she had insisted that Lauren wear no makeup. When they met a few hours later, she had led Lauren out of Harvard Square, still not disclosing her intentions, straight to this store, which Lauren had never even heard of. Just the sort of place Emily would know about.

"Okay," Lauren agreed, "but you have to let me treat you to dinner." True, the evening clothes had been Emily's idea, but Lauren had taken to it with all the enthusiasm of a convert. This was certainly a lot more fun than shopping for new tops with Cookie at the Cambridge Shop. "False mustaches," said Lauren, her eyes lighting up. "What do you think?"

"Handlebar mustaches," suggested Emily, twirling the air with her finger. But those the store did not sell, so Emily paid the bill, and they exited after making a great production out of who would go out the door after whom. "After you, my dear Emil." "No, after you, my dear Laurence."

Dinner was at one of Lauren's favorite Chinese restaurants in Cambridge. Hot and sour soup, Peking ravioli, shrimp with black bean sauce, twice-cooked pork. Lauren was delighted when the waiter asked, Do you want chopsticks, Mister? but Emily reminded her that considering the level of his English, he might just as well have thought he was saying, God save the Queen. Laurence and Emil wielded their chopsticks with the utmost care to protect the ruffled shirtfronts that concealed their breasts. Traces of black bean sauce, even the very best black bean sauce, would have detracted from the effect.

"Why," said Lauren, "is there going to be a big party at Radcliffe on a Monday night?"

"Don't you know?" said Emily. "It's to celebrate the big news. This weekend the president of Harvard announced that he was about to undergo a surgical sex change and he wants everyone on campus to share in his own joyous anticipation of a new life." Lauren's chopsticks clattered to the floor. "April Fools," said Emily. "It's an April Fools party. Waiter, can we have another pair of chopsticks."

Although neither Lauren nor Emily explicitly referred to the uneasy one-week hiatus in their friendship, their dinner conversation made it clear enough that they both felt there was some catching up to be done between them. "What's new with your distinguished professor of American history?" asked Lauren.

"Well, on Wednesday, I finally propositioned him after lecture, and since then we've been having regular sessions in his office in Widener. He covers his desk with a thirteen-star 1776 American flag, I lie down on top of it, and at the moment of greatest passion he calls out, 'The Redcoats are coming, the Redcoats are coming.' " Then, glumly, she said, "April Fools."

"Men," said Lauren, giggling, "they're all alike in bed."

"How about J.B.?" asked Emily. "Have you made any progress?"

"He's gay," said Lauren.

"April Fools?"

Lauren shook her head sadly. "I'm the only fool. I should have guessed—he's too gorgeous to be heterosexual."

"Wow," said Emily, "I don't even think Her Royal Highness suspects. I asked her this week whether he and she had ever et cetera, et cetera, but she's not even interested in him. She's still madly in love with—" Emily hesitated.

"With a certain member of the House of Windsor whose name we dare not mention," said Lauren. "Queen Elizabeth told me all about it and asked my advice, and I told her to write to Ann Landers, so check out tomorrow's *Boston Globe* to learn what Questioning Queen should do."

"And I suppose Prince Philip told you about J.B."

"No, actually I found out from someone I know whom J.B. made a pass at, someone *else*, I mean—I take for granted that J.B. has made countless passes at Prince Philip, all of which have gone some way toward livening up a dreary existence in Buckingham Palace."

"Who is this someone you know," asked Emily, obviously very curious but unwilling to put the question seriously, "this Ganymede whose undergraduate wiggle has attracted the attentions of our own Olympian Bond?"

"Ted Roosevelt."

"Oh." A long pause. "I take it you are not referring to the twenty-sixth President of the United States." How did Emily know he was the twenty-sixth? Had she been secretly studying to become worthy of a certain distinguished professor of American history? Or was it her father's career that put the presidency on her mind?

"No," said Lauren.

"I didn't know you knew him."

"I don't know him very well," said Lauren. And then she added, as if by the way, "We spent last night together in my room."

If Emily found this particularly interesting, her face certainly did not give her away. She didn't even stop eating, just paused with her chopsticks in front of her bow tie and said, "How was he?"

"There wasn't any American flag," said Lauren, "but I think he rated several stars."

"I've never really liked him," said Emily, as if Lauren had asked. "He plays games, all the time."

"I think that's why I like him."

"I knew him in Bangkok, you know, when we were both children, and then later in Washington. And once, he and I even—"

"At the foot of the Lincoln Memorial in the middle of the night, I know," said Lauren.

Now Emily put down her chopsticks. "I've never really liked him," she repeated, "but I had no idea he was so fucking indiscreet."

"Not his fault," said Lauren. "I pumped it out of him."

"Well, in that case," said Emily, "I suppose the poor boy

didn't stand a chance." She and Lauren both laughed, and
Lauren had the feeling that they had just made it through
a difficult moment between them. She also knew that
there would be other such moments as the evening moved
along.

The party was at Currier House, one of the Radcliffe
Houses, so-called for purely geographic reasons; once upon
a time, when Radcliffe had an independent existence, that
was where Radcliffe had been. Really, they were Harvard
Houses now, half male, entirely integrated into the Harvard
House system. There was dancing in the Currier Fishbowl, the indoor courtyard into which one could peer from
the second-floor railings that ran around the sides of the
bowl. Laurence and Emil leaned against the railing and
looked down at the dancers.

The party had been advertised as formal, though noone
had been quite sure whether that was an April Fools joke.
So there were men in tails dancing with women in jeans,
and women in gowns dancing with men in sweatshirts. It
was clear that Laurence and Emil would fit right in just as
soon as they decided whom they could dance with.

"See those two girls," said Emily, pointing to one side of
the dance floor. "They look a little out of it. I bet they're
from Wellesley, looking for Harvard men." Emily slipped
away from Lauren's side and reappeared a moment later
down below. Lauren watched her approach the prey, chat
with them both for a moment, then lead one of them onto
the dance floor.

Which left the other one looking rather forlorn. So
Lauren also descended, and lowering her voice and gath-
ering up her nerve, she said, "Wanna dance?"

The girl stared at her for a moment and then said, "Get
lost; what do you think I am, some kind of dyke?"

So Lauren retreated shamefacedly to the punch table,
resigned to the fact that she simply did not possess
Emily's talent for impersonation. At the punch Lauren
encountered one of the most repulsive football players
from her own dorm, one of Michael's neighbors up on
the third floor; his nickname was the Animal, and with
good reason. He, of course, was much too stupid and

unimaginative to recognize Lauren, but he seemed to feel that she looked familiar. He said, "Hi, buddy," perhaps supposing that he had encountered her at some time in a locker room.

Lauren did not risk responding, just grunted in salutation, knowing that such noises passed for conversation among the Animal and his friends.

"Think there are any Wellesley girls here?" said the Animal confidingly. "I don't wanna dance with girls from Harvard 'cause they think they're so smart."

Lauren pointed him in the right direction and was pleased to observe that he was not told to get lost. He danced like King Kong.

The song came to an end, the music stopped, the dancers wandered out of the Fishbowl, but Emily didn't find Lauren until a new record was just beginning. The Village People. "Macho Man."

"This is our song," said Emily, and before Lauren knew what was happening, she and Emily were dancing together alone in the center of the Fishbowl. Both from the sides of the dance floor and from the railings up above, people were staring and murmuring. Lauren was tremendously embarrassed and at the same time jubilantly titillated; she knew she was dancing up a storm. And Emily was completely unselfconscious, keeping an eye on Lauren and following her more dramatic turns.

And then Lauren realized that there was another couple on the floor, and as she turned, she saw that the two new dancers were both men. And then on the other side two more men. Then two women. Soon the floor was almost filled with couples of the same sex, though certainly not as filled as it had been before, and in the center were the two gentlemen in evening dress who had started the revolution. Out of the closet and into the Fishbowl, thought Lauren, reflecting that this was just the sort of thing that *would* happen when Emily was around. Lauren caught her hat just as it was about to fall off and give her away.

Several hours later, Lauren and Emily were sitting all alone in the center of the Radcliffe Quadrangle, surrounded by the dignified brick dormitories of a Radcliffe that no longer existed, the music from the Currier House party in the distance. They sat cross-legged, facing each other, and in the dark Lauren could make out clearly only the white ruffled triangle of Emily's shirtfront and the whites of her eyes; the dorm behind Emily was really just a shadowy rectangular form. They passed a joint back and forth and listened to a bell ring twelve times—midnight.

Lauren held the smoke in the back of her throat, then let it out gently and said, "I keep seeing you with the Princess. Does that mean we're going to room with her?" They had discussed men and sex over dinner, but now, stoned, after the dance, in the middle of the Radcliffe Quadrangle, Lauren knew it was time to talk about roommates.

"Yes."

"You've decided? She's decided?" Lauren intended the implicit reproach—why wasn't I in on this?

"I guess," said Emily, and then, responding to the unspoken reproach, she added, "I'm really not sure that we were the ones who decided."

"What do you mean?"

"I mean, my father met with one of her uncles in Cairo, and when he got back, he was visited by someone from the emir's embassy in Washington, and they agreed that they might have certain political and international interests in common, and he suggested it to me, and they suggested it to her, and then he met her when he was here this weekend, and at the Sheraton he met her cousin the heir and . . . " Emily's explanation sputtered and then died. "We were thinking of rooming with her, anyway," said Emily, almost pleading with Lauren to agree, "and I do like her, and you'll like her, too, and there will be J.B., though I suppose that's less of a reason now. . . . "

Lauren was definitely disturbed by the idea of her rooming situation being arranged this way, as a function of alliances and interests in Middle Eastern and American politics. On the other hand, wasn't this really to be expected if she was going to room with the daughter of a man who wanted to be President. And anyway, Emily was right. A week ago Lauren would have probably been

happy to room with the Princess—before Debbie was
murdered. But Debbie's murder had nothing to do with
this, of course . . . except . . . except that it was scary. And
wouldn't it be scary to live with the Princess, who had to
be attended by a security guard to protect her from
assassins, to live with Emily, who immediately thought of
assassination when her father knocked over a glass of
water. Suddenly the dark shapes of the Radcliffe dormitories seemed sinister, and the whites of Emily's eyes and
the silhouette of her hat. Perhaps, thought Lauren, perhaps I should leave them to room with each other.

"What are you thinking?" asked Emily, and Lauren
watched her suck in the smoke from the glowing remains
of the joint.

Lauren tried to come up with something, anything but
what she had actually been thinking. "What about Helena?"
she said. "She wants to room with us. Could she room
with us, too?" Only after she had spoken did she realize
what she was doing, that she was insisting to Emily that
she, too, should be able to introduce another person into
the group. And somehow the idea of having a fourth
person seemed less scary than just rooming with Emily
and the Princess.

"I'm sure that would be okay," said Emily, aware that
Lauren was looking for a token concession, relieved that
Lauren seemed to have accepted the Princess.

Then it's settled, thought Lauren, the four of us together for the next three years. But she said, "I'm so stoned."

"Me, too."

And with that they seemed to have passed through yet
another difficult moment and emerged on the other side,
still friends. Without thinking, Lauren stretched out her
arm, and Emily did, too, and Lauren drew her hand in
slowly, and Emily mirrored the motion. Lauren, cross-
legged, looked into Emily's eyes and lifted her palm to the
imaginary mirror; Emily's palm met hers on the other
side. They both removed their hats, almost in unison,
then put them back on again. And so they continued until
Lauren finally spoke one word, munchies, and Emily
echoed it in the night, munchies.

They returned to Weld with potato chips and M&Ms from the 24-Store. Entering Emily's suite, they found, seated on the couch in the living room, a pair of long, perfect legs and an enormous chemistry textbook. A moment later, Cookie emerged from behind the book, in one of her little nighties, her face covered with cold cream, ghoulish. "Hi guys," she said, "you really look weird, wow, like guys' clothing." Lauren thought Cookie looked pretty weird herself, even frightening, those dead-lizard eyes staring out from that white mask. And Lauren thought: if Debbie really got between Cookie and her chemistry, if she were seriously interfering with Cookie's ambitions, then Cookie would have been capable of anything. Capable of killing *me*, thought Lauren suddenly, and then made herself put the thought out of her head.

"Any mail today?" asked Emily.

"Nope," said Cookie, "none of us got any mail today— except Debbie, can you believe it?"

"Probably her term bill from Harvard," Emily suggested, "or will they send that to her parents?"

"Just a little blue postcard from the library." Cookie took it out from between the pages of her chemistry book. "She had a book out, and somebody else has requested it, and she's supposed to return it immediately."

"I have that book," said Lauren, "but I forgot to return it—I'll do it tomorrow. I'll take the card, if you like." She walked up to Cookie who parted with it readily.

"Why do you have the book?" asked Emily.

"I was helping Debbie's aunt empty out the room the other day," Lauren explained. "Remember, I ran into you and the Princess sitting here on the couch." She gestured toward Cookie and the couch.

"Did you find anything of mine in Debbie's room?" asked Cookie. A very odd question, thought Lauren. "You know," Cookie continued, "she stole my manicure scissors right before she was killed."

"Nothing of yours," said Lauren, thinking, what else did Cookie think we might find?

They left Cookie in the living room, studying, and in Emily's room Lauren collapsed on the bed, the same bed on which—but never mind that now. Emily took a Chinese porcelain vase from the dresser, and went out to the bathroom to fill it with water—potato chips and M&Ms would leave them desperately thirsty. Lauren, alone, asked herself: could Emily possibly have murdered Debbie because Debbie withheld the caftan? And of course the answer was no. But if Debbie had somehow seriously come between Emily and her father? Well, then, maybe.

Lauren rose from the bed and opened Emily's closet, idly looking for the caftan, but it wasn't there. She pulled open a dresser drawer next, and there she saw a snatch of maroon at the bottom. She reached in and took hold, and then slowly, very stoned, she drew the caftan out of the drawer and held it before her. Cut, slashed. Horribly, irreparably mutilated.

Even before she looked up, Lauren knew that Emily was standing in the doorway. She was carrying the vase, and for a moment Lauren was certain that she was going to drop it on the floor. But no, Emily placed the vase carefully back on the dresser, then turned and closed the door behind her. Jean-Louis Barrault peered over her shoulder, and the three stone Hindu deities seemed to look up from their sexual entanglement to stare at Lauren and her discovery.

There they stood, looking hard at each other, the two gentlemen in evening clothes, and one of them held in her hand a length of tattered, ravaged maroon cotton. Emily addressed herself to the question in Lauren's eyes. "Debbie did it," she said, so quietly that Lauren might not have heard if she hadn't somehow known what Emily was about to say.

Lauren mouthed but did not speak her next question. Why?

"You remember," said Emily, a little louder now. "You were there the night of the fire alarm when I saw the package in her room, my package from my father, which she had been keeping. And I was furious, and I, well, you remember." Indeed Lauren did remember how Emily had perfectly and mercilessly mimicked Debbie's ugly yawn, face-to-face. "You remember; she said she was going to kill me. And then that night, remember, I was Othello and the caftan was creased, probably because she'd kept it in the box for two extra days, and Cookie thought of hanging it up in the bathroom so the steam from the shower would take out the creases."

"Yes," said Lauren, "I remember."

"That night, while you were asleep, I went to the bathroom." Then she hadn't been sleeping in the bed all night; the alibi was worthless. "And the caftan was hanging there all cut up, just the way it looks now." She pointed, but she no longer seemed to care. And yet she had to care—or why would she have preserved it like this at the bottom of the drawer? "I knew it was Debbie who had done it—after what she'd said that afternoon. Instead of killing me, she destroyed the present from my father. And so I went into her room." Emily paused. "And I killed her." A longer pause, an endless pause. "April Fools," said Emily, smiling grimly. "Did you believe me?"

Lauren didn't know what to believe. Lauren was stoned. Lauren was planning a trap, a trap for her friend, and she was feeling guilty about it too, because, after all, Emily was her friend and she might be perfectly innocent and perfectly honest. Or was that no longer possible? "Maybe," said Lauren, "maybe Debbie cut up your caftan because she thought you cut the harp strings."

"Maybe," said Emily. The trap was sprung.

"You knew about the cut harp strings," said Lauren, and Emily's eyes admitted it even as they revealed that she was all of a sudden aware of how much she had given away. "You *were* in Debbie's room that night," said Lauren. "That, at least, was no April Fools joke. You were there; otherwise, you wouldn't have known."

"Yes," said Emily. She did not even ask how it was that Lauren knew about the strings. Emily was too busy thinking, plotting what she would say, and Lauren could not even waste time formulating questions.

She accused. "You cut the harp strings," said Lauren. "That was your revenge."

"Yes," said Emily. "I went into her room carrying that," she pointed at the caftan in Lauren's hand. "I thought she was playing the harp; I heard the music from outside her door. I didn't know what I was going to say to her. But there was no one at the harp. The music was coming from the stereo. And Debbie was asleep under the covers—at least I thought she was asleep. I saw Cookie's manicure scissors on her desk—you heard what Cookie said; Debbie had taken them—and I was sure she'd used them to cut up my caftan. Look, you see there are all those savage little cuts; that's why it all still hangs together in one piece. So I picked up the scissors, and there was the harp, and I cut through the strings one by one, snip, snip, snip." Emily snipped with an imaginary pair of scissors, and Lauren shuddered. "It was one of the most bizarre experiences of my life," said Emily, who suddenly looked even more stoned than before, "because I snipped the strings, snip, snip, snip, and the music didn't stop, just went right on playing, pluck, pluck, pluck, very beautiful. I didn't feel bad about it at all, because she could get new strings easily enough, more easily than I could replace my father's present."

"And then?" said Lauren. The stone deities also seemed to be listening to learn what happened next.

"And then I went back into my room and went back to sleep right next to you. The next morning, I found out Debbie had been murdered, and I knew I should have told the police what happened, but well, just by chance I happened to have an alibi, and as you can imagine, it was very tempting to keep quiet. So I succumbed to temptation. That's all."

Emily collapsed on the bed alongside Lauren, both of them in trousers and tails. "I'm so tired," said Emily. "I'm just going to crash. You can sleep here if you'd like." She closed her eyes and seemed to fall asleep on the spot.

Lauren, for some reason, preferred to go home to her own room for the night.

11
In the Audience

■

*Men in general judge by their eyes rather than
by their hands; because everyone is in a position to
watch, few are in a position to come in close touch.*
                                                    Machiavelli

Who would have thought that Augustine Wedgwood would
turn out to be such a mass attraction? True, the poetry
reading had been announced that morning to the three
hundred students in English 10, Harvard's famously bad
Introduction to English Literature—required for concentration in the English Department so that even Michael
was taking it—but such announcements were usually barely heard, let alone taken to heart. For some reason,
however, and despite the short notice, word had gotten
around Harvard that of all the famous people who put in
an appearance there in the course of an academic year,
this was the one who was absolutely not to be missed.
Harvard students who hadn't even heard of Augustine
Wedgwood two days ago were suddenly thrilled to have
the opportunity to hear him read.

The reading had been scheduled for four o'clock in the
Boylston Auditorium, and Lauren and Michael—at Lauren's

insistence—arrived early. At quarter to four, the hundred and fifty seats in the auditorium were all taken, the aisles were jammed, and droves of people were still arriving. Somehow the chairman of the English Department made his way up front to the stage where, after much frantic gesturing for silence, he announced in a barely audible squeak—the amplification, of course, was on the blink— that the reading was being moved to the Science Center due to the unexpectedly large crowd. There were groans from the people with seats, cheers from the people in the aisles, loud confusion from the back, where no one had heard the announcement and everyone was asking everyone else what that squeaky little guy had said, and general pandemonium as everyone gradually realized what was going on and rose to begin the migration to the Science Center.

A crowd of hundreds—Lauren and Michael clutching pinkies so as not to lose each other—moved out into Harvard Yard, then past Weld Hall, past University Hall, past Thayer Hall, out of the Yard, and into the Science Center. Finally, they began to resettle in that very lecture hall that was so tediously familiar to Lauren and Michael from International Relations, the same hall in which Senator Ravello had spoken on Sunday. They managed to find seats in the very back, even two seats together, thanks to Michael, who sweetly asked several grumpy professorial types if they would be perfect angels and just all shift over one place.

At ten past four the high-pitched chairman was once again seeking everyone's attention, this time to announce— his squeak now amplified to an extent that seemed to signal the imminence of nuclear attack—that the hall was full beyond capacity, that fire regulations were very strict. The people in the aisles were going to have to go to the adjoining lecture hall where they could watch and listen to Augustine Wedgwood on closed-circuit television. At Harvard, such technological wonders were possible only in the Science Center—but those in the aisles did not find the arrangement particularly wonderful. Groans from the aisles, a sprinkling of smug applause from the seats, harsh words, and then even blows between someone seated on the aisle and someone seated in the aisle.

"*Mon Dieu*," said Michael, "quite by mistake we seem to have ended up at the Rolling Stones concert."

"And there," said Lauren, pointing down below, "there is Mick Jagger." Two chairs had been brought out and set up next to the lectern, and Augustine Wedgwood—Lauren recognized him immediately from the photographs in the biography—was sitting in one of them.

"With Bianca," remarked Michael, referring to the chairman of the English Department, who was sitting in the other chair, trying to make conversation with the poet.

It was understandably difficult to create an appearance of casual conversation, since the two of them were sitting in front of a crowd of five hundred, never mind the television audience. Besides, the chairman was apparently on the verge of hysterical exhaustion just from having made his two announcements and presided over the relocation and displacement of the masses. Wedgwood, on the other hand, seemed quite at ease, perhaps even secretly pleased at what a star attraction he had turned out to be. He was a great and famous poet, but after all, he was not Mick Jagger.

"For twenty years now," said Michael, "his name has been popping up at Nobel time—but always a bridesmaid, you know. Some say it's because he belonged to the British Communist Party for two weeks in 1936, but really it's because he doesn't translate well into the Scandinavian languages." From Michael's tone one might have concluded that he read Swedish, Norwegian, Danish, and Icelandic, and that he participated personally in all the most intimate deliberations of the Swedish Academy.

The two elderly gentlemen, the poet and the professor, seemed so extremely exposed in front of that full house, and Lauren couldn't help reflecting that on Sunday there had been no such display of preliminary coziness between Senator Ravello and Professor Grasshopper. Senator Ravello had simply appeared from a side door at the end of the introduction—but he, after all, was too prominent a political figure to sit exposed in front of five hundred people for no good reason. Security had to be taken into account. Augustine Wedgwood, in contrast, was of no political interest—except perhaps for two weeks in 1936—and was in no danger of being assassinated. He wasn't even Mick Jagger. The tremendous turn-out for this reading was really nothing but an almost accidental moment of exceptional celebrity.

There was a commotion from the back of the auditorium where several young men—graduate students, no doubt— were refusing to go quietly next door to watch the television, demanding admission to the already full lecture hall. Everyone turned to watch them being firmly sent away, to hear their indignant objections, to feel smugly satisfied at having arrived early themselves.

Lauren didn't bother to turn around and watch the disagreeable scene in the back, and so she noticed what was happening down front, something no one else would have thought worth noticing anyway. She saw someone in the front row stand up—it was Helena—and approach the lectern with something in her hand. She set it down, and Lauren saw that it was a glass, and not a glass of clear water but rather—of course one couldn't be sure from the back of the hall—of iced tea. Wedgwood's eyes followed her with an intentness that was virtually rude to the chairman of the English Department. Helena's back was to the audience, but Lauren could tell when her eyes met his, from the smile that appeared on his face. The smile lasted only for two seconds, and Lauren may have been the only one who was really struck by it—who else, after all, would bother to notice Helena?—but it was a smile to be remembered. It was not so much lechery as a frank sexual welcome—not in the least incongruous on the face of this octogenarian—and Lauren found herself almost responding to it from all the way in the back of the hall. She must have introduced herself earlier, thought Lauren; she must have set their date for this evening. A long- anticipated evening, thought Lauren, and it looks to me as if Helena is going to get everything she's been anticipat- ing, and then some. When Helena turned away from the poet, her face gave no clue as to how she had responded to that smile. Her expression was almost childishly blank, and her new dress, well, that was really something: a simple white cotton shift with a Peter Pan collar. Lauren remembered what Emily had said, that Wedgwood was the model for Humbert Humbert.

The glass of iced tea stood inconspicuously alone at the lectern and waited with everyone else for the reading to begin. A very good idea, thought Lauren. Iced tea was so much more refreshing than water—Helena seemed to have every intention of refreshing Augustine Wedgwood. The sight of the glass made Lauren realize that she was thirsty, just as the sight of that smile had made her aware that she was, all of a sudden, filled with undirected lust. Not for Wedgwood certainly—even Emily's distinguished American history professor was too old for Lauren's taste—perhaps for Ted. Tonight, then . . . But no, tonight was the very last night to write the International Relations midterm. Tomorrow morning, in this very same hall, Lauren would be handing it in—hard to believe, of course, when she hadn't yet written a word.

Then a young woman with short hair and overalls approached the two seated literary gentlemen and spoke a few words—presumably to say that technical matters were now in hand, the television equipment was all set up—and she went away without a smile from Augustine Wedgwood. The chairman immediately rose for his third and last moment in the spotlight—obviously ready for the reading to get under way, presumably tired of trying to seem to be in conversation with Augustine Wedgwood. Without further ado, he launched into a completely incoherent introduction. Squeak, squeak, the great English poetic tradition, squeak, squeak, squeak, one of the greatest of modern poets, squeak, squeak. Nervously he reached for the iced tea, then seemed to realize that it was not for him. "Badly in need of strict sedation, our fearless chairman," whispered Michael to Lauren. "This great literary event seems to have done him in."

Then the poet rose, and the professor disappeared into the audience. Augustine Wedgwood looked frail as he moved to the lectern, but as soon as he began to speak, it was clear that his voice, and the spirit behind it, was very strong indeed. So confident was the tone that it almost seemed as though the volume had nothing to do with electronic assistance. Did he take his confidence from the ovation he had received? Did he realize that many of those applauding had barely heard of him two days ago? Or was he wise enough to know that people always applaud thunderously when an event finally begins after a forty-five-minute delay? Lauren was remembering his smile. "I haven't been in America in many years," Wedgwood was saying, "and I suppose I have never understood either America or Americans. I'd like to read you first a poem I wrote for an American friend during the war." ("World War One?" Michael was whispering, "World War Two?") Then Augustine Wedgwood, who had lived through both wars, began to read.

Lauren was thirsty and sleepy, and she was thinking, How funny that at Harvard I am constantly going to these lectures and waiting impatiently for them to begin just so I can tune out and think about other things until the lectures are over. Last night she had gotten home so late. She had folded her trousers and neatly put away her whole drag ensemble in the closet—it had been a present from Emily, of course, just as the caftan had been a present to Emily from her father. She had ended up lying on her bed, completely naked, looking up at the Klimt ladies, thinking about Emily. Emily, who at the same time was presumably still lying on her own bed, fast asleep, in full evening dress. Lauren had thought about Emily for a long time last night, and she was thinking about Emily now. And remarkably, as if to illustrate Lauren's thoughts, the back of Emily's head came into focus and became recognizable on the other side of the hall. The poet continued to read.

Now Lauren looked around the hall more purposefully, and her purposefulness was rewarded. Four rows behind Emily sat Ted—and was he watching her? Lauren's gaze wandered uphill, and seven rows behind Ted she saw the Princess—and was *she* watching Emily? Alongside the Princess sat J.B., and as Lauren watched, he looked up from his lap (Lauren was as sure as she had ever been sure of anything that there was a paperback book in that lap) and seemed to seek the back of someone's head in the audience—not Emily surely, but perhaps Ted.

"This poem," Wedgwood was saying by way of introduction, "was written for the most interesting woman I have ever known."

"This is a very famous one," whispered Michael to Lauren, "I'm pretty sure it's supposed to be Gertrude Stein."

It was nice, thought Lauren, that Michael was paying such attention to the reading—as if it made up for her own distraction. Helena, of course, Helena must be paying attention—or was she perhaps also distracted from the reading by thoughts of the evening in front of her. Lauren sought out the back of Helena's head, that gorgeous womanly hair covering the back of the disturbingly girlish collar. How many applications of how many herbal essences sufficed for Helena's first meeting with Augustine Wedgwood, their first encounter face-to-face? Next to Helena's hair was a very different blonde: long, straight, cheerleading, sunny blonde, Los Angeles blonde—who could mistake Cookie Fink? How did it happen that Cookie was accompanying Helena at the Wedgwood reading? For Helena was that not too devastating a combination of sublime and ridiculous? Cookie's head was tilted a little to one side, as if she were watching Helena instead of Wedgwood, and, Lauren supposed, the expression on Helena's face was probably a sight to see.

And, in fact, someone else was watching Helena from the other side; now Lauren recognized the revolting Frank Frosch, Helena's trollish, froggish lover, Harvard's own atrocious poet of suicide. Poor Helena, thought Lauren, this is her great day, and there she is with *that* on one side and Cookie on the other. But Helena was probably blissfully oblivious of everyone except one person. Lauren guessed that at this moment, for Helena, Frank Frosch and Cookie Fink didn't even exist, likewise the audience of five hundred at her back, and however many more were watching and listening on closed-circuit television in the adjoining hall.

Am I, thought Lauren, going to room with Helena next year? Lauren herself had proposed Helena to Emily last night without even realizing that she was about to do so, and Emily had agreed. It was an attractive foursome— Lauren, Emily, the Princess, and Helena—or at least it would have seemed attractive two weeks ago. One of the things that had kept Lauren awake in her bed last night was the question of whether now she could possibly room with Emily, even if Emily hadn't murdered Debbie, even if she hadn't cut the harp strings, even if everything Emily had said last night was a tissue of lies. In a way it was that last possibility, although it might mean that Emily was quite innocent as far as Debbie was concerned, which would make it hardest for Lauren to accept her as a roommate. But why would Emily lie in such a way as to incriminate herself, admitting to being in Debbie's room that night, denying that she had murdered her? Could Emily possibly be covering for somebody else? Lauren tried to think about the Princess, of everything she had learned about the Princess.

But she couldn't. Her mind kept returning to Emily, to the night before, to the progression of their conversation. They had discussed sex over dinner at the Chinese restaurant, they had discussed roommates in the middle of Radcliffe Quad at midnight after leaving the Currier House dance, and finally, inevitably, back in Emily's room they had talked about the murder of Debbie Doyle. Snip, snip, snip, remembered Lauren, pluck, pluck, pluck.

But then she remembered Laurence and Emil. I like Emily, she thought, I still like her. In fact, I'm crazy about her. Lauren thought about what Michael had said that morning when she had told him about the night before: "Lauren darling, I'm afraid it may be time to face the fact that your friend Emily is a murderer and she knows that you know she's a murderer, and I'm not sure what you plan to do about it or really what you even can do about it, but if you will permit me to give you a little bit of advice, for your own sake, don't room with her." And if I don't room with her, thought Lauren, does that mean I'm going to end up rooming with Helena? Is that what I want? The answer, deep down, was no. But why?

Because I want to room with Emily, thought Lauren. I love Emily. But if Emily murdered Debbie Doyle... Lauren thought of Arlie, of Debbie's comic fat aunt, of Arlie in tears in Debbie's room. . . .

Did you find anything of mine in Debbie's room? That was what Cookie had asked last night, and now the question popped into Lauren's head. Lauren looked down at Cookie, whose head was now turned farther toward Helena, almost in profile. Lauren could distinguish one lizard eye, dead but somehow very intent, watching Helena. Oddly chilling. Did you find anything of mine in Debbie's room? Could that possibly be Debbie's brother sitting three rows behind Cookie? Impossible to say—since all Davids look alike, from the front as well as from the back, from close up as well as from a distance. But wait a minute. Debbie's brother had been Cookie's lover. What if he had found out something terrible about Cookie, what if he had told Debbie, what if Debbie had been holding it over Cookie's head? Lauren had no doubt: Cookie would have murdered Debbie without blinking those eyes. And now, what if Helena had some inkling, what if Debbie had hinted to her before she died, what if Cookie suspected that Helena suspected? Why was she watching Helena like that? Lauren saw Helena's shoulders twitch nervously and was struck by the feeling that Helena was in danger.

Wedgwood finished a poem, and Michael whispered, "Now that Auden is dead, it's possible that Augustine Wedgwood is the greatest living poet, even if he is largely heterosexual." Lauren didn't even know who the other possible candidates were, homosexual or heterosexual, and for the moment she really didn't care.

"This is a poem that I wrote quite recently," Wedgwood was saying. His voice had become hoarse, and he cleared his throat before continuing. "It is called. 'For a Young Poet.' " Helena, thought Lauren, has he written a poem for Helena? I have to listen to this poem. But Wedgwood coughed first and cleared his throat again, his aged hand resting on the glass of iced tea.

Lauren stole a glance at Emily, who seemed to be watching the poet. Certainly she was not looking at her lap, as she had when her father had been speaking in this same room two days ago. Lauren remembered her own odd thought at the time: just as if he weren't Emily's father at all. Did Senator Ravello have something to do with the story of Emily in Debbie's room on the night of the murder? Surely, if Emily murdered Debbie, then it had to have something to do with Emily's father.

Lauren was tired and thirsty. She looked down at Augustine Wedgwood, who had not yet begun to read "For a Young Poet." Drink the iced tea, she silently commanded him, as if his drinking would somehow quench her own thirst. And, as if in response to her thought, he lifted the glass.

As if he weren't her father at all, thought Lauren. And then everything came to her all at once. Augustine Wedgwood. The biography. The handwriting. But there was no time to think it through, no time at all. Before she knew what was happening, Lauren found that she was standing up at her seat; except for Augustine Wedgwood, she was the only other person standing in that room of five hundred people. And Lauren heard her own voice, as if it were coming from someone else, absolutely clear, though without amplification, ringing with the natural acoustics of the hall. "Don't drink that."

Five hundred heads turned to stare at her in absolutely silent shock. But Lauren was barely aware of them, because her eyes were holding those of Augustine Wedgwood, and his were fixed on her, just as if they stood face-to-face, only the two of them. The glass was at his lips. Somewhere, in the very back of her consciousness, she heard Michael's whisper: "Lauren darling, sit down, you're completely mad." But Lauren held Wedgwood's gaze and just repeated her words, as clearly as before. "Don't drink that."

12
Poetic Imagination

■

> *But one must know how to color one's actions and to*
> *be a great liar and deceiver. Men are so simple, and*
> *so much creatures of circumstance, that the deceiver*
> *will always find someone ready to be deceived.*
>
> Machiavelli

"Augustine Wedgwood had never heard of Helena Dichter,"
said Lauren. "And Debbie Doyle figured that out. That's
why Helena murdered her; that's why Helena was even
ready to kill Augustine Wedgwood himself."

"Amazing," said Michael. "How ever did you fit it all
together?"

They were together again, in Lauren's room. She was
seated at her sturdy Harvard desk, her Olivetti electric
humming before her, makeup jars displaced to one side of
the big desk. But Lauren was looking away from the
typewriter toward Michael, who lay stretched out on his
elbows on Lauren's bed, a Smith-Corona where the pillow
ought to have been. The excitement of the afternoon—the
timely forestallment of murder intended, the apprehen-
sion of the murderer, the resolution of the mystery—could
not change the inexorable fact that tomorrow morning

Lauren and Michael were going to have to hand in essays on Machiavelli and the Cold War. To be sure, they had never been very enthusiastic about the assignment, and now, as the deadline approached, their concentration was hopelessly distracted.

"*According to Machiavelli,*" said Lauren, typing as she thought, speaking as she typed, "*the ancient Romans never avoided a war because they knew that war could not be avoided, only postponed to the advantage of others.*" She typed carefully, because she knew there would be no time to retype a second draft. "*And yet the Cold War was and remains, fundamentally, a war postponed.*" She turned away from the typewriter to the bed. "Michael, that is really stupid, isn't it?"

"Lauren darling, nothing we write can rival the stupidity of the assignment, and at least you've now begun." He looked at his watch. "It's just after eleven. These are due in twelve hours—I think we're going to be up all night."

"It was just a sort of crazy hoax," reflected Lauren, the Cold War forgotten, "and the funny thing is that it really wasn't doing anyone any harm . . . until . . ."

"Until she decided to start murdering people," finished Michael. "I don't think that can be considered entirely harmless."

"No, of course," Lauren agreed, "but it didn't have to turn out that way."

It was all so clear now, even obvious—everything fit perfectly—and yet it had all been so mysterious until this afternoon, so completely impenetrable, until Lauren had seen through the one great lie at the center of the mystery.

Helena had been a lonely, troubled, daydreaming adolescent from a broken family. She was beautiful, but she was deeply insecure and desperately eager to believe that she was better than other people. ("He's vulgar," Helena had said bitterly about her father that day in the Harvard Book Store.) She was beautiful, but she saw her own beauty as an illusion to be painstakingly preserved with hair conditioners and poses. Besides, she had to believe in a higher beauty, an inner beauty, an artistic, aesthetic sensibility, and that, too, she saw as something to be created and preserved, with images, poses, affectations, illusions, and ultimately, with lies.

"Think about it, Michael. Think of all the sensitive spirits in American high schools who write poetry and imagine that they are poets and believe that their poetic spirits make them better than all the other high school students around them, who are perhaps also writing secret poems."

"There was a quite lovely little boy at Exeter," reflected Michael, "who was always sending me poems. Some of them, I thought, were quite good...."

"But Helena," Lauren continued, "Helena was different. Her fantasies were on a grander scale, and she took the whole thing one step further... and then one step further... and then..."

Helena visited her father in London and acquired the biography of Augustine Wedgwood, and he became her special infatuation, her poetic hero. Perhaps she even sent him an adoring letter; more likely she wrote such a letter and never sent it. Yes, that must have been the beginning of it all, a series of passionately worshipful letters from Helena to her poet, unposted, pouring out her poetic heart and soul.

And then, one day, how tempting it must have been to imagine his reply and even go so far as to write it down in order to be able to read it back to herself. And then to compose longer, more intimate replies, letters in which Augustine Wedgwood assured Helena Dichter of her poetic talent. ("The poet you apostrophize is the poet you yourself will one day be. I can see that your talent is developing very rapidly indeed." That was the letter Helena had showed to Lauren and Emily on the night of the murder.)

And since the biography contained photographic reproductions of Wedgwood's poems in handwritten manuscript, Helena's obsession could easily have led her into efforts to copy his handwriting, to give herself the illusion that it was really he who was writing to her. Helena took an aesthetic interest in calligraphy, anyway; her handwriting was a part of her cultivated presentation of herself. Lauren remembered Helena's name inside the front cover of her collected works of William Shakespeare. ("If you ask me," Emily had said, "there's something a little psycho about writing your name so beautifully. Some kind of phenomenal self-obsession.")

"I suppose the really decisive step must have been forging that letter of recommendation for Harvard," said Lauren. "You know, forgery for personal advancement instead of just for ego gratification. Still, once she had perfected Wedgwood's handwriting, it must have been irresistibly tempting. No one in the admissions office would have checked the postmark."

"And it *was* ego gratification," said Michael. "Helena was from Newton, and those rich middle-class Boston suburbs are completely obsessed with Harvard. They all think that admission to Harvard is the sole criterion of individual worth. You know, at an aristocratic prep school like Exeter, people are really much more relaxed about that sort of thing."

"I wonder."

Yes, the letter of recommendation was a decisive step. ("He was the one who suggested it. I would never have dreamed of asking him." That was what Helena had told Lauren, and the second half, at least, was true.) But even more decisive was what happened after Helena was accepted, when she arrived at Harvard in September. Freshman year at Harvard is famous for bringing out everyone's insecurities. At orientation the freshmen are told over and over again that they are the most brilliant, most talented, most important eighteen-year-olds in America, and naturally they wonder if they really deserve to be a part of such a group. Helena started to *tell* people about her letter of recommendation from Augustine Wedgwood. She started to *talk* about her correspondence with him. She started to *show* people his letters. ("I hope he wouldn't mind my showing it to you," said Helena to Lauren and Emily the night of the murder. Timid reluctance, in order to disguise her trembling fear at her own audacity.) And so it was that Helena, too, became one of those extraordinarily talented and brilliant Harvard freshmen. Until Debbie caught on.

The telephone rang just outside Lauren's room, and her roommate, Carol, answered the phone, then knocked at Lauren's door. "It's for you, roommate." Carol mouthed the words, "Your parents."

Lauren took the phone into her room, and in a moment her parents were asking what was new. Well, thought Lauren, today I saved the life of England's greatest living poet, even if he is largely heterosexual. But Lauren had neither time nor inclination to recount such things to her parents right now. "I can't talk," she explained. "My International Relations midterm is due tomorrow morning."

"About the Cold War and Machiavelli?" asked her father. He never forgot one of her assignments. "What are your arguments?"

My arguments, thought Lauren. Jesus Christ. "My arguments," she said, "are too complicated to summarize in one minute."

Michael laughed out loud from the bed, and Lauren's mother said, "Is there a boy in your room with you at eleven-thirty?"

"It's my friend Michael," said Lauren impatiently. "Remember, I've told you about him; he's gay."

But Lauren's mother was not so easily satisfied. "Is he Jewish?"

"Michael," said Lauren, not bothering to cover the receiver, "my mother wants to know if you're Jewish."

"Tell her I'm the Grand Rabbi of Vilna," said Michael, tickled at the thought.

"Mommy," said Lauren, "he's the Archbishop of Canterbury, and could we discuss this some other time when I don't have a paper due in the morning?"

"The Archbishop of Canterbury," Michael was musing when Lauren got off the phone. Then he began to type on the bed. *According to Machiavelli, it is better for a prince to be feared than loved.* He paused. *And Cold War atomic diplomacy was based on fear, not on any genuine effort to arrive at diplomatic understanding.* Another pause. "Lauren, is that, or is it not, the stupidest thing you've ever heard?"

But Lauren's mind was on something else. "Roommates," she said, "if only Debbie and Helena hadn't been roommates, Debbie would never have been able to watch her at such close quarters, to realize that there was something funny going on with Helena and Augustine Wedgwood. . . ."

Lauren remembered watching Debbie and Helena together the night of the fire alarm. One plain, the other beautiful. One naturally unpleasant, the other unnaturally lovely. ("The worst of Helena is that she's such good friends with Debbie," Emily had said.) Helena had tried to explain the friendship to Lauren that day in the bookstore, aware that it somehow required an explanation, even after Debbie was dead, after Helena had murdered her. ("We both thought that art was the most important thing in the world.") Consider the roommates: the Princess was a princess, Emily was a mime and a senator's daughter, Cookie was a cheerleader and a perfect premed. But Debbie was undeniably an artist, and *that* is what Helena would have found most admirable—and most threatening. Helena must have talked just a little too much about Augustine Wedgwood to Debbie. And Debbie, with her nastily sharp eye, had noticed that something was a little bit off.

The friendship, no doubt, began with Helena's craving for artistic approval and Debbie's need for an ally within the suite. But there soon developed an increasing element of coercion, of implicit blackmail, as Debbie's suspicions were confirmed, as she gradually hinted at those suspicions to Helena. At the Wedgwood reading yesterday, for a moment Lauren had been sure that Debbie had found out, through her brother, some terrible secret about Cookie—and from there it was just a short mental leap to realize that the terrible secret was Helena's. Once Debbie was in possession of that secret, she could do whatever she wanted with Helena. Helena would have been completely destroyed if Debbie had started to tell people that Helena wrote herself letters from Augustine Wedgwood, after all

Helena's shy boasting. And Helena would probably have been kicked out of Harvard if Debbie had denounced the forged letter of recommendation—surely Debbie had guessed about that. But Debbie decided to reserve her options by asking Helena to room with her, an invitation that Helena dared not decline. In that sense, it was the pressure connected to choosing roommates that had precipitated the explosion: Helena must have realized that Debbie was planning to hold on to her for the next three years. In the bookstore Lauren had had that strange intuition, that Helena would have committed murder in order to room with Lauren and Emily instead of with Debbie. Lauren had been right—but then it had seemed preposterous, because there didn't seem to be any motive.

"But how could Debbie be sure?" said Michael. "And didn't Helena see that Debbie couldn't really be sure, that nothing could be proved?"

Lauren had thought of that. "The biography."

One last book, Arlie had called, as they finished packing up Debbie's things. ("I think that's a library book," Lauren had said. "I can return it; it's no trouble.") It was the book that Debbie had ostentatiously carried out with her the night of the fire alarm, and there it was again, at the scene of the crime, the biography of Augustine Wedgwood, the bookmark at the photograph of Wedgwood's handwritten poem. Debbie had taken the book out of the library not at Helena's friendly insistence but to complete her case against Helena. Debbie, who had in the past stolen Cookie's diary to read it aloud for the amusement of the roommates, would not have hesitated to take some of the supposed Wedgwood letters from Helena's room. Rooms within suites have no locks.

Comparing those letters to the photographic reproduction in the biography, she could have discovered strong evidence of forgery. Ironically, she was working from the same page that had helped Helena to construct her forgeries in the first place. Debbie must have hinted to Helena about what she was doing with the biography, and Helena went to Widener Library and requested that the book be recalled so that she could read it. ("Just a little blue postcard from the library," Cookie had announced. "Debbie had a book out, and somebody else has requested it, and she's supposed to return it immediately.") Lauren had glanced at the handwriting on the postcard, but had thought nothing of it until, during the Wedgwood reading, at the last minute, it had occurred to her that the card had seemed to be written in Wedgwood's own hand. A hand familiar to Lauren from Helena's letters. Helena, trying to disguise her own handwriting, had thoughtlessly written down the title of the requested book in the other handwriting she knew best. Debbie probably would have recognized it, but by the time the hopelessly inefficient Widener librarians got around to sending out the postcard, Debbie was already dead.

The phone rang on Lauren's desk. It was Cookie Fink. "Is Michael there? I called his room, and his roommate said he might be in your room." Lauren said that yes, Michael was there, but before talking to Michael, Cookie wanted to congratulate Lauren on "catching" Helena. "I was sitting next to her while that poet she likes was reading his poems, and I was watching her, and she looked like she was going to crack up." Lauren remembered: Cookie had been staring at Helena so intently that for a moment Lauren had supposed that it was Helena who was in danger.

"Anyway," Cookie continued, "now Helena really has cracked up. David the detective told me she's in the bin, and they're shooting her up to calm her down, and she says her name is Virginia Woolf. That name sounded familiar to me—I thought it might be the name of our old sixth roommate, the one we chased out—but I checked in the freshman register, and there's no one with that name in our class. Then I remembered that it was a name from a movie."

"*Who's Afraid of Virginia Woolf?*" suggested Lauren.

"Yeah, that's it."

Lauren passed the phone over to the bed, and Michael assured Cookie that he would return her January *Cosmopolitan* the next day with the article on "How to Make

Love to a Man." Apparently things were progressing apace with David the detective.

After Michael hung up, Lauren read him the new sentence she had typed. "*According to Machiavelli the Prince must fear internal subversion and external aggression, and during the Cold War these fears were linked: the execution of the Rosenbergs and the Korean War were manifestations of the same central concern with Communism.*" She grinned. "My father is going to be thrilled that I mentioned the Rosenbergs, but you have to admit it's the stupidest thing you've ever heard."

"I think some of my stuff is stupider," said Michael, looking over a page he had already completed. "Can you think of a way for me to get the Rosenbergs into my essay? Maybe then your parents would give their consent to our marriage."

"Are you ready to think about going to medical school?"

But instead of answering, Michael asked, "Was it premeditated? Did she plan the murder in advance?"

"Obviously there had to be some advance preparation for Wedgwood," said Lauren, "but I'm sure the murder of Debbie Doyle was completely spontaneous."

It was on the day of the murder that Helena had announced the arrival of a new letter from Augustine Wedgwood—his last to her, as it turned out. She had told Lauren and Emily about the letter in Harvard Yard the night of the fire alarm, right before Emily humiliated and infuriated Debbie by mimicking her yawn. And that evening Helena had come to Emily's room, wearing her Queen Anne's lace nightgown, bringing Wedgwood's letter with the invitation to visit him in Cornwall that summer. ("Affectueusement, Augustine Wedgwood"—really it was too much; they should have guessed.) No doubt she had every intention of going to the Oxford summer program so that when she returned to Harvard for her sophomore year, she would be able to allow her friends to coax out of her the intimate details of her encounters with Augustine Wedgwood in Cornwall.

After showing Lauren and Emily the letter, Helena had raised the subject of rooming, and Emily had made quite clear that if Helena was committed to Debbie, then any further combining among them was out of the question. No doubt it was alarming to Helena to realize that she was bound to Debbie, and to Debbie alone. Finally, Helena had left the room with her massive Shakespeare volume, the one that Lauren and Emily had borrowed for their impromptu *Othello*. After Helena left, they had joked about the possibility of her becoming Augustine Wedgwood's lover ("a notch on the bedpost of twentieth-century literature"), and afterward Emily had told Lauren the story of Debbie and the roommates and the wrong number. ("My theory is that if we all tried to control our bad thoughts, then Debbie would disappear".) Just as Emily finished her story, the music of the harp had begun on the other side of the wall, signifying—though of course they didn't realize it at the time—that Debbie was dead.

Had Helena, leaving Emily's room with the letter and the Shakespeare, encountered Debbie in the corridor? Was Debbie perhaps just returning from the bathroom with Cookie's manicure scissors after having mutilated Emily's caftan? Was it Debbie's rage against Emily that was turned against Helena, perhaps to punish Helena for being in Emily's room?

Debbie must have been lying on her bed during the interview, since that is where her body was found. Helena was left to stand alongside and hear herself accused. Lauren had no doubts: that was the night that Debbie had finally stopped hinting at her suspicions, that was the night that she accused Helena of lying and forging, explicitly and to her face, that was the night she threatened to denounce Helena publicly, unless... Unless what? Perhaps no conditions were stated for the moment. Perhaps Helena was ordered to think no more about rooming with anyone but Debbie. Certainly she was given to understand that she should consider herself to be at Debbie's disposal, that from now on Debbie would do with her as she saw fit, that from now on she must live in constant fear of denunciation and exposure. How easy, then, when Debbie turned her head, or rudely yawned, how easy to raise the heavy Shakespeare and bring it down on Debbie's head. Then to finish her off with a stray harp string and pull a blanket over the body.

The moment of genius came next: placing the five records of baroque harp music on the stereo so that they could drop one by one through the night. Helena got dressed and left Weld, she knew she needed an alibi as quickly as possible. Perhaps the trollish Frank Frosch had already indicated his interest; perhaps his advances had already been rejected. Now was not the time to be choosy.

Meanwhile, J.B. and the Princess were reading in her room, Cookie was dumping the Davids and setting off for the Sheraton, Lauren and Emily were dozing off to the harp music coming through the wall. In the middle of the night Emily woke up and found her mutilated caftan in the bathroom. She went to Debbie's room for revenge (rooms within suites have no locks) and by the light of the moon coming through the window, she cut the strings of Debbie's harp. Pluck, pluck, pluck. Snip, snip, snip.

"Emily thought Debbie was just asleep under the covers?" suggested Michael.

"Of course," said Lauren. "What else could she think? She figured that Debbie had fallen asleep with the stereo on. She cut the strings and then went back to her own room to sleep in her own bed—with me."

And just as Lauren said that, the telephone rang again, and this time it was Emily.

"I can't sleep," said Emily. "I keep thinking about Helena."

"I can't sleep, either," said Lauren. "I have my International Relations midterm due tomorrow morning, and I've just begun."

"Do you remember that night?" said Emily. "How she came in with the letter from Wedgwood and we were trying to decide whether we wanted to room with her."

"I was just remembering."

"Christ, she was insane," said Emily. "She could have killed us all."

"No," said Lauren, "actually I don't think she would have. Only Debbie."

"Yes, I guess you're right." And then she said, "After last

night, did you think I was the one who had killed her?"
Lauren was silent. "God, I hated her that night," Emily
continued, "because of the caftan, you know. The next day
I almost wondered whether maybe I *had* killed her and
just forgotten about it, or blanked out or something."

"Well, you didn't," said Lauren.

"You know, I almost feel relieved," said Emily. And
then, one last reminiscence. "Remember we were acting
out the murder of Desdemona, and then right next door—"

"I was just remembering," said Lauren again.

"I'll call you tomorrow," said Emily. "Bye-bye, good
night."

"Good night," said Lauren.

"Are you going to room with her?" Michael asked after
Lauren had hung up the phone.

"I don't know," said Lauren.

"She cut the strings," said Michael. "And she lied about
it. To the police and to you. And she used you as a false
alibi."

"Maybe that's what friends are for," said Lauren to
Michael. "If you ever need an alibi, feel free to think of
me. Emily's a friend, too—but I have to admit I'm not
sure I want to room with her now. I could reconsider
rooming with Carol"—Lauren gestured toward the adjoining room—"or I could even consider going it alone—I've
begun to have my doubts about the whole concept of
roommates."

"Tell me about the second murder," said Michael, "the
one you so brilliantly foiled. Lord, I was so embarrassed
there when you just stood up in the middle of the reading
and began to speak in tongues. I thought you were about
to announce the coming of the Day of Judgment."

"I was," said Lauren, "I was."

"Yes, I suppose you were," said Michael. "How could
Helena have brought herself to try to murder Augustine
Wedgwood? How could she have been so stupid?"

Helena could have gotten away with the murder of
Debbie Doyle. She really could have. The murder itself
was managed quite coolly and the alibi even brilliantly—it

was afterward that Helena lost control of herself and in the
end brought about her own downfall.

That day in the Harvard Book Store, when she had
every reason to keep quiet or talk about the weather,
Helena hadn't been able to keep herself from talking to
Lauren about those things that were most intimately
connected to the murder. It was almost obsessive. She had
led Lauren across the bookstore in order to show her the
biography of Augustine Wedgwood, the very book that
Debbie had used to detect Helena's secret. ("It was
published in England five years ago, and it's only now
being published in America. . . . This book was the beginning of the most important thing in my life.") And Helena
had felt compelled to explain to Lauren about her friendship with Debbie. ("Well, we understood each other. . . .
Debbie was very insecure. . . . About being loved, I
think. . . . And that's why she ended up doing things that
made people dislike her.") Helena had not been able to
resist inventing a suspect killer. ("When I came out, I
thought I saw someone standing alongside the front of the
dorm—I couldn't swear to it, just a dark shape in the night
really.") And Helena had been all too ready to proclaim
her alibi to Lauren. ("I went out around one o'clock. . . . I
remember the harp very clearly. It was as if she was
playing especially beautifully that night. . . . His name is
Frank Frosch . . . it was our first time together.") Lauren
had barely had to pry or detect; these were just the things
that Helena couldn't help talking about.

"After she killed Debbie, I think she really did begin to
go mad," said Lauren. "Otherwise she would never have
tried the second murder. Besides, you'd have to say she
was a little mad to begin with, I mean, considering all
those lies about Augustine Wedgwood."

"And now," said Michael, "she thinks she's Virginia
Woolf, and mind you, even if she really were Virginia,
she'd be mad, but considering that she's *not* Virginia,
well . . . "

"What I think," said Lauren, "is that her great lie may
have begun to turn into a true delusion after she killed
Debbie to protect it. I suspect that she may have started

to believe that she really did receive letters from Augustine Wedgwood, and somehow she tried to go on believing that even when she started thinking about murdering him."

The thing that drove Helena over the edge, of course, was the news that Augustine Wedgwood was in America. As long as the reality of Augustine Wedgwood was three thousand miles away on the Cornish coast, he could exist as pure fantasy for Helena at Harvard—but when she read in the newspaper that he was at an Auden conference in New York ... Her first fear was that if others learned he was in New York, learned from the newspaper and not from *her*, they would begin to doubt her intimacy with the poet. She actually went out of her way to tell Lauren that Wedgwood was in New York, told her as a whispered confidence. ("He wrote to me a month ago and told me he might be coming, but he asked me to keep it secret." What nonsense! Lauren should have seen through her right then and there!) And then, as if having him in New York wasn't frightening enough, poor Helena woke up Saturday morning to learn from a posted pale green announcement that Augustine Wedgwood would be giving a poetry reading at Harvard.

Lauren had run into Helena that very morning, when she came out of Weld and Lauren was waiting to get in. No wonder Helena had been in such a condition of distraction. But she continued to play her part. ("Excited of course," said Helena about the reading, "but not completely surprised.") Compulsively, she buried herself under new lies, claiming to Lauren that she had a dinner date with Wedgwood for after the reading. She seemed to feel that after all her stories, everyone who knew her would *expect* her to have dinner with Wedgwood, at the very least, and if she failed to satisfy their expectations, they would begin to doubt her. As Debbie had.

In fact, a minute before running into Lauren, Helena had been standing transfixed at the doorway of Debbie's room, watching Aunt Arlie try to pack things up. ("She sort of peeked around at Debbie's things, but real nervous, like she thought they were going to jump up and bite her. And when I say to her, how about giving a hand . . . she practically runs out of the room like a rabbit.") It was in that room, after all, that Helena had murdered Debbie a week before. But if only she had been able to bring herself to help Arlie pack things up! She might have come upon Debbie's library copy of the biography, and then it would never have fallen into Lauren's hands, and then Lauren might never have figured out what was going on.

"She told me she was going to have dinner with him," said Lauren. "For all I know she promised Frank Frosch that she'd introduce him. She really *had* to murder Wedgwood, if only to protect herself from herself."

"Yes," said Michael. "But how did she ever come up with the idea of poisoning the glass at the lectern?"

"Oh, I know that," said Lauren.

For Lauren, though unaware at the time, had been right on the spot as Helena received her inspiration. Senator Ravello had knocked over his glass of water, and the crash had been picked up by the Science Center amplification system; Lauren had seen Emily look up in terror at the thought of an assassination. Helena was sitting next to Emily and must have seen, too—and how easy to link the glass at the lectern to the idea of murder. Then, that evening, at the reception given by the Princess's cousin, Helena had been talking to the young Arab Oxonian who had met Augustine Wedgwood for two seconds at Oxford. Helena must have taken that as a personal challenge and no doubt outdid herself in telling stories about her tremendous relationship with Wedgwood. In the middle of her lies, nervous probably, aware that Wedgwood would be at Harvard in two days, she dropped her glass of orange juice on the Persian rug. Everyone was pretending that it was orange juice, but of course everyone was really drinking screwdrivers. The broken glass reminded Helena of the crash that afternoon, and the puddle at her feet started her thinking about innocent beverages secretly mixed with much more potent ingredients. Orange juice and vodka, iced tea and cyanide.

And cyanide she knew where to find. Frank Frosch, her lover, whose poems were all about suicide, had just published a poem called "Bitter Almonds" in the *Harvard Advocate*, a poem about suicide by cyanide poisoning. He possessed a capsule of cyanide as part of his suicide obsession, and he had probably showed it to Helena—just as boastful about his obsession as she was about hers. It would have to be mixed with iced tea, of course, instead of water to conceal the taste as the victim swallowed the lethal dose. The only warning would be the characteristic odor of bitter almonds, and probably he wouldn't notice. He would pass out and die in twenty seconds, in front of the whole audience, and in the case of such an old man the sudden death might well be attributed to a stroke. Helena stole the poison, mixed the potion, and placed it beside the lectern herself just as the reading was about to begin, just when everyone's attention was conveniently distracted by a commotion in the back of the hall.

"I think she thought of the murder as an act of passionate adoration," said Lauren. "You know, the climax of her fantastic obsession."

"Finally taking possession of the adored object," said Michael.

"Yes," said Lauren, "and I'll tell you the most terrible irony of all. When she brought the glass up to the lectern, he was sitting alongside the chairman of the English Department, and he looked up at her and gave her the most incredibly sexual smile I have ever seen in my life. It was more than just an invitation; it was like complete consummation right on the spot."

"The old goat," said Michael. "I know that smile."

"But the point is, if Helena had gone to his hotel room that night, I'm sure she could have had him; she could have made all her fantasies and lies come true. But it was too late. She could only go back to her seat in the front row, sit down in her innocent white dress, and wait for him to drink and die."

Lauren and Michael were both silent for a minute, she at the desk, he on the bed.

And then Michael began to type. *"According to Machiavelli, one must be a great liar and deceiver, and since men are so simple the deceiver will always find someone ready to be deceived. Is this not Stalin at Yalta?"* Michael looked up at Lauren. "Really it's Helena, isn't it?"

It's everyone, thought Lauren, it's everyone who's insecure and wants to deceive people, who wants to exaggerate talents and accomplishments. Everyone who wants to impress people ends up telling either little lies or big lies. And here at Harvard everyone wants to impress everyone, because we deceive ourselves into believing that everyone else is so impressive. And besides, there are so many people here with famous connections. Ted really is a Roosevelt. Emily really is the daughter of a famous senator who may one day be president. The Princess is really a princess. Who could guess that Helena's connection to Augustine Wedgwood was a complete fabrication? Maybe Helena really was a talented poet. Just as Debbie was a genuinely talented musician. Hell, even Cookie is remarkably talented—at collecting dates and getting A's in premed courses. The point is that for Helena the possibility of possessing a certain talent was not enough. Especially at Harvard it wasn't enough. She had to be a great liar and deceiver, and even at Harvard we were all simple enough to be deceived. Maybe because we're all so preoccupied with how impressive everyone is and how impressive we want everyone to think we are.

"Sometimes," said Lauren to Michael, "I think Harvard is an evil place."

"Lauren darling," said Michael, "you'll feel better about Harvard after you've finished your essay. Help me think of something else to say about Stalin."

13
Completed Assignments

■

*Time sweeps everything along and can bring good as
well as evil, evil as well as good.*

Machiavelli

Lauren and Michael arrived at International Relations the
next morning feeling very bleary indeed. They had been
through the proverbial Harvard all-nighter, but they had
been through it together, which made the whole miserable
experience more bearable. Lauren had gone out to the
24-Store at two in the morning for chocolate Häagen-
Dazs, and Michael had gone out at four-thirty for boysen-
berry. With ice cream and each other to sustain themselves, they had emerged triumphant, each with ten pages
of utter nonsense about Machiavelli and the Cold War,
both fiercely insistent that what they had written was far,
far stupider than anything else that had ever been written
by any college student anywhere. And even while they
were creating these masterpieces of scholarship, they had
found the time to analyze in fascinating detail the murder
mystery and its solution.

Now they stood at the very top of the Science Center
lecture hall, where yesterday Augustine Wedgwood had

been reading his poems, where Augustine Wedgwood had almost been murdered, and they looked down upon a scene of chaos. Two hundred students, all dead tired, were either waiting in the aisles to go down to the lectern and hand in their essays or straggling back up the aisles to their seats empty-handed. The focus of all this dispirited traffic was an enormous brown cardboard box beside the lectern, slowly being filled with essays on Machiavelli and the Cold War. "The garbage barge," muttered Michael as he and Lauren, with their offerings in hand, joined the line of students descending in the center aisle.

To one side of the garbage barge stood Professor Grasshopper, grasping his lecture notes. He seemed rather pleased with himself, pleased no doubt to think that it required but a few words from him to generate the stupendous heap of undergraduate gibberish now accumulating before him. He alone in that great hall seemed well rested and at ease.

But wait, surely there was one other person. Lauren looked over her shoulder, back to the last row where, sure enough, J.B. was reading a book. The Princess, of course, had to be somewhere in the crowd with her essay—no hired assassin would be clever enough to mingle with a mob of Harvard students handing in their take-home midterms. Perhaps one day the Princess would be assassinated, thought Lauren, perhaps while J.B. is reading a book. But if it ever did happen, it would have nothing to do with roommates, with Radcliffe, with Harvard.

J.B. seemed to become aware that he was being watched, and he looked up and caught Lauren's eye. Dark suit, as always, dark tie. He's so attractive, thought Lauren, but he, too, is not quite what he seems to be. Or at least not what I imagined he was. When I thought he was up on the roof in a purely professional capacity, watching for snipers, checking access from the roof to the windows of Weld, in fact he was also hoping that Ted might happen to reappear. The same thing I was hoping for, actually. And then when, by great good fortune, I found myself alone on the roof with him, I somehow thought I could have my way with him—but of course he was immune to my charms. Which goes to show that just because you name someone James Bond doesn't mean that he can be counted on to chase after Pussy Galore. No, people are not what they seem to be. Lauren was very sleepy.

But not too sleepy to recognize the young man who was coming up the aisle in the opposite direction. "Good morning," said Ted. "Don't tell me; let me guess. Those papers you're holding deal with Machiavelli and the Cold War; I'm clairvoyant when I've been up all night." Actually his usual elfin charm was considerably subdued. "I thought I was going to get two hours of sleep, but when I finished, I realized that I'd only written six pages, so I had to retype the whole thing with two-inch margins on both sides."

"I just left out page seven," said Michael conversationally. "Skipped from six to eight. There's nothing like mispagination."

Lauren was suddenly overcome with a sleepy, irresistible urge to place her hand on Ted's ass. This was not unconnected to her sense that J.B. was watching them from his seat. She slid one hand beneath Ted's army pants and gave him a playful caress; with the other hand, which held her essay, she waved to J.B. Turn green with envy, she thought, because I've got him.

Ted said, turning to Lauren, "Who's that? You, I hope."

"Well, it certainly wasn't me," said Michael.

"It certainly wasn't," said Lauren.

"Why don't you come sit with us for the lecture?" said Michael to Ted.

Lauren eyed Michael sharply but repeated the invitation. "Yes, why don't you come sit with us?"

"I couldn't," said Ted. "I never sit through lectures; it's a matter of principle. I only came this morning to hand in my midterm, but now I'm heading out before the class starts—I think it's rude to walk out in the middle of a lecture. Going right home to sleep." He brought some life into his sleepy eyes for Lauren's benefit. "I'll be up by this evening. Shall I come visit?"

"Do," said Lauren. As he went off, Lauren thought about the curve of his ass beneath her hand. She thought about Ted naked on the roof, about Ted naked in her bed.

Now Harvard didn't feel like such a terrible place, and spring seemed full of promise.

Standing before the box of papers, Michael tossed his on the pile with an air of good riddance. (It came back two weeks later with a grade of B-plus. The grader commented, "Good insights; needs more detail to support generalizations.") Lauren gritted her teeth and dropped her essay on top of Michael's. (It came back with a grade of A-minus. "Interesting discussion, good organization, nice point about the Rosenbergs.")

"It's the stupidest thing I've ever written in my life," said Michael as they made their way back to the top of the hall to take seats for the lecture.

"Mine is stupider than yours," said Lauren one last time. "We'll be lucky if we pass." They found two seats in the last row and waited glumly for Professor Grasshopper to begin.

About an hour later Lauren woke up, unsure where she would be waking—in Emily's room? In her own? But she found herself in the Science Center lecture hall, and the hall was quite empty. Except for Michael, who sat beside her, rereading *Death in Venice*.

"I've slept through the whole class," she said, rather pleased.

"You certainly have," said Michael, "slept like a baby. The lecture ended ten minutes ago—you didn't miss a thing, believe me—and when everyone trooped out, I shushed them so they wouldn't wake you."

"My guardian angel," said Lauren. And she meant it.

She looked over the huge empty hall, all those empty seats, and her imagination filled in some of the places, working from her memory of yesterday's poetry reading. The Princess was right back here with J.B. And Emily was over there. Helena was way down in the front row— Lauren remembered her beautiful hair from behind. And Cookie was sitting next to Helena. And there, at the now abandoned lectern, Augustine Wedgwood had been reading his poems. Lauren remembered how his eyes had met hers during those final moments, when she saved his life, without even quite knowing what she was doing—it had all happened so fast. Yesterday he had been so real, and today he was just a phantom in her imagination. As he always had been for Helena.

Yesterday's moment of realization came back to her with great intensity. The moment when everything had suddenly fit together, when she rose to her feet without knowing what she was going to say, when she spoke and everyone in the hall turned to stare at her. Which hadn't mattered at all, because all at once she had understood.

"I feel very close to Debbie," said Lauren to Michael.

"Debbie?" As if he had almost forgotten her.

"Yes, Debbie was the only other person besides me who figured out what was going on with Helena. She figured it out before I did, but she was Helena's roommate. She was sharp, Debbie Doyle—unpleasant but sharp."

"If only, like you, she had used her sharpness for good instead of for evil."

"Let's go," said Lauren, rising, feeling a terrible sense of déjà vu at standing up in that hall. "Let's go back to Thayer and get some sleep." She noticed a discarded copy of the *Harvard Crimson* on the seat beside Michael. "Pass me that paper," she said.

"Oh, leave it be," said Michael. "It's such a rag."

"I want to see if they say anything about me," said Lauren, and she took it with her as they went out of the hall. The big headline was POET SAVED FROM KILLER FRESHMAN. "Christ," said Lauren, "it *is* a rag."

But before she could read any further, Michael distracted her. "Cookie thought the old sixth roommate might have been named Virginia Woolf. Isn't that a scream? Cookie is definitely not Miss English Literature, but she does know a nice nose when she sees one." They stepped out of the cavernous Science Center and into the spring sunlight.

"You'd better watch out," said Lauren. "One day Cookie is going to decide that your nose is so perfect that all you need is a name change to spend the rest of your life taking her out to dinner."

"Nonsense," said Michael. "Cookie does realize that I am out of the question for her."

"Because you're gay?"

"Oh, no," said Michael, "not because of that. Because I'm too short."

Lauren and Michael were just the same height, and so their smiles met at the same level. Lauren stopped in the open air, between the Science Center and Harvard Yard, and she looked closely at the *Crimson* in her hand.

But Michael distracted her again. "Are you going to room with Emily next year?" he said.

"No," said Lauren, who hadn't quite realized that she'd decided until he asked. "I think I'd rather have her as a friend than as a roommate, and I'm not sure I can have both." She looked back at the newspaper.

"Do you think your friend Ted has found a roommate for next year?" asked Michael provocatively.

Lauren bristled, and then thought, Oh, what the hell. "Why don't you ask him?" she said sweetly.

Michael seemed slightly taken aback at such noblesse oblige.

"Here's my name," said Lauren, finally finding herself in the newspaper story. She read aloud. *"Lauren Adler, a freshman of Thayer Hall, warned Mr. Wedgwood about the danger and probably saved his life. Our* Crimson *reporter contacted Adler by telephone last night to find out how she felt about the day's events. Adler said, 'I did it for English Literature. . . .'"* Lauren looked up from the newspaper in amazement. "I would never say anything like that!" she exploded. "Nobody called me last night from the *Crimson*! What the hell is going on here?!"

Michael was looking extremely sheepish.

"Michael!!" cried Lauren.

"Lauren darling," said Michael, "calm down, please. You know, when you went out for the chocolate Häagen-Dazs last night at two in the morning, well, that's when the *Crimson* called. And somehow—must be something about my pitch or my intonations—they thought *I* was Lauren Adler. And I couldn't bring myself to disappoint them by telling them you'd gone out, so I just came up with a few statements for the press." Michael's sheepishness had already collapsed into giggles. "I just said what I thought you'd have wanted to say if you'd been there."

"I did it for English Literature," muttered Lauren, rolling up the newspaper, thinking that she would start swatting him with it around the ears. But an adjoining trash can was too convenient, and so, with the same motion that she had employed an hour ago to drop her midterm essay on the pile in the box, she now deposited the *Harvard Crimson*. And at the same moment she broke out laughing.

She took Michael's arm, and together they walked on into Harvard Yard.

ABOUT THE AUTHOR

VICTORIA SILVER graduated from Radcliffe *magna cum laude* and now lives in San Francisco where she enjoys a certain notoriety. She also enjoys chocolate, cowboys, murder, and suede, in various combinations. She is the author of the wildly acclaimed *Death of a Harvard Freshman*.

MURDER MOST BRITISH!

FROM ANNE MORICE:

☐ **25647-5 MURDER IN OUTLINE** $2.95

Actress Tessa Crichton finds she has mixed reactions to an invitation to be on the panel of judges at the annual inter-house competition of the Waterside Drama and Ballet School, her not-so-beloved alma mater. When she arrives on campus, she finds her earlier premonitions of disorder are mild compared to the reality: the headmistress is having an affair with the founder's husband, a kleptomaniac is on the loose among the budding thespians and Connie Bland, the beloved and bewildering foundress, is suffering from a most mysterious illness. When Hattie McGrath, a student with a penchant for drawing very compromising caricatures, is found dead, the picture is one of murder most academic.

☐ **25652-1 MURDER POST-DATED** $2.95

Nobody knows who started the rumor that James McGrath murdered his wife Rosamund. Certainly no one had seen her in a while and she *had* gone off to visit a sick cousin without mentioning a trip to the neighbors. Still, everyone was inclined to accept the story, that is, until one of the neighbors meets the cousin in town—in excellent health and eager for news of country cousin Rosamund. By this time, Tessa Chrichton is on the scene and fascinated by this series of events. Fascination soon turns to a neat bit of detection when James McGrath comes to her with a very strange confession.

FROM JOHN GREENWOOD:

☐ **25574-6 MURDER, MR. MOSLEY** $2.95

It was sometimes said of Jack Mosley that he knew everything in the 12 miles by 12 miles of moors, cloughs and valleys that were his territory, and the bizarre murder of Brenda Thwaites Cryer well and truly had its roots in Mosley soil. Brenda, after a 17-year absence from Parson's Fold, had returned, accompanied by a shadowy reputation, a failed marriage and money which seemed to have no particular source. It was there in tiny Jackman's Cottage that she was killed. The only possible witness, her invalid mother, was missing. Why were Brenda's brother and sister-in-law showing such uncharacteristic concern for her? What was the source of her mysterious affluence? And most baffling of all: just where had the very dead Brenda Cryer spent the last eight years?

Look for them at your local bookstore or use this handy coupon:

HARDCOVER FICTION FROM BANTAM

*From the author whose books have sold more than
2 million copies world-wide*

BRIAN FREEMANTLE

comes a thriller rich in espionage and intrigue

☐ **THE BLIND RUN** (05161-X • $15.95)

Crafty and argumentative British Secret Service agent, Charlie Muffin has crossed swords with authority perhaps once too often. Now he's found himself jailed for something he swears he did not do and, not surprisingly, his Intelligence bosses have chosen to ignore him. Faced with the frustrations of prison life, Charlie fights back . . . until twists in his situation develop to snag his interest: an elusive Russian mole has been uncovered and sentenced to prison, the same one that now holds Charlie. When his new prison mate reveals his daring plans to escape to Moscow, Charlie's attitude turns from one of antagonism into one of peaked interest. And when the Secret Service uncovers the plan, they stop ignoring Charlie long enough to enlist him on a most daring mission: to escape with the Russian, posing as a defector, in order to rescue a British mole in the KGB and bring him back to the West.

The mission is a daring one, but simple . . . until the ever-cautious Charlie finds himself in love and faced with the most agonizing choice of both his career and his life.

The mystery is revealed

Barbara Vine *is* Ruth Rendell

☐ **A DARK-ADAPTED EYE** (05143-1 • $14.95)

Here is the stunning first novel by Ruth Rendell, one of the greatest living practitioners of the British mystery, writing under the pseudonym of Barbara Vine. In this chilling novel, a once adoring niece delves deep into her family's psyche to uncover the circumstances surrounding the murder for which her aunt was hanged. Sifting through layers of time-honored illusion, Faith Severn must expose her own image of the family to the harsher light of day, a light which reveals just how a suffocating affection can become twisted into something deadly.

Look for them at your bookstore or use this coupon for ordering: